You, Dracula

Praise for I, Dracula, by D.S. Crowe

A visceral, gripping tale of life, blood, loss, and painful self-discovery.

Dr. Madeline Potter

Dracula scholar

Atmospheric, wonderfully detailed and beautifully written.

Jason Figgis

Film director

A powerful reimagining of Dracula as a tragic character.

Conor Kostick

best-selling author of Epic

A beautifully woven gothic tale about a tumultuous life lived in pursuit of love and acceptance.

Ulrike Ascher

author of Magic of the Elements

You, Dracula

D.S. Crowe

For my parents, Stela and George,
whose love, support and generosity
have never failed me.
Thank you for bringing books into my life

Hungary
Bucovina
Transylvania
Moldavia
Hunedoara
Sibiu
Fagaras
Brasov
Banat
Targoviste
Walachia
Bucharest
Serbia
Bulgaria

OVROBOROS

Cneaja

"*I will soon be forgotten, and my name will
never be known.
Will you, Dracula, remember me,
your mother?*"

Cneaja, Sighișoara, 1430

"I am with child, my lord."

The words I had repeated over and over in my head came out in the end. I uttered them with more assurance than I felt. Your father's face opened with a tentative smile, the first one I had seen after our rushed union only weeks before.

"You have to rest, Cneaja. I will send ladies-in-waiting for you. You will be the mother of a *voievod*. This child is yours to look after for now, until you give him to me and his country."

His joy was short-lived, like the rippling of water on a still lake touched by a raven's wing. With the smile gone as if it had never been, your father's face turned back to the stillness of before, and he took a heavy step towards the door. My step behind him was small and quiet.

"My lord, are you happy with this news? Does it please

you?" I found it hard to ask, but I was craving some reassurance from the man who had taken me as his wife. I didn't know much more about your father than the harshness in his eyes, which he carried from his throne hall into our bed. I was as scared of him as I was of my father. They both seemed old to me and always so stern. I was eighteen, not that anyone counted or cared. Eighteen and with child.

"It is good news, and one day this baby you carry will make a great *voievod* for *Valahia*." He closed the door behind him and left me there, alone, hoping for just another good word.

I stood in the middle of our room, looked at the bed we had shared for a few nights and wondered about the seed left inside me. Was the baby going to become a man like my husband said? Would I be able to make him grow into a strong ruler, as my mother said I had to?

What if the seed in me was going to grow into a girl, small and shy like me, with dark, long hair that I could comb at night like my mother used to do for me? A girl who would sing with me while we knitted mittens? A girl whom *Valahia* wouldn't claim and I could keep for myself?

I couldn't tell. I hadn't even known there was a baby until one of the women from the courtyard talked to me. These were women I saw every day in the morning, leaving the house with the washing and bringing it to the riverbank and coming back when the sun was high in the sky with heavy loads of soaking fabrics on straining mules. They would then hang the long sheets and tablecloths in the courtyard to be windblown like flags on the battlefield, and the soldiers' uniforms would waff and puff around in the breeze. This whole cloth army would then march aimlessly for the rest of the afternoon with no trumpets and no beat until the women came back and released it from its trials.

The day before I gave the news to your father, I was picking sour cherries from the bottom branches of a tree. I could have gone up that tree in no time, but your father had seen me once and forbade it; he said it was not ladylike, not fit for the wife of a *voievod*. I preferred the cherries at the top—their flesh was softer and their colour a deeper red, and when you bit into one, the ruby juice would burst inside your mouth and trickle freely between your lips. That was when I could go and get them myself, because when other people were picking them for me, they just didn't taste the same.

I heard the woman coming towards me, her long skirts brushing against the blades of the scorched grass in the orchard. *Phshhh, phshhh.* I kept picking my cherries and I turned to face her only when her shadow was upon me.

"Your dirty clothes my lady, I need them, we are going to the river. Can we go fetch them from your room?" she asked, putting down a basket full of black tunics.

I looked at her crumpled face, dark and dry from the sun, her short arms relieved of the weight of her load. The thought sneaked into my head just as her eyes rested on me and her right hand opened its skinny fingers to grab my shoulder.

"There are none," I mumbled, shaking her hand off. That was when I knew it myself, right then and there, at the same moment the wrinkles on her face stretched in disbelief, then shock, then recognition.

"You must be… I think you are…"

She didn't need to say 'with child'. She only brought up her hand to cover her mouth. I hoped she wasn't going to say anything at all because I had to say it to myself first, to let the words sink into my mind and fill it with that idea of a child in my belly.

"What if I'm not?" I tried, but she dismissed me with a wave of her arm, which she withdrew then quickly, took hold of her skirts, and ran back to the house.

I sat under the cherry tree and fiddled with the fruit I had picked earlier. The cherries smelled sweet and bitter at the same time, and my mouth watered at the thought of them. I put one in my mouth and squashed another through my fingers. The red juice burst through its skin, smearing my own skin like blood. The sun resting low on top of the trees seemed to set the orchard on fire. It suddenly became very quiet. The silence that surrounded me was soft and choking like the red wool of my husband's royal cape. I could hear my heart beating.

That night, I waited for your father to come to our room, alone in the big bed, wondering about him. He didn't always come to me at night, and sometimes I was glad to be left alone to just sleep and dream my dreams. But sometimes he came, and his business with me was done quickly and without words, and I never knew if it was good or bad or just so. I sometimes wondered how it was for him as I knew my pain myself. The nights he came smelling like all the barrels of *rachiu* from the cellar were the worst, as nothing pleased him. In the end, he would fall asleep on top of me, and his snores would keep me awake till the morning.

He didn't come at all that night, but I wasn't worried about him—it was the worry about the child in my belly that was keeping me awake.

"Nothing to worry about, my lady; a *voievod* needs heirs in times of war. He needs boys to keep the country safe and the throne in the right hands, boys ready to die for the country," my maid said the next morning while helping me get dressed.

Mioara was only a little older than I was. Her skinny face had no beautiful features— the nose was too long, and her chin was too pointy, but the bushy eyebrows hid gentle eyes that were easy to look at, and her words were playful. She was a great comfort to have around as she seemed to know the way the house was run and by whom, and she helped me know my place among those people. She also made me laugh, and I wanted to tell you this so you know I used to laugh. Before you came.

"Why have a child if you send him to death?"

"Death comes with the kingdom, my lady. It is a *voievod's* honourable duty to die for his country. And his sons will have to die too if the country needs it," she continued while fastening my bodice looser than other mornings.

"My mother talks the same about duty, but my country, Moldova, hasn't been at war during my father's reign. Isn't a *voievod* better if he keeps the peace for his country rather than dying for it?"

"Maybe so, my lady, but if it comes to it, if peace is gone, a true *voievod* has to be ready to die fighting."

This was the way my mother spoke, too, but she never had to send my brothers to the battlefield. I looked down at my belly and gave it a gentle stroke.

"Ready now," said Mioara, smoothing the dress along my arms. She spun me around and made me look into the heavy mirror hanging on the wall opposite the window.

"You are glowing. Maybe just a little something for your cheeks." She reached for the powder on the dressing table and started to spread it on my face with a small brush. I wished I didn't have to leave my room. It was quite bare. The bed in it was too big when I was alone and too small when my husband came, and yet, I would rather have stayed in there than trumpet my news in the throne hall. Or anywhere else.

"Do I have to tell him? Can't somebody else say it to him?"

Mioara started to laugh behind me and then spun me around once more and held me by my shoulders to face her.

"If you know you are with child, you have to say it to everybody, or the child will be born mute. We don't want the child to be mute now, do we?" she said, arching her black eyebrows and starting to laugh again. I arched my eyebrows, too, and laughed back, imitating her. She ruffled my hair and tied a loose bow.

"All ready to go, my lady. We'll wait in the throne hall until the *voievod* comes."

I waited for your father that whole morning until the sun rose so high in the sky that there was no other place for it to go but down. And only then he came; he listened and went again. Shortly after that, four older women came in and bowed their heads to me with reverence and stern faces. They sent Mioara away—she wouldn't know what to do for a childbearing woman, they said—and that was the last I saw of her.

Those women were not gentle and caring like my mother or friendly and joyful like Mioara. They seemed older than anyone I had seen before but not hunched over like most old women. They carried themselves straight as if their necks were tightly stuck in the tall collars of their black vestments. Their moves were never rushed, and their talk was as measured as a reading from the Bible. I felt lost around them and lacking.

Only days after I was given into their care, that murder of crows came into my room with grim faces. With one breath, they seemed to have sucked all the air around me. There was no smell from them; I would always remember that, because it made me think I was dreaming. Yet they were right there, unyielding as ever. They helped me sit up in bed, propped me against the wall with pillows, and told me you must have been conceived on a holy day, the day of Saint George.

"And this is a good thing, isn't it? A holy child with a patron who slayed the dragon?" I said, full of hope.

The women looked at each other from the two sides of the bed and shook their heads, questioning my innocence. I felt stifled under their better knowledge of life and apologetic although I didn't know what wrongdoing I was guilty of.

"This baby was conceived on a saint's day, so he will be marked," muttered one of them.

"Marked how? Will he have a mark on his body? What do you mean, marked?" I wished I knew more of these things, women things and church things, to help me grasp the meaning of their furtive looks. They looked at me in disbelief, and I could see pity in their eyes too.

I didn't get the answer to that question until later, when you were born, and I saw there wasn't a single mark on your body.

That day, those four women in their long, dark garments welcomed me to my womanhood with their rigid faces, took over my small life, and ruled it with iron chains. And I let them.

Of course I was the lady of the house, I was higher in the hierarchy of our small household than those women, higher than all the women in my husband's small country. But I felt of no importance because all of them had more knowledge than me. It wasn't knowledge of wars or trade or diplomacy that I craved, although that would come later too. I just wanted to know how to govern my life so I didn't feel wrong all the time and repentant. It wasn't a feeling fit for a princess. I didn't want to settle for it, and neither would my mother.

I wish I could say he loved me, but the truth is your father acquired me for my valued bloodline and nothing else. I was a descendant of the Mușatin Dynasty who ruled Moldova, a long line of kings and boyars who fought and won many battles in its name and kept the peace for its honour. I was a true princess—a prized trophy to carry an heir.

The spring of my eighteenth year was just turning into summer when I was told he had demanded me for his wife, and his visit was forthcoming. I didn't waste much thought on it at the time, refusing to grasp the urgency of the situation, busy as I was with being my parents' daughter and a sister to my brothers as well as a princess to the country. My life felt full.

It was only the night before his arrival that it suddenly dawned on me what marriage could bring and take from my life. That was when I lost all sleep with worry. I lost it to the branch hitting my window, told off by the summer wind, and to its shadow creeping along the wall in front of me. I lost it to the caw of crows outside and to the crawling spiders inside. But mostly to the fear that engulfed me with every hour passing.

When the morning finally arrived, I had been watching the door of my bedroom, eyes opened wide for a long time, waiting for my mother to come in and hoping to hear that my suitor's visit was annulled. Her words instead, when she peeped through the door, slapped away all hope.

"Vlad Dracul is here. Get ready."

I did not see his face in the courtyard as he dismounted his horse and handed the reins to a footman. I watched the short and stocky figure being welcomed through the heavy entrance door of our house, and then I sat on my bed and worried myself into a frenzy. What was going to become of my life? Would there still be laughter without my brothers? Would the bread still be soft and sweet when I dipped it in the cream of that new country? Would I still be able to sit idle in an orchard without a care in the world and look at the clouds? And what about my mother? Would she ever come to stay with me at night, embroidery forgotten on her lap, telling me stories of the great men and women who sat on the throne of Moldova for hundreds of years?

My life in my country was full of good things, small things that made it warm and safe. These things made it seem important to me because I was made to feel important, looked after with care, listened to with consideration. Everywhere I went felt like home. But a strange country in a strange man's house? How would I fit into his home? Would I even want to? All I wanted to do was run. I just wanted to keep wearing my childhood as a cape that could shield me from whatever life was planned for me.

After a while, my mother came into the room and sat with me on the bed.

"It is done," she said with an encouraging smile. "Your father is pleased."

She placed a hand on my shoulder and squeezed gently. Heartened by her warmth, I put my head against her palm and hugged her. Surely, she'd listen to me and call it off, whatever it was they were planning.

"I'm scared, Mother, and I don't want to go."

"Of course you are scared, Cneaja, but you are a brave girl and we raised you well, like a true princess."

"Must I go? There are handsome young men in this country who have asked for me. I could be married here, close to home."

My mother sighed, wiggled her hand out from under my cheek and took hold of my chin, turning my face towards her.

"That is for common girls, not for princesses. Women of our stature must do what is best for their country. I came from Bucovina to marry your father. This was what I had to do."

"But father is a nice man and a good *voievod,* and you are happy here."

"It wasn't always like that," she whispered, turning her face away from me. "It wasn't like that at the beginning. It is now, because I knew my place and I did my duty. You will find your own way."

"And what if I don't? What if I don't like him and he doesn't take to me? What if he is stern and there is no laughter? What if I'm lonely and I miss you? What if I miss my brothers and our home? Can I come home then?"

When she looked back at me, there was no warmth left in her eyes, only a cold stillness.

"You don't have a choice anymore, only a duty—to our country, which will be left in peace if this alliance is sealed—and to your new country, which will welcome you as one of their own and to your husband, who will trust you with his children. You have to understand, my sweet girl, from now on, you will not be you anymore; you will be the lady of a country, the wife of its *voievod,* and the mother of all its future kings."

"But I can do all that here, near you…"

"You don't have to be near me to make me proud. Your duty is now to your new country, to *Valahia.* Serve it well. Look well after your husband so he will look after the country today. Look well after your children, raise them brave and just and kind, and they will look after the country's future. And after yours in your old age."

I was hurt. I didn't understand how my mother was willing to give me away to a stranger. And all that talk about children and duty and old age! I always knew it would come someday, but this was too rushed, it came too soon, and I was being sent too far. Only yesterday I was listening to my mother's stories about great men and women of this country, and today I was told to be one. There had to be a way out, or at least a delay, at least until I felt ready or willing or worthy. Or at least not so scared. Surely my mother had the power to do something.

"Do you not love me anymore?"

The tears were gathering at the back of my eyes, ready

to burst the locks.

"Love has nothing to do with it, Cneaja. I did right by my own parents, by my husband, and by my country. I did everything in my power to give good children to the country. My whole life will be judged by my children, so don't make my life seem worthless."

With this she stood up, straightened her dress, and looked at me as if our conversation was over. I followed her outside into the courtyard where the footmen were waiting patiently. The horses were drinking water from a trough, smacking their lips with delight, and the apricots in the apricot tree were bathing in the sun, gathering its nectar. It was peaceful out there. There was no peace to be found inside me. I started to tremble in the hot afternoon, the cold spreading in me like the winter wind through the trees.

After a while, your father came out, looking ahead with confidence, like a conqueror. My father followed, looking preoccupied but content. It was a powerful shake of hands between them, fuelled by the power they held. My fate was sealed with a heavy pat on the shoulder. As my mother had said, it was done.

My husband-to-be glanced towards me fleetingly. Such was his haste, in fact, that for days, I couldn't remember anything about him other than a big beard. With a curt nod he muttered, "I'll be waiting in Sighişoara for you." He mounted his horse without another word and galloped away, swallowed by the dust the hooves lifted in the dry afternoon.

I was left there, pinned down by the sun and by my

parents' eyes, melting in hopelessness.

"Why me? Why now? He doesn't seem like a nice man," I mumbled, my words smothered in the tears that ran freely down my face.

"We are honoured he wants to marry you, Cneaja," said my father. "Your mother did well to raise you like a true princess. She did well with all of our children, all good people for their country. You make sure to do the same."

"Why is everyone talking only about the children? What children? There are none," I looked about me, gesturing wildly with my arms. "What about me? Have I no say in this? I thought I was important to you."

My father looked surprised and my mother pained.

"Of course you are important," said my mother sternly, "you will be the lady of the country."

"What if I can't? What if I am weak and unworthy of all of this?" My words sounded more like a plea than a question.

My father took his eyes off me and sighed with an air of exasperation.

"Of course you can. Every woman of your rank has to. It's your duty."

You were growing inside me, taking me over bit by bit. Not just my belly with your body, but my heart with love for you, my mind with hope for your life, my limbs with tiredness, my time with church-going, and my freedom simply because, being your mother, I couldn't be or do anything else.

The four ladies-in-waiting were hovering over me all the time, capable, decisive, restless like worker bees over their queen. But I didn't feel like a queen. I felt like a prisoner in my body. My house was my cage. The town of Sighişoara was an inhospitable place full of strangers. No friendly faces and no warm people, especially not the women around me.

We went to church every day. There was no rest from the rosary and the liturgy. My talk became a subdued whisper, and I seemed to have forgotten words other than those from the scripture. The holy water was clinging to me like a sheath, the smell of incense and candles were stuck to my nostrils, and I often dreamt of a creature clad in dark clothes walking towards me.

At the beginning, the creature was far, and its steps were small and measured, just like our priest's around the altar, creeping slowly from inside his long vestments. As the weeks passed, the creature was getting closer to me, and the closer it came, the more alarming the dream, because I couldn't see its face and I couldn't even tell was it man, woman, child, or beast that haunted me. I hated this dream, and I would wake up in a sweat, the cold drops searing my goosebumps.

I wasn't a stranger to the church. I used to go with my parents every Sunday in Moldova. My father was a pious man, and he built many churches around our small country. When they were ready, he would go and visit them, and the people in the villages were happy to see him, greeting each other like good friends, talking about their business and the affairs of the country.

"If there is no rain, my lord, we are all starving," they used to say, "if there is, we are all well fed. And that is all there is to it."

Too much sun or too much frost would bring them to church to pray for forgiveness. Too little of these and they would come to pray for mercy. And when everything was right and the corn was tall and the sunflower bright like the sun, it was still the church they came to, giving their thanks and paying their respects to a God who listened. "That is why they need churches," my father would say.

I liked those times best when a whole village gathered to dance a *hora* after the sermon in front of the freshly painted church, and people generously gave away smiles and pats on the shoulder to children and neighbours and *voievod* alike. People weren't afraid of the church or the priests, they were afraid of God. He was the only one who could punish.

It wasn't like that in *Valahia*. The small church in Sighișoara wasn't painted on the outside like the one in Voroneț with the beautiful blue of the Moldavian sky. The plain stone was cold and uninviting, more like a crypt for the dead than a welcoming place for the living. The echo of the steps when coming in was deafening in the deadly silence, and every step sounded like a sentence. The paintings inside were of angry saints looking down on people unforgivingly. I couldn't find salvation there, only grief.

You, Dracula

One morning we were walking to church, the four women marching around me like the bars of a cage, when a wretched man crawled in the dust from a corner and begged me for a coin. I didn't get to see much of his face, but I remember his lips being too small to cover his teeth, which were coming out of wet, red gums like those of a wolf.

As I reached for the purse tucked at my loose belt and picked a coin to throw at the beggar, I was entirely unprepared for the commotion that followed. In an instant I could feel my human cage closing on me. One of the women grabbed hold of me and started to shout: "Don't look—close your eyes, Cneaja!" She reached out, smacking my face with her palm to cover my eyes.

I could hear the other women cursing the man and kicking him. His moans were laden with sadness, not anger, and his gasps were smothered in self-pity. The women abandoned him and turned to me, rushing me the last few steps into the church.

They let go of me only when we stepped inside, and suddenly dignified, smoothed their skirts, readying themselves to attend to me. But I was furious.

"What happened out there? Why did you treat that man that way? He is just a beggar wanting for food," I said, pushing their hands away as I would push a swarm of locusts.

But they were undeterred, smoothing my cape and straightening my bonnet.

"You can't look at ugly people, my lady," said the

oldest of them, crossing herself three times. "If you look at ugly people when you are with child, your child will be ugly, my lady, you should know that. Did your mother not teach you anything? These are important things…"

They nudged me through the small door and all the way to the front of the altar, and the priest threw more holy water at me and started to mumble his litany. I wasn't listening. Images of the rushed goodbye from my parents in front of our house while the carriage was waiting to bring me to Sighişoara paraded in front of my eyes. The memory of my mother's embrace and her tears digging into her skin brought tears to my eyes too. The two days we were allowed together before my wedding didn't make room for many words of advice on a fruitful marriage; they were filled with my sobs at such a hurried union.

Your father had the purse taken from me the next day. I guess the *voievod* of *Valahia* couldn't accept an ugly child then. Later on, he had to settle for you.

As I was coming closer to the day you were going to leave my body and enter my world, my anticipation about seeing you and holding you and looking into your eyes kept growing. And the more infatuated with you I became, the more constraints were imposed on my life.

Eating became a conundrum that tangled my everyday

life in unforeseen ways. My ladies-in-waiting were hovering over me with food all the time, so I didn't crave anything. If a craving came upon me, I had to ask somebody to fetch at once whatever I wanted and never take it myself, as it was deemed stealing. Stealing anything meant a birthmark on the baby in the shape of the stolen food, and that was the last thing we wanted.

I was allowed to eat all I wanted but I was not to skip, jump, or climb, and lifting something was a deadly sin. I had to lie down every few weeks with my belly sticking to the skies, and the women balanced a golden ring over me to make sure you were still a boy. Every time there was a full moon, I was confined to my bed because, they said, more babies are born ahead of their time on a night with a full moon.

My husband wasn't coming into our bed anymore. In fact, I hardly saw him, and when we met in the house, he would nod his head with a sharp movement. Invariably he would say to me. "Get some rest, Cneaja" and to my ladies-in-waiting, "Look after her well."

That is all I was for him: a body of valuable descendancy and strong upbringing to carry an heir for *Valahia.* I couldn't be more than that, not his wife, not his woman to share a bed with.

There were other beds he went to share, though, and other women were finding their way in and out of our house. Not young like me, mourning their childhood, but versed women, unapologetic for their looks and at peace with their status. Women who gave him pleasure in a way I didn't know how to and who stood up to him in a way I couldn't have dreamt of.

You, Dracula

It was such a woman I heard one night when waddling my belly around the house to ease the pain in my legs after a horrible dream. It was the same nightmare that kept coming back to haunt me with its faceless creature. That night, the dark shadow of a being was very close, hovering back and forth over my belly. I could hear its heavy breathing, and I could smell it too—a stench of dead leaves and rotten fish. With each heave of the creature, the baby was getting more restless in my belly, turning around, punching me from inside. I knew I was caught in a dream, but I couldn't find the way out of it, so I gathered my courage and reached with my hand for the shroud that covered the creature's head. When I touched the smooth fabric, I touched nothing else. No creature, no body, only a black veil and lace that fell suddenly in a mound over my belly. The weight of it pressing on the baby made me jump with terror, and unable to draw air anymore, I woke up in a cold sweat, only to be hit with the burning pain that slashed my stomach with the baby's every new kick.

I left my room without a torch, and I was crawling, feeling my way along the walls without making a sound. The night was young, and under the rolling clouds, the full moon was making its way up to take over the sky. A red light came through the windows, and my shadow danced on the walls like wild flames in a fire.

I wasn't meant to be out of my room, not on a full-moon night. Not until you were ready to enter the world. But I knew you were ready by the way you were pushing your fists through my skin, fighting me, fighting your way out of me. We were both ready.

You, Dracula

Your father's voice, low and loaded with menace, took me by surprise, a thunderous whisper creeping from under the door. I wanted to run back to my room, but another voice made its way through the corridors: a woman's voice, harsh and full of spite.

"You can't send me away. I will stay and be the mother of your child," she said.

"The child has a mother. I married Cneaja to carry him in her belly. There is no place for you in this house."

"You made a place for me in your bed, Vlad. You called for me every night you craved the touch of a ripened woman, not that of a raw girl. Now you have to make a place for me in your life."

Your father wasn't a weak man, Dracula, but then, neither was that woman.

"Get out of my house," he muttered in a low voice.

"Make me," she hissed back, and when I heard the harsh sound of his palm landing on her cheek and the noise of a body hitting the floor, a puddle of warm water drenched my feet while the clouds rolled over the full moon, and my eyelids sank heavy over my eyes.

I felt strong arms pulling me up and dragging me along the corridor. They barely settled me on the bed when the baby from my insides slid with ease and landed between my legs. I remember somebody screamed.

"The new *voievod* of *Valahia* is here!"

Anastasia

"I thought I knew who I was before you,
Dracula, made me your wife."

Anastasia, Târgoviște, 1456

"What a day, my lady, what a day this has been…"

The maid finished pouring the water into my tub, bowed discreetly, and closed the door behind her with a soft touch. The room was now quiet and warm, the fire gorging on the dry wood with crackles and spews. Finally, alone. The yellow flowers hanging over the fireplace sneaked into my memory and unearthed from there what I hid and bolted with seven locks earlier that day.

My secret was pulsing in the rhythm of my heart, and my skin tingled on the inside as if I were the keys of a harpsichord touched gently by a master musician, and resonating with its melody, I embraced the sweet stupor that invaded me. I stayed like that for a while, aware of my body, floating in the bathtub like a velvet red petal forgotten by the wind in the middle of a lake. Nobody to watch me.

I was desperate to decipher that mystery, to touch it

with my fingers, roll it with my hands, hold it in my palm, to make it real—if even for a moment—and then hide it again where it belonged, deep in my belly. I could feel it there, ready to be opened, on the verge of blossoming, and I parted my legs.

My hand found the way to the place where it was kept. My fingers hurried to ruffle the hair and uncovered that minuscule part that contained all of me. One touch awoke me from the sweet stupor of before, and another one sent me sliding like a burning coal on an icy slope. I was going fast, cascading, the flame never lessening, every touch smoothing the way, one coal ready to meet the whole fire, trembling from the cold and ignited. Heaven and Hell at once, both in my chest and my belly. I felt in Heaven, but I knew I was probably going to Hell. It was all I wanted.

When the last sparks died down, I fell back, suddenly aware of the tub's unpleasantly sharp edges and the lukewarm water. My secret, locked away, was safe.

It was when Bogdan touched me at the river earlier that my body started to speak to me. It was the precise moment when his lips brushed against mine and left the bittersweet taste of discovery lingering on them for all those hours. Just that one touch and one glimpse in his dark eyes. I ran from him then and wished I hadn't. I would stay now while knowing I shouldn't.

Ever since the midsummer's day celebrations had ended earlier in the day, moments of my life were full of these contradictions, my body opening to its desires and my mind closing on its boundaries. And the secret was mine to keep and live with, to unearth and touch, to cherish it or loathe myself for it.

I was thinking of the night before, the *Sânziene* night, seeing Bogdan throwing the yellow flower headdress in front of our house. My heart was beating so fast, finally free of the worry he wouldn't come. I had been fretting all night and ten times more when seeing the hours of the morning almost upon us and no headdress on my doorstep as was the tradition on midsummer's night.

It had been a long wait staring at the shadow play the moon was setting up in my room and listening to the echo of young men's steps along other streets to throw the headdresses on other doorsteps while our street stayed lonely and deserted and my doorstep bare.

I could already see from my window the sun peeking over the steeple of the church and setting the heavy bronze bell on fire when, at last, Bogdan came down our street with a perky step. I wanted to stay hidden, but I also wanted to show myself and smile and shout, *I'm here, in this house, throw the flowers here, for me—I have seen you before and I was hoping you were going to come.*

Maybe I wished him so badly to do it, or maybe he was going to do it all along, but when I saw the headdress landing at our door, I gave a little cry of joy. Maybe he heard me, or maybe he was going to do it anyway, but he looked up and I thought he saw me and smiled, and maybe there was a wink too.

I carried that smile in my head the whole morning while two maids were getting me dressed in a beautiful white blouse, an *ie* made of the finest linen my father could pay for.

"Did you hear the owl last night in the elm tree?" asked one of them, fixing my skirts.

"I did," said the other, "how could I not? It wouldn't shut up, the stupid bird."

"Why do you call it stupid? I thought owls are wise."

"People say that about them, don't they? But they also say that when you hear the call of the owl, it's a call for a death in that house," she said and nearly bit her tongue trying to take the words back.

"I am sorry, my lady, I shouldn't have said that. I am sure it's just old folk talk that nobody believes anymore. Please forgive me, I shouldn't have said anything, my mouth sometimes speaks without my head."

I didn't care about her mouth or the owl. I cared about the dance that afternoon and about seeing the man who left the headdress for me. The yellow flowers were so fresh, and they had pride of place on my dressing table, smiling at me from all their small blossoms covered in the morning dew. I felt my lips parting into a smile too.

"What are these flowers called?" I asked just to hide the grin that was taking over my face.

"The lady's bedstraw, my lady—it's a wildflower that comes out only now, at this time of the year. The fairies gave it magic powers last night when they had their dance in the forest. Now you'll wear it yourself at your own dance today."

The maids were fussing around me, plumping the white blouse and combing my hair.

"Can't we go now?" I asked with hope and

impatience.

"No, my lady, we are waiting for the dew," said one of the girls, and she sent a know-it-all smile over my head to the other one.

I didn't mind, it was my first year to be given the headdress, and I was hoping it would be the last. I wanted to be married. I wanted to marry the dark-eyed boy.

"What dew? What does that have to do with the *Sânziene* dance?"

Just then, somebody else came in, an older woman, and by her stature I could tell she was the maid who served my mother before she died. I couldn't see her face; her head was buried down between her shoulders and covered with the hood from her long cape. My maids were bustling with anticipation, but Petra kept looking down, avoiding their stare, her own eyes focused on a piece of white cloth in her hands.

"Did you meet anybody?" the girls wanted to know, and she shook her head. No she didn't, the ritual was observed and safe, no words exchanged with strangers. They seemed pleased, all of them, with her undertaking.

"Can we wash her, then?"

Petra handed them the cloth, and I noticed only then that it was wet—not dripping wet but heavier than it should have been and limp with the moisture. One of the girls took it from her hands with great care and came towards me.

"This cloth is wet with dew gathered this morning from the lady's bedstraw flowers in the forest. If you wash your face with it, you will be healthy and you will know the love of a man this year. Take it, my lady."

She offered me the cloth and I took it, careful not to seem too eager. I could feel my heart pumping hard, as if the touch of the fabric were Bogdan's hands, the young man I had hoped to come to my house to give me a flower crown and make me his queen. I wiped my face with the cloth as if it were the holy water in the church. It felt precious to me. It was going to help me make a special life for myself. And this life was going to be together with the man I chose.

When my face was washed, my two maids lifted the headdress and fitted it on my head with some pins, then stepped back and looked at me with affection. The old woman took off her hood and looked me up and down with pride.

"I am allowed to talk now, and I can see you and by God, you are so beautiful. I wish your mother, God bless her soul, was here to see you on such a fateful day, with your fresh headdress, ready to go and find the husband you wish for." She stepped towards me and gathered me in an embrace, which took me by surprise.

I hoped she didn't know—how could she know of my lie, the secret I kept buried in my heart since I was little? The lie that made my mother die.

I wish somebody knew about it if only to tell me, did she die because of what I did? Was it me, my dishonesty that wintery day many, many years ago when we couldn't play outside because of the snowstorm that made her stop holding and kissing me and then made her stop breathing?

You, Dracula

The big vase had always been on the round table at the entrance hall in our house. Ever since I could remember, I was told it was made in Murano and brought to Târgoviște all the way from Venice, which was a rich place across many seas full of people who went to parties with masks on their faces and rode to church in boats. I liked that vase; it had colours I didn't see in our dusty town, and they glowed and sparkled when the candles were lit around it. It must have been important, too, because it came from such a great distance. I had never seen a sea, but they told me it was far and wide, and sometimes it was warm like the water in my bath and sometimes stormy like the Argeș River.

I didn't mean to knock it down. It was an accident, a mistake, an unfortunate moment of too much glee when one of the young servants was playing with me, chasing me around that table howling like a mad dog in the middle of the night. We watched it tilt, and before either of us could reach it, the vase lay in smithereens on the rocky floor. We looked at each other, and I could see the fright taking hold of the other girl's face at the same time as tears found free run on mine. We were both petrified in the middle of the hall, surrounded by such colourful proof of our dark deed.

When I heard my name being called by mother's maid, I started to shake and tremble as if I had just come back from the storm outside.

"She knows... she knows already," was all I could utter. "How did she find out?"

"Nobody knows, nobody saw anything, they didn't know it was us. They can't know. Please, be strong and don't tell."

The girl was now so close to me I could see the terror in her eyes. She reached out for my hands and squeezed with all her might.

"They can't find out," she pleaded with me. "I will be thrown out, please, I can't lose this work. Please don't tell."

I started to climb the stairs to my mother's chambers, slow, sluggish, my steps laden with guilt. I waited outside the door for a moment in the hope my tears would dry out. After a moment or two, the door opened suddenly and the maid, ready to call my name again, got a fright seeing me right in front of her, like a ghost in the middle of a dark corridor. She opened the door wider and gestured for me to come in.

Mother was in bed as she had been for weeks now, still wearing her kind and loving smile on her still beautiful face, only thinner and paler by the day. Petra pulled me gently into the room while she stepped out and closed the door behind her. I shuffled towards the bed, ready to burst out with my terrible news yet thinking of the girl's plea to keep it a secret. I was terrified because I had never had a secret before, but the thought of having one was also tempting and made me feel important, with the servant's work hanging on my every word.

Mother's eyes opened slowly, and I thought she would guess then, she would know just by looking at my face that I had done something wrong. Should I say it before she guessed it? Should I forget about the little girl's trouble and confess? Stay honest as I was always told?

We both opened our mouths to speak at the same time, but her hand's gentle touch on my face made me hesitate.

"I am going to go soon, my love, on a trip, for a while…" she whispered.

Should I tell her now? I was thinking. *Should she know about the vase before she goes on her trip?*

"When are you going, mother? When will you be back?" I asked, thinking that maybe it would be better to tell her when she returned.

She started to speak slowly and with great effort, but I wasn't really listening, my mind full of the colourful pieces glistening on the floor in the hall. I hoped the girl had cleaned them up quickly as she promised. Next moment, I decided I couldn't live with that secret for however long she would be gone so I opened my mouth to talk. My mother squeezed my hand.

"So, Anastasia, even if I am gone for a long time, you have to remember that you are perfect in every way, and I love you with all my heart. You are so beautiful that my eyes can't get enough of you, so smart that I would listen to you speak all the time, so joyful that you light up everybody's heart. Learn new things all the time, stay honest, and obey your father because he only wants what is best in the world for you. Stay perfect as you are, and you will be so easy to love."

I didn't grasp much of what she meant by telling me all that, but I understood she loved me because she thought I was honest, and that was when I knew I couldn't tell her about the vase anymore. It was too late.

You, Dracula

Later on, when my father broke the news that mother was dead, gone far away and never coming back, I regretted my hasty decision. I was only five years old then, and for a while, I thought it was me and my lie that sent her away. I thought she tested me on my honesty, that she must have known about the vase, and she was waiting for me to tell her, and when I didn't, she had no choice but to stop loving me. She must have left, I thought, because I was not perfect anymore.

Over time I was shown care and deference from all the women in the house, but it didn't feel like love. Petra, my mother's maid, hovered over me all those years, making sure things were done right for me and that I was well looked after. Yet her embrace from earlier took me by surprise because it had never happened before.

I knew my father had loving thoughts for me although he wasn't able to talk about them or show me his love. And that just wasn't enough anymore. I wanted to feel the presence of love. I wanted to feel love in my stomach and in my chest and no guilt in my head.

We had a big house in the best neighbourhood of Sighișoara. A coveted street where some of the most important people of the country lived. Marele Vornic, the Great Judge, lived in the house next to ours. His house was even bigger. But then, so was his job. The *hatman,* the chief of the army, was a few doors down, too, and he was always in our house talking about important things with my father, who was a *dregator*, the governor in charge of the country's safekeeping.

That morning, the maids led me straight into my father's rooms, where he seemed buried in papers. The smell of the warm wax that he used for his seal was forever clinging to the walls of that room, and sometimes I thought my father himself was covered in its distinct scent of tobacco and incense. I don't remember my mother's smell if she had one. She was too long gone. When I thought about her, all I remembered was guilt.

I went to kiss my father, but he stopped me, holding my shoulders at arms' length. He looked at me with a mixture of wonder, pride and worry, the kind of all-at-once emotions that only a father can muster for his daughter.

"You got your flower crown," he said with relief at my being courted and uneasiness at my being sought after. "Your first crown… Are you not too young to get a crown?"

I started to laugh because he was most certainly jesting.

"At eighteen, I'm already old for my first crown, *tată.* I thought it would never come."

"Well, it did, and I still think it's too early. I was hoping you were going to stay with me here in the house for a little longer." He touched the yellow flowers in my crown gently, and then he touched my face. "You know

I want what's best for you, never think otherwise."

I laughed again and then broke the tender moment with a noisy peck on his cheek.

"I'm going to do whatever I have to do today to get a husband, and you can't stop me."

"I'm not trying to stop you; I know you can't be stopped. I just locked away all the young men of Sighișoara," he laughed. "You know, to protect them from you…"

We parted with good humour, and the gaiety of that moment put me at ease with the day ahead.

Petra was the one who knew the order of things and the meaning of everything for the celebration of *Sânziene*, and I was happy to follow her lead. We passed through the long corridors of the house, and I held my head high and my smile wide. My father's many subordinates, going about their business, bowed with a kind smile when seeing my headdress. I was light on my feet and opened my heart for whatever the day would bring.

The old maid brought us out, and the warm June sun enveloped us with its glow. The long white blouse I was wearing was caressing my body, fluttering in the breeze. We walked past the corner of our street, and once in the *piața*, I saw other small groups, just like ours, of maids or mothers surrounding a young girl with the yellow flower crown. The older women were purposeful in their stride. The younger ones, like me—a little shy, a little fearful— some willing and some rather scared, walked with their heads down, stealing a glimpse every now and again at the other girls from under the yellow flowers.

You, Dracula

The main square seemed brighter today and cleaner. The people didn't seem sad or preoccupied like they did on any normal day, and nobody was rushing. The lady's bedstraw flowers were adorning the tradesmen's stalls and doors. A group of *lăutari*, three musicians, were tuning their instruments. The fiddle didn't seem to be wailing as it did on other occasions but seemed to dance when touched by the bow. The sense of celebration was hanging from that bow and from the musician's hand, from the yellow flowers dressing up the windows, from the smiles on people's faces, and it was covering me. I was drenched in it. *Sânziene* had arrived, and I was wearing a crown.

We came into the *piaţa* from different corners and alleyways and from different walks of life. Yet rich or poor, daring or shy, beautiful or less so, we were all made equal by the long white blouses and the flower headdresses. All young, zestful, innocent, and curious to walk the path of discovery. And we were all going to church.

I felt strangely naked when we had to remove our headdresses in front of the priest. I thought my yearning for whatever was to come, my longing to see Bogdan, my desire to stare into his eyes and read my future were written on my forehead for everybody to see and judge just as I could see it on the other girls in the church.

The priest was blessing the crowns, and I couldn't wait to get mine back. He was slow and his mumble was the only thing that didn't seem like a celebration that day. The movement of his hand spreading the holy water over the flowers was as slow as the sign of the cross at a funeral, not joyful or jubilant as it was for betrothals or weddings. I most certainly wasn't there for a funeral.

When we came out of the church, things were new again. There was a lot of fuss around a cart full of golden wheat that was settled now in the middle of the square. I remembered this from other midsummers when, as a girl, I could come here with bunches of wildflowers and help the young girls to weave them in their crowns. And now it was my turn. Other girls were bringing the flowers to me, helping me weave all the good things in my crown so my marriage would be lucky and healthy, prosperous and fertile and full of love.

Two little girls came to me with their fresh bunches: wheat for prosperity, chamomile for colds, jasmine for an abundance of love and money, mint for the eyes, rosemary for bearing children. They were all there, in the tiny fists, offered to me with kindness by hopeful girls, just like I once was.

We started to work around the cart, helping each other, sharing the bounty of fresh flowers that were enchanting us with their smells and their colours. We were laughing, careless, and happy, weaving stems and words into the story of that day.

When my crown was finished, it looked perfect, and the two little girls helped me replace it on my head. I looked around me. The other young women, like me, looked more self-assured. We exchanged smiles and held hands. Behind us, small groups of young men were gathering. Some daring. Some tall. Many smiling. A lot willing and appraising. All of them impatient.

You, Dracula

That was when the musicians started the *Drăgaică*, the music for the old dance of the fairies. We gathered in a circle and started the slow dance. I had seen the moves all those years before when I was helping with the flowers and watching from the side. When the music started, my legs knew what to do, my body taken by the rhythm, my heart keeping it. I was finally dancing the *hora* I had been dreaming of.

The old women in the town were saying that even the sun rests in the sky at midday to watch our dance, and that is why the day is the longest in the year.

We kept moving around in the circle, and that was when I saw Bogdan again. I recognized his broad shoulders and his determined walk. His eyes were following me and spoke to me of a secret. I suddenly became so conscious of my every move, my back became straighter, my hips undulating, my breasts hard under my blouse. I let myself sway with the music, unaware of the other girls, my eyes closed, my lips hot.

But then I felt a hand grabbing my arm and pulling me away from the *hora*. I stumbled and tripped on my long white dress. It was Petra, my mother's maid, with a pained look in her eyes and an anger I hadn't seen before.

"What did you do? Who gave you this?" With a quick move, she snatched the crown from my head and showed me one of the plants in it. It had small white heads of fragile flowers and delicate leaves. She pulled it out of the crown.

"What is wrong with it? What are you doing?" I asked full of dread.

"It's hemlock, *cucută*, Anastasia, it brings death! It should never have been in your crown—it's poisonous and it brings bad luck. Who gave it to you?" she cried.

I didn't know. Was it one of the little girls, was it one of the young women? Was it meant for me, or had it just found me amongst all of us there?

Petra ripped the flower away and threw it on the ground. Her long and bony fingers mended the rest of the crown, adding more wheat and jasmine, but the spell was broken for me. I watched the other girls finishing the dance, swaying to the rhythm of the music, their faces reddening from the effort, the heat, and the emotion. I was stone cold and petrified. The only emotions running through me were humiliation and dismay.

"I want to go home," I said, turning around to my maids.

But Bogdan was suddenly there, right in front of me, his eyes still enticing me into a secret, his hand reaching for mine.

"Nevermind the *Drăgaică*," he said, "it's time for the swim. Let's go," and with one smooth move, he circled his arm around my waist and pulled me along with all the other couples.

I was easily convinced. I could feel the strength of his arm leading me, his breath skimming my ear, his broad shoulders inviting. I looked behind and saw Petra scolding my two maids and trampling the white flower in the dust, but I didn't care. It wasn't important to me, could harm me no longer.

You, Dracula

The Târnava River was quick and its waters cold, never lingering in the sun long enough to warm up. It sparkled in the afternoon light and was inviting, promising to cool down the fire that was burning within us.

"I am Bogdan," he said, starting to loosen the wide girdle from around his waist. I was mesmerised by his large palms touching the small buckles, and a shiver ran through me as if he were undoing mine.

I could feel his gaze over me, but I was unable to look back at him or to say that I knew of him, that I had watched him many times learning the skills of the sword and the arch in the town *piața*, that I had asked to do all the chores I could only to pass through that square and set eyes on his broad shoulders and strong arms, hoping he would take a look at me, too, and that I did it every week for the past winter and spring.

The girdle fell in the grass at his feet. He wasn't moving anymore. He was waiting.

"Bogdan, I said, that's my name. I hope you remember me from the *piața*. I certainly remember you," he said, and my heart jumped in surprise and delight.

His voice was deep, and the words sounded distinct and precise. I gathered myself and lifted my eyes. He was smiling. I could see that much. There was a glimmer of delight on his face, the way his lips were lifted at the corners. His manner was sweet but cavalier.

I grabbed my crown and deposited it on the grass beside his belt without a word. I sprinted towards the water, shaking my sandals off. Last thing to go before jumping was my belt. The river welcomed me, and its rapid waters swallowed me quickly up to my waist. I was fighting to stand in the middle of the current, and I struggled to turn around to see how far behind I had left Bogdan.

It was that moment, when I turned around, the moment his lips brushed my ear, when my body spoke to me and whispered about secrets that it held and fires that were waiting to be sparked inside. He was standing now just a breath away from me. Our shirts were wet and clinging to our bodies, which were craving a touch, a caress, anything but nothing. Bogdan's arm moved, his big palm reaching out. He could have covered my face in it, he could have enveloped the whole of me between his shoulders.

"Anastasia!" Petra's voice reached me from the shore, worried, upset, pleading.

My legs were soft, and they wouldn't carry me through the current. I wanted to remain there in its midst, to be swallowed by the water and travel with it fast, hitting the shores, whirling in its banks, following its urgent flow until the final outpour.

"Come back, Anastasia! You'll catch your cold."

I started slowly, battling the rush of the river, suddenly feeling the chill taking hold of me and becoming conscious of all the eyes that were escorting me to my maids. Let them look, I didn't care about their stares. I cared about Bogdan's, fastened on my spine, clinging to my neck and brushing my hair.

Petra wrapped me up in a large white cloth, picked up my crown, and pushed me gently towards the path back to the town. Before the two young maids closed in behind me, I turned around and searched for Bogdan. Coming out of the river against the setting sun, with water dripping from his long black hair, he looked like a creature made by gods.

"This is the last custom of *Sânziene*, Anastasia," said Petra when we reached our house that late afternoon. "The throwing of the crown."

The other two maids seemed eager to pursue this, whatever it was.

I was unsure: "Throw it? Can't I keep it? It's beautiful."

Petra mumbled something about hemlock and death and the bad luck it could bring, but I wasn't paying attention to her.

"You have to throw the headdress on the roof of your house. If it lands and stays there, you are going to marry this year. If it falls, you have to keep trying until it stays there, hooked on the roof, and that's how many years you'll have to wait for your wedding," said one of the maids with excitement.

The four of us looked at the house, and for the first time I didn't like that we lived in such a big one. From where I was standing in the street, it seemed too tall, the two stories impossible to conquer. The fox at the heart of our crest on the door seemed to be appraising me to see my worth. The headdress in my hands seemed suddenly too heavy.

I stepped back as far as I could. I squeezed the crown at my chest and wished it luck and then threw it with all my might. It didn't make it to the roof, not even close. We all gasped, and in the silence that followed, I was sure I heard my heart tearing like a piece of paper. The fall was imminent, and with it all my hopes for marriage that year, but then, by the grace of God, my father opened a window, and the crown got caught in its lock.

We all looked at Petra, the keeper of all traditions and the knower of all answers. There was no heart left in me to beat its drum.

"It counts, it's hanging by the house, it will be this year," she said with confidence, and I smothered her in a shameless embrace. My father was smiling too.

"And who is this young man?" he asked.

"It's Bogdan Spătaru, master; his father is Mare Spătar, the chief of cavalry," said Petra. "She did well. Our girl did very well."

There was a sense of celebration that evening in our house. A pig was slaughtered, the silver was brought out, the candles lit, and the keys to the cellar changed hands. People came to the house, and the red wine was flowing from beautifully painted glasses. I was happy that they came. I was even happier when they left. I loved their joy for me, but I was eager to find my own joy, to uncover my secret.

And I did as soon as I was left alone.

The water in the bathtub was getting cold, but the memories were so alive, my body so in tune with them that I wanted that evening never to end. I closed my eyes, searching for my secret again. I didn't want to open it, I just wanted to know that it was still there.

My hand was finding its way between my legs again when the door flew open, and the maid came in screaming.

"The new *voievod* of *Valahia* is here!"

Mara

"I wanted to be your lover, but you, Dracula,
Took me for a fantasy and made me a slave."

Mara, Poenari, 1456

Our hut was dark and stuffy. I was lying on my bed, listening to my father's snores from the other side of the makeshift curtain, just like every other night. I could hear my mother talking to my brother, trying to sooth him and his scorching lips. I knew she had the wet cloth over his face, dripping the cold water onto his lips, trying to cool down his burning body and murmuring sweet lies, "You are going to get well, Gheorghiță. I will look after you and you will be well again. Drink the water, come on, drink it."

I could hear his delirious mumbles, "...the horse is going too fast, can you stop it...? I'm going to fall... somebody, please, help..." His rumble was constant in my ear during the night, and it had been for days now, since he got sick. There was no escape from his babble or from his sickness.

You, Dracula

The mattress was hard; the straw in it was pressed down and didn't give me any comfort. Every time I moved, it popped through the worn linen and stabbed me in the back like any enemy would do. I put my other dress under my head as a pillow, but the difference it made didn't matter. There was no other place for the dress anyway.

Overwhelmed by the cries beyond the curtain, I got up and crawled out through the small window. The forest was quiet except for my steps on the dry kindling. I tiptoed through the leaves and cones of last autumn and ignored the pins that were prickling the soles of my feet. They weren't hurting me as much as the straw in the mattress did. Nothing could hurt me as much as the poverty we lived in.

My father was a woodcutter, and we had a mule. The mule always got to eat more than us because, my father said, without the animal carrying the wood to Târgoviște, we'd be no more. They were working hard, man and beast together, but no matter how much wood got cut and carried, it was still not enough.

There was little food unless my father caught a deer, and there were no clothes unless some of the townspeople showed some mercy seeing my father's torn rags. I had two dresses, but sometimes, in the summer, I had to do with one.

The summers were always harder because townspeople didn't use the wood to keep themselves warm. Should I be upset at the sun for shining? Or should I be upset at the blacksmith for taking most of my father's wood and giving him pots and pans in return?

We had a lot of those but very little to put in them. Why didn't the seamstress need more wood so we'd have new dresses, or the shoemaker to give us some shoes? We had no use for pots and pans.

I would have loved to have shoes. In the winter, my mother would use all the old rags and wrap them around our feet to keep them from freezing. Walking through snow was painful, but how else would I get from home to the church to clean it?

When I finished my chores the first time I was there, I went looking for the priest to get my pay, and I was hoping it would be food or money. He inspected in all corners, wiping his finger on all the walls and paintings, looking for dust or dirt. He was a young man, but his thick and dark eyebrows gave him a stern look, and I couldn't tell, when he finished, if he was pleased with my work or not. He came close to me and gave me a blessing. I had been blessed before in the church, and I didn't have to work for it, so I stood in front of him waiting still for my pay.

"Well, young girl, you did a good job here."

"Thank you, Father. Can I get my pay now?"

His eyebrows moved together in a frown, and he seemed suddenly upset.

"I told your mother that we don't pay in money or things, but in salvation," he said. He turned around and went inside the sanctuary.

When I recounted the story to my mother that

evening, she said that I should think myself lucky. Not many girls could clean the house of God like I could. And this was how I got my first lesson in kindness at eight years old.

The forest was opening to me as it always did, calm and dark. I never ventured too far away during the night, but it wasn't for fear of it. It was my home more than the hut we lived in. The hut was made out of its wood and sat on its land. The forest could swallow us or grow its branches over us anytime, but it didn't.

The shadows were dense, the full moon wasn't coming for another few days, and not much of its light was piercing through the canopy of the trees. I didn't need the light to guide me, I knew my way. I was coming close to the meadow when the cold breeze caressed the leaves of the linden trees and made them flaunt the scents of their delicate flowers. The jasmine responded from the bushes, and for a moment, the forest smelled lush and lavish just like the perfume shop in Târgovişte. The smell dreams were made of.

When I returned to the house, there was more than the light of the fire flickering through the windows of the hut. Could it be a candle? We couldn't afford candles, so one would be lit only on special occasions. I could see my mother's shadow collapsing to the floor, and then I heard her scream.

"Don't leave us, Gheorghiţă! Don't go, it's not your time, my son, my baby…"

Was he dead already, did he die while I was in the forest? This was so much faster than my other two brothers who died before him. It took them a week to give up on living. They wanted so much to stay alive, and they were screaming when their turn came, "Mama, please do something! I'm burning, don't let me die," begging her for water and air. And she kept saying, promising them, she wouldn't let that happen, but she did.

The two of them left us last winter, just around the time the priest said we should celebrate the birth of Jesus. We were happy for Jesus to be born but also sad for my brothers' deaths, so there was no celebration for us that year. The priest wouldn't have their dead bodies in the church because he couldn't honour a birth and two deaths at the same time, but he came to bless the graves at the side of the house, and that was special. The two small graves had big crosses made of the most expensive wood, *pădurea veche*, the Old Forest had to offer. My father wouldn't skimp for his sons.

I went into the house through my window, not wanting to step through the door straight upon the dead body. The curtain was still pulled, just as I had left it. My mother had hung it there when my breasts started to grow under my dress and I started to bleed every month. "You're a grown woman, now, soon to be married. Don't let your brothers see what you have. It belongs to your husband when we find one for you." I was eighteen now, and there was no husband. And I didn't want one that my parents could get me—hard-working or even honest but poor. He'd better not be poor at all.

My mother pulled the curtain just as I steadied myself. She stepped aside with her head down, sobbing. I was petrified in my place, my back against the window, taking in the stillness that had overwhelmed our house. His small body was there, white like the jasmine flowers in the forest, but he wasn't. There was nothing in his place, no joy, no anger, no fear, not even surprise in the face of what was to come. Nothing. Just stillness, but stillness couldn't replace my brother.

I was just about to step farther into the room when my mother gave a sharp scream and pushed me hard until I fell down as if struck by a scythe.

"Your shadow, Mara—your shadow was over him, over Gheorghiţă! What a curse to fall on us!" she lamented. "Our family is cursed. You better take us all, Lord. Why live, why live with this curse?"

Gheorghiţă's twin brother started to cry, frightened, and my father grabbed my mother by the shoulders and shook her hard. I pulled myself up and watched her torment. What else could I do?

"What is it, woman, what happened? I know Gheorghiţă died, but this is not a curse, it's a blessing for him, his pain is gone. No more suffering for him…"

My mother squirmed out of his hold and looked at me with anger.

"Mama, you're scaring me, what did I do? I don't understand."

She let out a cry and then collapsed near my brother's body. Between sobs, she uttered:

"If the shadow of a man falls upon a corpse, the dead will become undead."

In the morning, my mother sent me outside to pick wild garlic, and that was when the meaning of what she had said started to seep through my mind. People were coming to the church from time to time with stories of *strigoi* and *moroi*, vampires and ghosts, asking the priest what to do about this dead or that long-gone aunt who kept coming back to steal the milk from the cow, a lost child who torments his mother's other children, or awful-looking people who climb up on the belfry of the church and call the names of folk who would be found dead the next day.

There were stories and there were cures. The priest would say to pray more, but the people who knew the cure would mount a young girl on a young mare and lead her through the cemetery over the graves. If the mare would not go over a grave, they were sure to have found a vampire. And then they'd take that body out and chop it and burn it and bury it again at a crossroads. People were praying, too, but God had no power over *moroi*. Only the Devil did.

I went into the forest to get the garlic. It was growing freely on the floor of the woods, and the delicate flowers left a sticky liquid on my fingers. It smelled familiar, of a dish my mother used to make when we had deer. The earthy smell brought unwanted memories of all my brothers when they were alive and roaming about the Old Forest to pick mushrooms for that broth.

Three gone, lost to the big cough. No coins to buy the medicine to cure them. Was I next? Was I going to lie on my bed of straw, as white as the jasmine and the garlic flower, as still as the bark of the trees and empty of all my dreams?

I pulled the garlic from the soil with its roots and brought the bundle back home. My father was gone. Two women from the village whom he must have called were helping my mother wash Gheorghiţă's body. He was awfully skinny and small for a boy of five. His twin was a bit stronger, but he was always the one shovelling the last crumbs from the table into his mouth and eating the wild blackberries when they were still green. He wasn't anywhere to be seen.

"Where's Voicu?" I asked. The three women were silent and preoccupied.

"He is outside digging the grave. I couldn't have him looking at Gheorghiţă dead and naked like that. The upset of it all," my mother said, shaking her head without lifting her eyes, "and the curse…"

I gave her the garlic and she took it without another word and gestured for me to leave again. I was halfway to the door when I heard her give a little scream full of pain and horror. I turned and when I set eyes on that sight, my mouth filled with a vile concoction that my stomach had churned. The sudden spasm shook me from inside out, and it all came out, spilling on the ground.

"Mara!" screamed my mother again and pushed me outside. "Go, go, you've done enough already. Your shadow did enough already…"

I was relieved to go; the sight of that woman shovelling garlic into my dead brother's mouth had broken my heart. I stumbled outside, barely catching my footing, and went to cry at the side of the hut. Gheorghiţă's twin, Voicu, was scratching at the surface of the soil trying to dig the grave. He threw the shovel to the ground, ran into my arms, and started to cry with me.

I stayed like that for a little while thinking, *When was the last time I held him? Maybe not since he was a baby…* and I remembered having to carry him while my mother carried Gheorghiţă. I heard her steps coming towards us, but I didn't let go of Voicu—I needed to hold onto him like I needed to hold onto life.

"When somebody dies, their spirit leaves the body through their mouth, and this is how we know they're dead," I heard my mother saying. "But your shadow passed over Gheorghiţă, and his spirit might be taken by the dark shadows to make him a vampire." She took another step and put her arm on my shoulder.

"If they do, well, there will be no way for his spirit to come back in." I lifted my eyes and looked at her.

"Vampires hate garlic," she said, wiped a tear from my cheek, and gathered us both in a loose embrace.

We didn't have money for a coffin or for a funeral or

for bread to break with neighbours as was customary. The priest said he would say mass for Gheorghiță if we brought him to the church, and he would do it without charge because I was cleaning the church so well.

So the next morning my mother took down the curtain that separated my pile of straw from the rest of the hut and wrapped Gheorghiță in it. There was a lot of curtain for such a small boy. We ate a handful of berries, and the mule got some stale bread saved for him from the previous day.

My father lifted the body onto the cart, and we left the house in silence, a mule and four tearless ghosts. We had cried ourselves to sleep the night before; the tears were all gone, yet the pain stayed. Even my father, when he came in after the day's work and saw the tiny man on the table with a garlic leaf escaping from his mouth, shed a tear. "Only a few of us left," he said, put his head down on the mattress, and turned his back to us all.

I don't remember much from the church; the smell of incense made me pay more attention to my empty belly, and a growl made the priest jump. I had seen this church many times, and I had prayed to the saints on the walls for food or for clothes sometimes and shoes and honey and maybe a necklace. I always prayed for a kind man with money in his purse to marry me and share with me what was his, and sometimes, if I closed my eyes, he would come. But today's prayer was different, without me knowing it at first, until its words formed inside my head one by one.

"Please, God, don't let me die. Not today, or tomorrow, not ever. I am scared of not being, scared of the stillness, scared for my spirit to leave my body. Please God, don't ever let a breath of mine be the last one I take."

When I opened my eyes, the mass was over, and the priest was putting out the candle.

"Take it home and light it again at the grave and say another prayer for his soul," he said, putting the candle in my mother's hand. "I can't come all the way into the forest; you'll have to make do without me."

We left the church as we came, with heavy hearts. We followed the mule and made sure Gheorghiţă's body was not falling off the cart. My mother picked up the curtain every time the wind blew it away with a sigh. My brother's steps got smaller and smaller, and my father scooped him up in his arms, where he fell asleep, his head dangling.

When we arrived back home, he settled Voicu on the ground. The boy screeched a little when his tiny body touched the musty leaves. He opened his eyes, ready to start crying, but seeing my father's face looming over his, he changed his mind and went back to sleep. The old man set himself to finish digging the grave. The soil was always cold and hard, hidden from the warmth of the sun in the shadows of the Old Forest. Cutting into it was hard. My father wasn't a weak man, and he could put down a big tree with a few blows of the axe, but the battle with the earth seemed to consume him and drain all his power. My mother and I sat by him, listening to the sound of the shovel thumping in our ears, wishing it to end and yet never, ever to end.

The hole was only a little wider than Gheorghiţă's body when my father put the shovel away, worn out.

"It will have to do. Wake Voicu, get him up. It's time," he said.

My mother went into the hut to light the candle from the fire, and I whispered Voicu's name to no avail. The poor boy was still fast asleep. I called again, and when I saw he didn't hear me, I went over and gave him a little push. He jumped in fright, and trying to pick himself up, he lost his foothold and slipped into the grave.

His cry and the terrified look on his face tore my heart apart. My parents rushed to pick him up, and he scrambled straight into my mother's arms, watching me with fear and reproach.

I stepped back in shock, and searing tears got free rein on my face. My father lowered Gheorghiţă's body into the ground with rushed moves, accompanied by Voicu's desperate sobbing. My mother tried her best to shush him but gave up. She put him down again and reached to the back of her skirt. I couldn't see what it was at first— it looked like a piece of metal reflecting the pale light of the dying sun. It was only when she lowered herself into the grave that I could see the sickle in her hand, and when she fitted it around my brother's neck, I felt my legs weakening. My father and I looked at each other, bewildered.

"I had to, in case he wants to leave the grave, if he becomes a vampire… his neck will get caught in it." Then she smoothed her skirt and her hair and climbed out of the grave.

"Let us pray."

The whole forest fell quiet, the badgers and the leaves with the worms and the wind. When the first shovel of soil hit Gheorghiţă's face under the curtain, it seemed like an avalanche, a whole mountain falling on top of me, collapsing my whole world.

"Please, God, don't ever let me die."

I was happy when my father said I was to clean another church. It wasn't the scrubbing that made me happy but the promise of food he was given in exchange for my work, and I hoped there would be enough for us and the mule this time.

This other church was in Târgovişte, and hadn't I always wanted to be out of the forest, living in a place that had more than one street and one church? Târgovişte had three churches, and the streets were so many that they had to give them names to help you know where you were.

I had been to Târgovişte four times during cold winters when my father needed extra help to deliver the wood, but now I was going to go with him every week, and that meant walking its many alleyways just like all the other people who seemed busy and important and had places to be in their expensive clothes.

The priest in my new church wasn't different from other priests, but the church was. It was built with stone from the Făgăraș Mountains instead of timber from the Old Forest; it had paintings covering the walls and coloured glass in the tall windows. It was big. It needed a lot of cleaning, and I was doing it all as quickly as I could because after that, I was free. Free to roam about the place, free to notice colours and fabrics and dresses, free to take in the smells of roasted pigs and baked breads, free to listen to whispers about money and fame, people who ruled, and the others, like me, who were ruled.

Something wasn't right when we came into the city for the fifth week. There was an unusual stillness. There was no bustle at the gates, no scared horses, no beggars grabbing at the wheels of our cart. There were guards, though, and unlike any other time, they asked us about our business and looked under our logs in the cart.

"Just wood for the fire," said my father, baffled by all the fuss.

As we made our way through the cobbled alleys towards the centre of Târgoviște, my father pointed at the black cloths hanging from the windows of each house like menacing flags after a lost battle.

"Death," he said, "it looks like death to me." There was a chill in the air, not only the autumn chill, but something dire, a sort of thick darkness like soot that was dampening the morning light.

He dropped me in front of the church. While climbing the steps to the door, I could hear him swear at the mule.

You, Dracula

It was not in an angry way; it was more like begging the animal to remove them from there.

I opened the church door slowly, my heart pounding as I took the first small steps in, my head trying to tell my heart there was nothing to be scared about—just another day of cleaning just another church. The candles in the centre were lit, their murky light crawling on the walls. I fixed the door back on its latch, determined to finish my jobs quickly, to go out again on the streets, to find the people who had not been swallowed by the stillness, people who made loud noises and moved around with a spring in their step.

I hadn't seen the corpse, not at first, not until I had my dusting cloths out and the bucket filled with water from the fountain in the corner, not until I put my scarf over my head to tie my mane of hair and blessed myself three times. Only then, I took my steps inside and looked in front of me at the altar and inside the box that was sitting in the centre of the church guarded by the candles. That is when I saw the corpse and its face streaked with cuts.

He didn't seem peaceful like my dead brothers did, as if they had just been embraced by the angels. The man lying in the box was fearless and stubborn and ready to fight the darkness in front of him. The cuts on his face made him appear cruel and ready for revenge. Mad and thunderous. He didn't seem to have been finished with life when it left him.

I circled the box, unable to take my eyes off the body, contemplating this new kind of death that takes you unawares and leaves a mound of useless flesh behind for the worms to eat. In the end, after I shed a tear for my dead brothers and another for my parents who were getting ready day after day to welcome their own deaths, I pulled the blanket that was covering the body over his face, too, and went to the big cross at the altar where Jesus was hanging in pain, and I prayed.

"Please, don't ever let me die," I murmured.

"Oh, but that is a silly wish, girl."

The two small doors of the sanctuary opened, and the priest stepped out through them, clad in black. He was polishing the chalice he used for mass. He had to do that himself because women were never allowed near the altar in our church. My mother said it had to do with our cleanliness in the face of God, but I never understood why I was clean enough to scrub the rest of the church yet not that spot and not that goblet. I didn't mind because it meant less work for me, less time spent in the darkness of that death place full of ghost saints and more time spent in the brightness of the bustling streets with their lively people.

"I'm sorry, Father," I said, startled, as he had never spoken to me that kindly before. "It's just that, you see, my people die around me, and it makes me scared to see them like that, with no life left in them, no thoughts, no joy, no sadness, nothing left of who they were. Just the body. They were my brothers, and then they were nothing."

"But think of all the people you will see dying if you are alive forever. Think of all the pain and the sadness you'll go through again and again. But when you die that once, you can go to the right of our Father and stay in his light forever."

The priest came closer and pulled me gently to look at the body in the box.

"Look at this man. The *voievod* of *Valahia*, killed on the battlefield. This man has done things for his country and left children behind who will remember him as he was in his life."

He turned around then with a swish of his black robes and went back into the sanctuary.

"This is the right way to die, young girl, after you lived and left something behind to be remembered by."

I could see his head poking above the swinging doors, and I thought about my young brothers who died before they could make or do anything to be remembered by, only the three small crosses at the side of our hut, but I didn't dare say anything about that.

"Hurry up and finish now, we have a funeral and a wedding to officiate today, God help us all," and after he crossed himself arduously, he dismissed me with a wave of his hand.

It was different now in the streets, different from when my father and I arrived that morning and were taken aback by the stillness and the emptiness of the town. The sun was looking for its place to rest for the evening, and the lamp men started to go around, lighting up the torches set on their poles along the alleyways.

There was movement, and farther away there was noise. I was to remain in front of the church until my father passed by with the cart to take me home, so I sat down on the steps waiting for him. People started to come into the church one by one, their black silk and velvet garments brushing past me, a handful of sombre and quiet people, stepping firmly with an air of duty and respect. Duty to their dead *voievod*. Respect to themselves, the ones left behind, if I were to believe the priest.

The sunlight was now nearly gone, and an early autumn chill was getting through my flimsy dress straight to my bones. I was watching the people gathering in the town square and thinking about their prosperous businesses and their big houses and their children who were surely polishing their shoes, when a small woman of about forty years of age, wearing the mourning attire, came towards me up the church steps. Her face was drawn, her eyes sunken in the despair of crying, and still sobbing, she put her hand in her purse and handed me a coin. I was surprised by it. I heard about the tradition of throwing coins at the corner of the roads ahead of the hearse, but I never saw it happening. How could it ever happen in our forest or in the poor village I came from?

I bowed quickly.

"Thank you so much, my lady," I said, feeling the weight of the metal in my hand. "*Dumnezeu să-l odihnească*, God rest his soul! You must be very sad."

The woman stopped for a moment and looked at me with those sunken red eyes.

"Little do you know, girl, very little. I'm losing a husband and a son today, and there is no coming back from where they're going."

I was at a loss for words, and I just followed her silhouette climbing the steps towards the church, her velvet skirt shimmering in the light of the torches. The priest came out to meet her.

"Lady Cneaja, my lady, may you be blessed by our Virgin Mary and may she wipe your tears and give you strength on this fateful day of your husband's funeral and joy for your son's wedding."

The woman started to murmur, a prayer, or maybe a curse, and entered the church.

On the other side of the *piață*, something different was happening. More people were gathering, townsfolk in their work clothes and village people in their Sunday best, and bottles of *rachiu* were secretly passed around. There was an air of joy and mirth but not quite shown on their faces or spoken in their words. Not until the *lăutari* came and started to tune their instruments.

Once the band began to play two fiddles and some pipes, people seemed to loosen a bit. Bottles of the hard liquor were not hidden anymore but offered openly for others to share. I even spotted a boy no older than my second dead brother taking a glug then passing it to his father, who jokingly hit him over the head. My father arrived.

"It's time to go—let's go before it's so dark we can't see our road anymore."

"Please, *tată, te rog*, can't we stay for another moment to watch? Look at all these people," I pleaded.

"We have to go now, we are working people, so we have to keep working, we don't just stay to watch."

"But there's music, too, and maybe there will be dancing, please."

"Working people don't have time for dancing." He gestured for me to get into the cart. "Unless you want to go to the funeral of the old *voievod*, like you haven't seen enough death already."

I got into the cart as I was told, but the town square was busy now, and my father found it hard to lead the mule through the crowd. I felt like I was gifted that little more time and wanted to fill it with everything worth remembering from that day.

That was when I saw the bride, a gentle girl no older than me, dressed in a beautiful white blouse, long, all the way to her toes. She was very pale in the light of the torches and seemed sad, or the shadows were making her look like that because who would be that sad on their wedding day?

I couldn't take my eyes off her when I heard a voice, a roar cutting through the crowd. A woman's wailing.

"*E Dracul*, the Evil is here, right here at this unlawful wedding!"

I tried to see her but couldn't because of the commotion that followed. More people screaming, stones thrown in all directions, bottles broken, *rachiu* spilt, people pushing for a better place in the spectacle.

Then, suddenly, silence. I couldn't see what was happening; I was too small among all the bodies that surrounded me who were now swinging backwards, shuffling their feet and lowering their heads. I grabbed and squeezed my father's hand.

"What's happening, Father?"

He looked up through the crowd once more and then down to me.

"The new *voievod* of *Valahia* is here!"

Cneaja, Sighișoara, 1431

They took you from me straight away. My ladies-in-waiting grabbed you from between my legs before I had a chance to set my eyes on you. Maria, the oldest one among them, lifted you above her head and proclaimed: "It's a boy! Vlad Dracul has an heir! God bless him and the Kingdom of *Valahia* in the prosperous year 1431!"

You were screaming, a piercing protest, and your small limbs were struggling to free themselves from the strong hold.

"Go fetch the master!" said that woman to one of the others as she was bringing you down. I didn't like her touching your little body; her scrawny fingers seemed to grate your skin, but what was I to do? I felt weak and nauseous, small and spent, and I desperately wanted to see my baby, to hold you in my arms and fall asleep until the end of time.

Instead, they propped me up against many pillows, and Maria put you on my lap as if you were the finest, most delicate china. The baby I carried in me for nine months, the body that seemed so big in my belly, was now in front of my eyes, a small and helpless creature with a mighty cry. There was a part of me desperate to hold and protect yet another afraid you might shatter under my eagerness; sweet words and lullabies rushed to the tip of my tongue and sweet caresses to the tip of my fingers, all asking to be bestowed on you while a fierce doubt was holding me back. I thought I ought to do so much with all that love and fear that was bubbling in me, but the thought itself had me paralysed.

Maria fiddled with my nightgown and grabbed one of my breasts with one hand while the other supported your head and guided your mouth towards my nipple. You latched quickly and firmly, with a sort of raw knowledge I seemed to lack or had forgotten. You were beautiful, my baby boy, with dark skin and a head full of hair that shone in the light of the torches like ebony. You were ravenous and impatient and pressed on to conquer me sip by sip. I surrendered to you with joy. It took me only that one moment to decide I was going to love you forever, and there would be no room left in my heart for anybody else.

I could feel your gums rubbing on my nipple and your lips caressing it into obedience. That was how strong my baby boy was. I was happily lost in your eyes and in my admiration for you, but at the same time, I started to become aware of the pain your sucking was causing me, and a sense of guilt started to sneak in. Was I supposed to feel anything else but happiness and ecstasy, gratefulness and adoration? Was I flawed? How much should I endure for the small and helpless being in my lap?

Except you didn't seem helpless. You were frustrated and demanding. And although I felt important to you, I also felt used. And at fault for feeling all that. And pierced by pain.

In the end I couldn't take it anymore and pushed your little mouth away. It felt like I severed a thousand leeches' teeth off my skin, and I was terribly thankful for the relief that overcame me. It was only when one of the ladies-in-waiting shouted, "Look at his mouth! *Sânge*, there is blood on his lips!" that I looked at my nipple and saw a rivulet of blood where there should have been milk. My heart sank and my adoration for you faltered.

The other women started to shout, panic took over. You started to scream again in my arms, and I just lay there dejected, not knowing what to feel or fear anymore. The door opened in the commotion, and a few more people came in.

"We have to bring in the witch," somebody said.

"A witch is no use, she wouldn't know! She wouldn't be able to say," a woman's voice proclaimed. "I was born on a Saturday. I know. Show that baby to me! Show it to my green eyes."

This woman was small, but her hoarse voice

commanded the attention of all, and they parted to make room for her. She came towards the bed, old, hunched, her face dry and wrinkled like a raisin, her mouth closed tight in a sly smile. Only her eyes seemed alive, unnerving as she kept them set on me, unblinking. She mumbled something to herself, grabbed you from my arms, and wrapped you in some fabric.

"Come to Tinca, little baby. The rest of you, go, go, leave us alone."

My ladies-in-waiting seemed to be mesmerised by her and, obedient, made their way to the door. Although their presence seemed stifling most of the time, the old woman oozed an ill-fitting air that I couldn't trust.

Tinca—if that was her name—put you on the bed near me, and although I wanted to take you and hold you tight and protect you from this woman, I was in fear of you too. She blew over you three times, but then she came towards me and started to shake my shoulders.

"The child has the evil eye, my lady, *e deochiat*. I will take him away and untie him of his curse."

Was it true, what she was saying? Was it true that you had the evil eye? What had I done wrong while carrying you in my belly to bring a curse upon you? There were so many rules to abide by… so many bad omens to avoid… so much advice to listen to…

Suddenly I missed my mother desperately. I missed her taking charge and always knowing what to do, telling me what was proper or fair or just. The thought of my mother's voice telling me about the duty I had towards my country and the care I owed to its future *voievozi* strengthened my will.

"I am not giving you my baby."

I questioned my judgement that night when I heard the word *vampir*. It was Tinca who said it first, and it floated in the room between us for a short time. Then, when she called the people who were waiting outside, she said it again to them, pointing at my bloody nipple, and the word *vampir* made room for itself in those people's minds and on their tongues and they said it. They uttered it to themselves first and to each other after. And it must have sounded good to them because they kept saying it louder and louder until it exploded in my mind with fear and grief. The beginning of our end, my son.

I didn't know what to make of your father's decision to keep you. Why did he refuse to give you to that woman, to Tinca, if you were indeed a vampire? She told him of the poison you would bring to our lives, and he didn't care, he refused to see, blinded by his pride. And how did Tinca know?

I never brought you to my breast again. The warm blood you drew from me that stained my skin and my nightgown also smeared my mind, and I couldn't wash the memory of it. I tried to cover it with new memories of you that would send our first encounter into oblivion. Sometimes I thought I could.

You, Dracula

Month after month I watched you grow, feeding on the pain of other women's breasts. Nurse after nurse started to reject you and refused my coins, no matter how many I was trying to pile into their hands. They were talking. The rumour about your taste for their blood and their pain was spreading. The word *vampir*, tucked away at the beginning in the far corners of our house, was now raising its head in the middle of the corridors. While people grew weary, I was sinking deeper and deeper into confusion and anguish. Not you. You were new to the world and wanted to gain whatever place you had in it.

There was no reprieve from you or from the guilt I felt looking at you. I wanted to love you, I thought you deserved to be loved by someone, and I wanted that to be me. Not being able to give you love after I gave you birth seemed wrong. My mother's words kept ringing in my ear—"You need to raise good boys for the country"—and I knew that was my duty, but were you a good seed for me to grow?

The dark bundle I held in my arms at birth, plump and bouncy and alive, was not there anymore. When you started to walk, a year or so later, you were stretched and skinny, like no other little boy I've seen. Your face was long, your eyebrows were large, hiding the eyes in a perpetual frown. You always seemed upset. You lingered. Your eyes lingered on me.

"Why do you keep staring at me?" I asked one day when your eyes bore burning holes at the back of my neck. The sight of you when I turned, pale and gaunt and deadly still, stirred a revolt that had been smouldering in me for a while.

You, Dracula

"Tell me, talk to me, why don't you say something?"

You were coming close to your third year then, but not even three words had come out of your mouth in the whole of your life. You jumped and jested, climbed and crawled like no other, but you never talked.

Your silence was exasperating because I thought you could but chose not to speak, and sometimes you were saying more with your eyes than I cared to hear from your words. I didn't know if it was love you wanted that I couldn't spare or attention you craved that I couldn't give you. I kept trying to get away from you and from the guilt you were carrying with you.

"Say something, do you hear me?"

You kept staring at me unabashed. We were in the kitchen alone and had been there the whole morning. Just as with every other meal, this one, too, took you a long time to eat.

"Eat your food and be done with it."

I covered the distance between us in two steps. I could feel the revolt in me transforming into anger.

"I will let you starve," I cried and grabbed the bowl of porridge to throw it away. You didn't flinch and your eyes kept following me, empty of any emotion. Suddenly I couldn't take it anymore. I wanted to cover those eyes and wipe away that glare.

There was no hesitation on my part and no recoil on yours when the porridge landed in your eyes. The cold mush stuck to your face like a second skin. Pale and dry. I thought I should regret it, but I didn't. I glared back at you, our eyes locked, neither backing down.

After a moment you stood up and pushed back the chair with a force I didn't think you had.

"I don't care for your food." And these were the first words you ever said.

Your father wasn't talking about any of this. He was away a lot, spreading his loyalty very thin between the sultan and the pope, getting trapped in the vice they kept tightening with the power handed to them by their gods. Swearing loyalty to these archenemies when needed had been easy, but proving his allegiance to both when asked to do so was not. I could picture the outrage my father in Moldova would feel to see the cunning alliances my husband made and broke. As for me, I was curious how long his deceitful tactics would last before he was caught in the web of his own lies. All I could do was pray to my own God that my life would be spared when it happened.

On the rare occasions he came home, he made sure to visit my bed.

"We need more heirs. *Valahia* needs more powerful men," he would say before collapsing on top of me. I kept squeezing my legs and hoping his seed would never enter me again, because what good would I have been to anybody if I gave birth to another one of you?

"Garlic, my lady, the peasants, they use garlic."

I hadn't told Maria about the fear that whispered in my ears at night or the guilt that I felt every minute of the day when looking at you, but she must have known herself from the way she was shielding me against you. I had started to take a liking to her, the oldest of my ladies-in-waiting, the woman who proclaimed you to the world. She never asked why I was looking out my bedroom window without doing anything, why my words refused to leave my mouth most of the time, and why my tears seemed to never end. She didn't ask any of these things, but she brought a pillow to put against my back on the chair at the window, she told the servants what to do when they stayed idle, and she changed the handkerchief in my fist when it got too wet.

"What good would that be, Maria? Would it undo the things that are done?"

"It doesn't have that kind of power, my lady, but garlic makes them stay away…" she whispered without meeting my eyes, glancing at the door as if afraid you could hear us.

I pondered over her words for a while, and then I let them go, resigned to bearing the cross of being your mother. It was me who brought you into this world, and it was my duty to carry you through it, if only I knew how. Should I summon love to guide me, or should I follow the easy path of rancour?

You, on the other hand, kept coming back. Kept lingering around me. One day I was sewing some embroidery, a scene from the Bible, Pontius Pilate judging Jesus Christ. I had been at it for a long time as I found working at anything tedious and draining. You were curious, you wanted to know about my colours, my reds, my oranges, my golds. You asked questions about Pilate and the meaning of punishment, and you were meddling with my needles on the floor in front of me. You picked things up and put them back and asked even more questions. I found you tiring. I kept my head down and hoped you would go away. You were relentless. I could feel my blood boiling with frustration and my skin crawling with antipathy.

Then I sensed you getting up, looming over me like a lanky spider, and a chill started to wrap around my shoulders. Your eyes were merciless, and I didn't seem to be able to pull myself from under their scrutiny. I abandoned the work on my lap and watched helplessly the grin that opened on your face as you knotted my balls of wool.

When you finally took your eyes off me and settled them back on the needles, the chill lifted as swiftly as it came, and a wave of relief swiped over my mind.

"Leave my work alone, you're messing everything up," I scolded, and I reached into your hands to take my things back.

Your small face, a boy of four, became rigid and unkind, and it made me regret my impulse. I was going to withdraw my hand, but you caught it in yours, and with the other, you stabbed one of my needles in the back of my hand. The shock petrified me, and in that one moment, you stuck out your tongue and licked the blood that was oozing from the tiny puncture. I withdrew my hand before the nausea took over, but even after a few days, looking at you made me squeamish. The coldness of your hands when they held mine and the eeriness of your coarse tongue on my skin have stayed with me to this day.

After you left, I screamed for Maria.

"Bring me the garlic, please."

"We need to have more heirs," was your father's croon when he happened to stop by our house and burst into my room smelling like a cellar.

I watched him one of those nights, starting to undress himself. I watched him failing again and again to undo the laces of his trousers, and I thought I ought to help. It was what my mother would have expected of me, after all, and that was why I tried hard to convince myself it was my duty to prop this man up so he could stump into me and muddle my life. But when I heard him swearing at his own impotence, and I smelled the garlic from under my pillow, I went quiet and pretended I was asleep. I heard him falling over, picking himself up again, swearing, mumbling and then, suddenly, his weight landed on my bed.

I jumped and sat up, wrapped in all the covers I could get.

"I think you should go to sleep; I think you are very tired," I said to the heap of flesh near me.

"We need more heirs. Come here." Your father grabbed my arm and pulled me towards him but, for the first time, I resisted. I shook his arm off me.

"No, we don't. We don't need any more children like him. He's a monster. We made a monster."

"What are you talking about?" Your father lifted himself up and sat beside me. "What do you mean, monster? What did he do?"

It was for the first time I had his undivided attention, and I was faltering, not knowing what to do with it. How much did I know for myself that wasn't my imagination and how much of that was even close to the truth? Had I transformed my revulsion of you into a story that could be told to others? Or maybe I just made myself believe something that was nothing. But, most importantly, how much of it could I tell your father without enraging him?

"He is cold and white. He doesn't say much, just stares at me all the time. When he smiles, his gums are red, and I don't like his smell," I said quickly, in one breath, before he could intervene.

"You don't like his smell?" Your father was laughing, but his temper was not light. "Wash him, woman, wash the child if he smells!"

"He doesn't like water, and he screams in the bath like a devil," I tried again. "That woman, Tinca, who came at his birth, she said he is a…" I tried hard to say the word *vampir* but couldn't. Your father started to laugh.

"Don't you mind that woman, do you hear me? That woman was in my bed once, and she thought she'd be forever, and now she wants my child too. That woman has no power over me. Or over you, or my son. Don't let her drag any of us in her web of lies. She is a dangerous woman, that one."

Murmurs came back as fleeting memories and shadows and roars too. Was it Tinca's voice I had heard in the corridor of the castle the night of your birth, who claimed you and my place in my home? The same woman whose face your father slapped? Was it the same Tinca who then brought the word *sânge* into my house, said you were *deochiat*, with the evil eye? Was it her who called you a *vampir*?

I wanted to ask him all that, but he lifted himself off the bed and pointed a finger at me.

"You stop this nonsense right now. You and all your half-witted women who believe in fairytales. That boy is going to be the *voievod* of *Valahia* one day, and he doesn't need unholy rumours spread about him. Wash him well and bring him to church." He straightened himself a little, and I thought he was going to get up and go, but instead he said, "Now, let's make another one."

The following day I told the ladies-in-waiting to scrub you well, and when everything was set out for your bath, I watched you slither out of their arms like a snake, kick the tub with the force of a boy twice your size, and then run away like you'd never even been there.

As for the church, that wasn't a place for you. And your father knew it.

The night of your birth, soon after that awful woman left us with the word *vampir* hanging as a curse upon us, he brought you to the church himself to have you baptised. He wanted to present you in front of God, hoping that the Almighty would have your sins washed and forgotten and help you sit in your rightful place at the *voievods'* table. But God rejected you that day—or maybe you rejected Him.

Three plunges in the basin with holy water was all you needed to become a Christian in our Orthodox faith. You barely had one.

When the priest tried for the second time, your father told me, you started to cough, gasping for air like you were drowning and became cold in his arms all of a sudden, pale and stiff.

"He is dying, my lord, the baby is drowning," he pleaded and tried to give your still body back to your father in haste, as if it was burning his hands. Your father refused to take you.

"He has to die a Christian. Try again, Father, we need him to be baptised, to give up his sins. You have to try again."

It seemed to your father the priest kept hesitating, caught between the fear of you and the fear of his *voievod*. He just wanted to be rid of your body and waved his arms nervously, mumbling prayers. Your father lost his patience and started screaming, trying to grab you from him and dunk you in the water himself. He said he missed holding you by a moment when the priest let go, and you ended up on the floor between them, dropped with a thump.

Both of them were stunned to see your little body

broken, with the limbs sprawled on the hard stone following unusual lines. They kneeled in silence and started to whisper a prayer over you. The sharp cry that your body let out then sent them both into the pits of terror. When your arms and legs came together again and you wiggled them like a bug trying to escape, the priest shot up and ran away as if he was struck by the Devil himself. That was why your father had to bring you out of that church neither Christian nor pagan, but the kind that you chose.

Soon after your father's visit to my bed, I knew I was with child again. The fear grabbed and held on tight to me for nine whole months. This time around, I did everything to abide by the unwritten book of superstitions that my ladies-in-waiting inherited from all the wise women before them. I tried hard to believe that what I had inside me was going to be a child like any other: neither beautiful nor ugly, tall nor short, witty nor stupid. I desperately wanted a boy who would make a good *voievod*, a boy I could teach about courage and honesty, mercy and justice, just like my mother taught me about sacrifice and loyalty. Then I would know I had fulfilled my duty and could finally hold my head high.

But every time I set eyes on you, my hopes would crumble and my heart would sink and a cramp would take hold of my belly as if to punish me for my credulity. I cried a lot in those nine months, tears of regret and of fright, tears for you but mostly tears for me.

When the time was so near that I could see the little toes trying to break through my skin, Maria—my old and protective maid—came into my room one night. I wasn't asleep. I hardly slept those days, too busy worrying about the birth and the child that was to come out of me.

Angry clouds rolled over the full moon I had seen earlier, and the crepuscule had taken over my room. I didn't like the darkness. The shadows were unsettling me, and I imagined creatures of nightmares hiding in the corners. Sometimes I imagined you lurking under my bed ready to pounce when the unguarded sleep might take hold of me. I didn't like to sleep either.

Maria didn't carry a candle and didn't close the door behind her. She tiptoed around the room, careful not to make any noises. She sat on the bed with me and leaned close to my ear. When she spoke, her voice was low and secretive.

"We have to baptise this child. We have to get God's blessings upon the child before Evil sneaks to claim him."

I looked at her in fright and in hope, and I nodded for her to continue.

"It is a night blessed with a full moon, and you came full circle and the baby inside you is fully grown." I kept nodding.

"I have talked with the priest. He is waiting for us, and he thinks it is the right thing to do."

"What is this right thing? What are we doing?"

She brought a finger to her lips to shush me and put a cape over my shoulders. She led me out of the room through the dark corridors of the servants' quarter, and then we stepped outside. The clouds had dispersed after having dropped down a quick rain over our sleepy town. The air was crisp and smelled raw, and the full moon, heavy with a warm light, made the *piața* glow like a room ablaze from a mighty fireplace.

We took the way of the shadows, tiptoeing against the musty walls, careful not to wake up the few drunks who were snoring under the cover of the night. Maria didn't seem old anymore but agile and stealthy. Squeezing my hand slightly, she led us with resolve and gave a sigh of relief when we made it to the other side of the square, to the church.

A figure came out in front of the door, darker than the darkness itself. From the long black vestments and the bushy charcoal beard, the priest's eyes popped out, startled. Without a word, he went inside, leaving room for us to follow.

The screech of the door closing behind me locked in the unpleasant smell that hit me when I stepped in. Acrid, sharp, vinegary, with a bitterness I hadn't encountered before, the heady smell didn't come from the many candles that were flickering in a circle on the floor of the church.

When the priest handed my old lady a small bowl, the odour became even more pungent.

"Drink it, my lady, you have to drink this."

The nausea that hit me when she brought the bowl to my mouth made me gag.

"What is it? It's vile."

"Castor oil to urge the birth, my lady, you have to drink it. We need the baby out quickly, tonight, before anybody gets word of its arrival. This will help. Come on, now, be good and drink it."

She kept prompting me and bringing the bowl close to my mouth. I took it reluctantly and lifted it to my lips. She pushed it from underneath.

"All of it. All in one go. It's easier this way."

When the slimy liquid touched my tongue, it felt like a worm started crawling on it. I wanted to spit it out, but the old lady kept pushing the back of the bowl, and when my mouth was full of it and more kept coming, I had to swallow and let the worms slide down my throat.

I felt dizzy and sick, but the woman told me to walk, to keep walking and never stop until I felt the pains of the baby coming. So I started to put one foot in front of the other and hold on to pew after pew, and I kept swallowing the gelatinous thing that covered the whole inside of my mouth.

The priest busied himself with the holy basin for the baptism, and every time I passed by, he nodded approvingly. I couldn't say how long I walked or how many times I circled the benches. It didn't seem important. Nothing seemed of any importance until the baby was out of my belly.

The first spasm took me by surprise and made me fold

into myself from the middle. Shortly after that came the next one, enraged, spiteful, inflamed with the pain of many knives stabbing. All the ones after that came fast, and Maria wouldn't allow me to stop walking.

"It's for the baby, my lady, keep walking to keep him away from Evil," she said, taking out a knife from the deep pocket of her dress.

Needles stabbing, steps taking, tears dropping, prayers coming, dread, fright, stabbing, step, cry… and then he came. I only had time to sit when the baby dropped out of me, and Maria rushed towards me with the knife.

"Don't, what are you doing? You promised!"

An image of my first born, of you, in Tinca's arms, her scrawny fingers on your skin, the word *vampir* coming out of her toothless mouth, made me feel powerless, painfully incapable of protecting my babies, so I pushed the old lady away, trying to kick the knife out of her hands.

The priest stepped towards us then, and my struggle lost its momentum; its strength lessened and so did my wish to live.

"Kill me then, kill us both," I begged, staring at the knife.

Maria stopped for a moment, stunned.

"It's for the cord, for the baby's cord, to cut it, my lady, nobody's killing anybody. Why would you think something like that?"

I fell back on the floor exhausted and watched her sever my baby from me.

"You have a beautiful baby boy," she said, lifting him.

"Can I hold him, Maria? Please, give him to me," I begged, but the baby was already given to the priest.

"Later, my lady, not now. Let's have him baptised first; we don't want him to get the evil eye. Someone might come, something might happen any moment. He needs God's blessing."

As I watched my baby boy disappear into the basin once, twice, three times, I knew she was doing the right thing for him and for me. I could barely hear the priest's mumbled incantation and Maria's loud prayer above the boy's high-pitched cry. Tears started to cascade down my face, but for the first time in what felt like a lifetime, they weren't tears of sadness or anger, but of relief and joy. My baby was going to be safe, and maybe I could be too.

I allowed myself to relax and my mind to calm down, soothed by the rhythm of the prayers and incantations. The sweet lullaby got quieter and opened a door to a world wrapped in cotton and wool, and just as I wanted to go through that door, I felt arms poking me and pulling.

"Wake up, my lady, we have to go. Your little boy is baptised and safe—let's go back to the house and announce him to the world," said Maria, pulling me up with one arm while holding the baby with the other.

I stretched out my own arms and reached towards my baby, but she shook her head disapprovingly.

"You are too weak. We need to bring you back to the house and into your bed. You can hold him then."

You, Dracula

She propped me up and I started to shuffle my feet along the church floor. I was counting my steps trying to stay awake. I was looking down at my feet just to make sure they were coming out from under my nightgown, not feeling them, not feeling anything else but a desire to sleep. Left, right, the feet were moving, and they carried me to the door of the church and then outside. The crisp air woke me up only to remind me of the pain I was in.

The *piața* was quiet and felt watery, shadows running with the rain and washed off by dawn. Maria's steps were small, measured, after mine, and I could hear her breath, shallow and fast. I could hear my baby's breath, too, deep as the sleep he had fallen into, and then suddenly, another one, wispy and throaty, close by, too close.

I lifted my eyes to see whose it was at the same time as Maria's frightful gasp. The woman who stood firm in front of me was old and small, and she seemed poor in her patchy black cape, but her stare was unyielding and the green eyes unforgettable. I pulled Maria with the baby behind me.

"You came too late this time, Tinca, the baby is christened. There is nothing you can do, he is in God's hands now."

The joy I felt saying those words warmed up my heart, but the chill brought in by doubt was a powerful shackle. *Please, God, don't let this woman take my child*, I kept praying in my head.

Tinca's face remained still, her eyes unabashed.

"Hm," she mumbled finally, "you can have this one to yourself."

I let out a deep sigh of relief and turned around to take a look at my baby in Maria's arms. He was still asleep, happily unaware. Maria tightened her grip on him and smiled. When I turned to face Tinca again, she was gone. I looked around the *piața*, but there was no trace of her. She seemed to have been washed away by the dawn's glowing light.

We started walking again, left, right, blood dripping on the ground from under my nightgown, with every step forward a dark red puddle left behind.

Radu was everything I hoped for you to be. His cheeks were rosy and his lips full, his blond curls were soft to the touch, and his toes were made for tickling. He stopped crying when I sang, and his smile filled me with the love I always knew I was meant to give. For the first time I felt like a mother and not ashamed of failing to be one.

After Radu was born, you took the habit of leaving the house at night. I was worried at the beginning about drunkards coming at you in the street or rabid animals attacking from the darkness. I was afraid you might be cold or hungry or lost somewhere, frightened and all alone. But I shouldn't have worried. Fear wasn't something that crossed your path or your mind. You seemed to relish the shadows.

You, Dracula

One night I saw your head and shoulders hanging out from one of the windows of our house. I was in the nursery feeding Radu, rocking the chair in the rhythm of the song I was humming, contemplating the sky, the tops of the trees touched by a mild wind. I was taking in the smell of gardenias from the pots at the door and feeling light in my head and my heart.

Your face popped out in the window frame across from mine, and for an instant I thought you looked straight at me, and I froze. It took me another moment to realise you couldn't see me from behind the curtain, and a sigh of relief left my chest. You seemed alert, wary of something known only to you, your nose held high in the air, driven by whatever you knew lurked out there. Your skin seemed even whiter and rather transparent, with a sheen that reflected the glow of the moon. An animal on a hunt was what you brought to my mind, not a child.

You stayed like that for a short while, vigilant and stern, waiting. At the beginning there was only one crow. It came in a quiet and calm fashion, the flapping of the wings imperceptible, and sat on your windowsill. You started to pet the bird, and its neck bent down towards you as if bowing with reverence. The second one came shortly after that, and then more arrived. I didn't dare move behind my curtain, engrossed by the power you seemed to have over those poor creatures. You stroked them with your fingers on the feathers of their wings, on their tail, and they pitter-pattered in front of you, chirpy and obedient, hungry for your attention.

They continued to come, alone and in pairs, quiet and

undeterred, fighting for a place close to you. When you grew bored, you dismissed them with a wide gesture and watched them squirming on the narrow ledge like an angry hive, wings flapping noisily, beaks hitting the rock in an infernal rhythm, the caws and croaks loud and menacing like a storm. The silence descended into cacophony.

Afraid Radu might awaken with all of the clamour, I made an attempt to get up from the chair, and at exactly that instant, your eyes shifted from the birds towards my window, and I thought they clung onto me. I didn't dare move anymore for a while—I just stayed there petrified, watching the murder of crows disperse in a black cloud. When the last of them was gone, you closed your eyes and stepped back into the shadow, and I could finally breathe again.

I thought that seeing your new brother might change your ways. He had adored you since he was a few weeks old, and he always smiled when he saw you. But I had to stop allowing you near him the day you brought in a mouse you had killed and threw it on his small chest.

"Small present to play," you said, "for small baby…"

I never knew if you were naive enough to think that the dead creature was a heartfelt gift, or you were smart enough to hide your cunningness under false pretence. Did you do it because you didn't understand the workings of the world like the rest of us whose lives were entangled with feelings, emotions, and rules? Or was the mouse for me? To see if I paid attention, if I grew scared, and if I could forgive? I did all of these. Many times. Until one day when you cut Radu's face with a dagger, and I witnessed in your eyes the sudden shift from the abyss of darkness to the fire of Hell: your extraordinary rage.

I brought a mirror to show you. I wanted you to see for yourself what I saw, the beast that you were becoming when giving in to that rage. I hoped that, watching yourself as the monster I watched, you would understand why loving you was difficult and being your mother was painful.

You refused to see, and in the end, you gave in to the rage, slashed my arm with a shard of the mirror, and didn't stop until you drew my blood and feasted on it. You were a boy of ten.

"You have to lock him away, my lord, you have to allow it, he is going to kill Radu. He nearly killed me."

My husband inspected the wounds on my arm, and for the first time, I detected something in his eyes, a warmth I had never seen before. I thought it might be compassion or even love, but it was pity. That's all your father had for me, and I took it then. Pity was better than nothing.

"Please, my lord," I pushed.

But by then even the pity was gone; your father's eyes were steeled once more against emotion. The apathy was taking residence once again, and I knew then I didn't mean anything to him.

"The sultan asked me to go and see him."

Your father pulled out a missive from his pocket and handed it to me. I recognised the seal. I used to see letters with the golden crescent in my father's court in Moldova when he allowed me to stay in the throne hall. I had to plead with him to be granted such a privilege, but sometimes he said I could. Sometimes he would even allow me to stay while my brothers were taught how to read and write despite everybody's belief that it wasn't necessary for a young lady to know anything more than embroidery.

I took the letter from him and looked over it quickly. The sultan was summoning him to Constantinople for his disloyalty to him. The tone was friendly, but I could sense the implications were not. One sentence at the end caught my eye: "*Bring your boys to me so I can see them and tell them about all the good that comes from being my friend.*" I knew too well what that meant.

"Don't take Radu, please—not Radu, he is still a baby. Your first born would please the sultan much more. Take Dracula. The sultan would love to kill him because he is the first in line after you…"

But your father brushed me off like you would a fly.

"Madwoman. The sultan asked for both of them, Cneaja. I can't bring only one."

"Please," I kept begging. "Take somebody else, you can pretend, take another woman's child, don't take Radu…"

You, Dracula

When the door closed behind him, I mumbled something that I had never said out loud until then.

"I hope the sultan kills you too."

I didn't come out of my room for days after your father returned from Turkey without my sons. How could he have left you two there, pawns in his ruthless plan to prove his loyalty to Murad? I filled my days with memories of Radu being kind and gentle and smart, smiling at me from all the corners of the house. My nights were populated with nightmares of him being tortured, cold and lonely with nobody to whisper a good word of reassurance.

I cried, I wailed, I sobbed, I stayed silent, I ate too much and very little, over and over again. Out of my window I watched the young cherry tree in the garden losing its leaves in the autumn wind after losing its fruit earlier in the year, and I saw myself already barren, young and empty just like that tree.

Your father, as usual, expected much more from me.

About a fortnight after he came back from the Turks, defeated and sonless, he stepped into my room reeking of alcohol and the same sense of entitlement as always. He looked small, smaller than I remembered him, and desperate. He was conciliatory. His presence, at other times crushing, didn't make me fear him anymore.

"Let's make another heir. If the sultan kills the two boys, we must have another to get the throne back from whomever dares steal it," he said, mumbling. "The Turks are coming closer and closer; we have to be prepared with soldiers and heirs."

He reached for his groin, and I found that revolting. He didn't know how to be a father, and he most certainly didn't deserve to be one. I pushed him hard out of my room, and before I slammed the door in his face, I hissed, "You don't get to touch me until you bring Radu back."

I knew he wouldn't. He was cowardly; his loyalty was always misplaced and served only him. And, above everything, he wasn't cunning enough. And he didn't care. But I did.

After four years of incessant struggle with myself, drowned in self-pity and overwhelmed with guilt, feeding myself only with anger and blame, when the hope for Radu's arrival lost the grip of reality, I packed a bag.

What I had in the bag was of no importance, but what I had in my heart did: the love, the longing, the determination, the sense of duty, they were all travelling with me to get my Radu back. I also took Maria and a guard, whom I paid handsomely to watch over us.

Your father was told I went to a monastery to pray. As he didn't see me capable of anything else, he was pleased to hear I put myself to good use.

We started our journey over the Danube and into Turkish land, riding on the less travelled paths, wearing less fanciful clothes, hiring a quieter boatman and a faster caleche. The money I had opened gates and bought silence. At the sight of gold, people stopped asking questions and made our way smoother.

In less than a fortnight I was in the heart of the pashalic and sent word that I wanted to see the sultan. The first day they said he had affairs elsewhere. The second day they talked about an indisposition. Third day went quiet. Fourth day brought the news that he left the town. Three days after that, they said I could see the sultan at the end of that week and no sooner. I had time. I had all the time in the world to bring my boy back.

I wasn't accustomed to the heat of the Turkish plains. I missed the breeze that was ruffling the trees back home and the sun happy to take a rest in the middle of the day behind a cloud. There were no clouds to be seen here, and no one could take a break from the relentless sun.

The first night we spent in town, we kept the windows open but to no avail. The hot air from outside had taken residence inside, clinging to the bedsheets, to the curtains, and to our throats. We had just dozed off when a mighty scream burst outside, like a song with no melody in a deep, throaty tone. Maria gasped in surprise, and we held each other tight, not knowing what it meant. It sounded menacing and we were grateful when it stopped soon after it started. The following day the guard told us it was the call to prayer, the rhythm by which Muslims lived their lives. We heard it then during the day, too, and we saw the men taking down their rugs and kneeling devoutly, praying with ardour in the direction of the Kaaba, but it never sounded quite so menacing as that first night.

You, Dracula

Our lodging was on one of the narrow streets in the bazaar, and there was no rest from its bustle either. Short commands, harsh admonishments, screams of victory, bargaining, insults, children screaming, went on until the call to prayer. After that, the world died slowly, suffocated by the nauseating smells of the spices and melted by the heat, only to be awakened the following day by the pungent fragrance of a bitter brew brought in by the Syrians. They called it *cahve*, coffee, and they boiled it in a tall pan called *ibric*.

In the end, it took the sultan seven days to see me and send me away with a flick of his hand.

When I stepped into the vast hall of the harem, a cool breeze enveloped me like a caress, a slow music insinuated itself into my head, and the smell of incense made me mellow and dreamy, ready to recline on one of the immense cushions scattered around. But that was not why I was there. I kept my sight fixed on the sultan at the end of that hall, and I kept walking towards him, ignoring the gentle murmur of the fountains and the lush shadows of the strange-looking trees.

Murad had very small eyes barely squinting from a fat face. He was covered with silks and velvets and sprawled on the throne, still too small to fill in its grandeur. As he kept quiet and looked at me with a touch of amusement, I started to talk.

"My son, Radu, is everything I have left in this world. These four years I have missed him like I missed my eyes and my hands and my heart. My life is empty without him. Keep my oldest, keep Dracula, but let Radu come back to me. I am begging you for your mother's sake."

You, Dracula

"My mother is dead," said Murad with indifference.

"Maybe she is, but her spirit is still with you, I'm sure. And you remember her love, don't you? She must have loved you very much."

I really wasn't sure if I should have said something like that, and I wondered for a moment what you would have answered if somebody asked about my love for you. I hope you would have said "She tried," because the truth was that I did.

A shadow passed the sultan's face, and for a moment I thought he might consider it, he might give in to my imploring.

"No. I like Radu. Radu stays with me. You can have the other one. That one is wild."

"I don't want that one," I said, ready to throw myself and kneel in front of him, but he dismissed me with a flick of his hand and a frown.

"You dare talk to me about a mother's love. How can you call yourself a mother choosing one son over the other?"

You see, I didn't think I was choosing Radu over you. I thought it was my duty to choose the one who could lead the country.

When you came back a year later without Radu, I

wished the entire earth would split in two to swallow me whole. You were taller, whiter, there was even more emptiness in your eyes. When you came through the door fresh from the Turkish prison, I looked behind you hoping to see Radu's shape, and I listened to the silence hoping it would come together as his voice. But he wasn't there.

I tried to hide my disappointment and my grief with an embrace, but the coldness of your touch, the indifference in your eyes, the absence of emotion I felt when I was holding you were unbearable. I let go of you and indulged in a memory of Radu, unblemished by you and your stench.

"You shouldn't have come without him," I shouted at you with malice, and I saw your taciturn mood swinging from indifference to rage in an instant. I was glad about it because I wanted you to bathe in the same sea of sadness as me.

For the next year I watched you going around the house at night like a ghost, sneaking up and down the darkest alleyways of Sighișoara, climbing the walls of the tower like a spider, and catching bats in mid-flight, all in silence, so quiet as if you didn't exist. You didn't talk to anyone, especially not to me. You were scaring the horses when you went by the barn, but a touch of your palm on their mane would make them purr like a cat. There were always owls where you went, perched on the windowsills and on top of the houses, on the tree branches, white and quiet like you, bad omens like you.

You, Dracula

Your father didn't come home all that time. Was he afraid of your wrath? Was he ashamed of his cowardice? In all likelihood, he was feeling sorry for himself somewhere on a battlefield, in a tent at night, scared of the shadows of his past and trembling at the fallout of his future. It was of little importance. He didn't come to see you, and you didn't ask for him.

And then, one day, you disappeared. There was no word from you and no trace, and with no master, the owls went back to the woods.

Reports were coming that you went to your cousin Ștefan cel Mare in Moldova and helped him in his battles; that you were brave and daring and your power with a sword was unequalled; that you were merciless, and no living creature was left behind your trail of destruction.

News was coming from *Transilvania,* too, that John Hunyadi, king of the province, took you under his wing and taught you everything he knew about the art of war and the art of diplomacy, about the riches of the pope and the cruelty of the sultan, the austerity of the cross and the opulence of the crescent. They said you were a fast learner, and your loyalty to him was unwavering. They said he trusted you with his country and gave you two duchies, Făgăraș and Amlaș, in the heart of Transylvania.

With you gone, your father returned home, but our house in Sighișoara was too small for him and the soldiers he needed for protection, too easy to reach by the temporary allies he made if they turned into foes, and too exposed for his own boyars who preferred him dead. That is why he moved us all to Târgoviște: far away from all the borders and, on one side, with unimpeded views over the plains so he could keep an eye on the Turks if they arrived. On the other side, the town was protected by the loyal chain of the Carpathians.

One thing this new capital couldn't protect us from, no matter how hard I tried, was a fast-spreading rumour. And when the one about Radu started to drop its poison along the back streets of Târgoviște, nobody could stop it before it reached me. I wished I had never heard it; I wished for people to have dropped dead before they spread it.

The thought of Radu and the sultan together in the lewd harem I had visited was inconceivable: not the delicate Radu I knew with his angelic skin and blond curls against the sultan's fat cheeks and bulbous nose. Surely not my Radu. I was certain it was just a rumour spread to throw mud in the face of a country that he would rule one day.

And who would be served by such a denigrating rumour if not your father, who wanted to keep the throne to himself, or indeed you, who wanted to gain it? The betrayal seemed so obvious and the plan so devious that I immediately took it upon myself to stop it, to smother it back into the filthy mouth where it began. I owed that much to Radu as his mother.

I set myself to work trying to find out who started the rumour and who spread it, who needed to be stopped and who needed to be bought to stop it. While trying to erase the trail of their lies, I realised I could replace their evil rumour with one of my own making.

"I hear there are stories about my first born, about Dracula. People are talking about things he does in battle for Hunyadi, have you heard these rumours?"

The ladies-in-waiting had their heads down, their eyes set on their embroidery, and their mouths shut as a gaol's door. But I could tell I had their attention.

"Did you not hear? I can't even remember who told me about this…"

"About what, my lady?" asked Maria, tuned as always to my needs and intentions. During the years we had spent together I came to rely on her devotion, and now I needed all the help I could get to spread my rumours about you.

"The prince, my son, is said to have received an ambassador from the sultan and told him he wants to put all of the soldiers he commands in the sultan's service, and he would personally march them into his land to place themselves at his disposal."

"Is this not treason to King Hunyadi of *Transilvania*?" asked a young girl whom I didn't recall seeing before in my entourage. The other four women threw poisoned looks at her and frightened glances at me. I continued my story.

"The sultan then sent word to all of his people and throughout his land that no one should harm Dracula when he comes into Turkey, but they should all honour him and receive him well. This way my son travelled for nearly five days into their land, and then he turned around and began to rob their cities and impale their people and cut them in two and burn them."

I could see a shiver of fright and disgust sweeping through my small audience.

"He allowed no one to remain alive, not even the babes in arms," I finished with a sigh.

"So, he is still on the side of the Christians then? He didn't give himself to the sultan? That is good," one of them tried to console me.

"If he were a real Christian, he wouldn't lie and kill like he does. It is a shame, and I am sad to say it, but he won't make a good *voievod* if he behaves like that. Radu, on the other hand, would make a merciful ruler, I know that."

The women looked at each other, and I knew by their faces that my news would spread fast. It was a good tactic to start denigrating you. What I didn't know was how its meaning would be twisted and how it would work against me after all. What I pointed out as savagery and treachery was taken for bravery and wisdom. People were talking about a cunning and fearless Dracula who stood his ground in front of the Turks and played into their own pride and credulity.

"You know people want Dracula to be their new

voievod," I said to your father during one of his rare visits to our house in Târgoviște.

"That's good," he told me, "he would make a good *voievod* if he comes back from Hunyadi."

I wasn't afraid of him anymore; his stalky presence in a room didn't make me stiff with anticipation or fear, his raspy voice didn't make me silent. You see, I had very little to lose in those days, only wishes and hopes. Everything hurtful that could happen to me had already happened. But I had something to gain. And, because your father didn't know that, I had to play my game with care.

"He is too cruel; people will hate him. People want justice, not persecution. They want food, not punishment," I said.

"You need to show no mercy these days, otherwise people will step all over you. It's good to live in fear of your *voievod*," said the man nobody was afraid of anymore, the ruler who clung to his throne by torn threads.

"Radu will make a better *voievod*. Bring him back from the Turks and let him rule the country with their help. He'll keep peace for the people and money in their coffers."

"Maybe he could keep the peace but only if he gives the sultan these people's blood and all the fruit of their labour and their children too. Besides, didn't you hear about Radu and his good times in the sultan's harem?" he said, and a smirk started to take over his face. "He has the sultan on his side, but on top of him too."

I hated that rumour so much—my insides were

churning at the thought of that image.

"That couldn't be further from the truth, and you know it, you are his father. It is just a rumour spread by bad mouths who have their own interests to pursue. They don't want what's good for the country. Who is to say that Dracula himself didn't start this rumour about Radu to hide some of the things he is guilty of?"

And indeed, who was to say? Nobody knew I made up these stories myself to make people think less of you and more of Radu. They were lies, but they were good lies. They were serving a good cause: that of the country.

"Dracula is the first born, woman, he doesn't need to slander Radu. The throne is his as it is." The smirk on his face was widening, and although at the same height, he seemed to look down on me.

"Did you even hear what the devil, your first born, did to that woman?" I asked and quickly crossed myself.

Your father looked at me blankly.

"He was with a woman, a mistress he took. And she wanted to please him and told him one day that she was with child. But Dracula didn't believe her. She kept saying it was true, and wasn't it wonderful news for him? He got very angry at her, and when she still didn't stop, he unsheathed his sword and cut the woman open and looked at her entrails to see for himself. And he shouted so the dying woman could hear him. 'I told you, woman, it cannot be, there's no child in you,' and he left her there to die."

Your father looked at me with a mixture of disgust and disbelief.

"Is this the demon you want to leave the throne to?" I pressed.

"Nobody is taking my throne from under me, Cneaja. They'll have to kill me first," he said, full of confidence. Why he thought that would be hard, I don't know.

There was a time when you were still away in Hunyadi's camp when another rumour started to make its way through town, whispered in taverns and muttered at crossroads: that the sultan was bringing Radu back to put him on the throne of Wallachia. God had finally answered my prayers. This truly was a rumour I didn't start myself, but I was very happy to help spread it.

Images of Radu and me ruling the country in peace and prosperity were appearing before my eyes when I put my head on the pillow. Those days I slept better than I had slept in years. The more I believed that such a reign was possible, the more I became convinced that I owed it to Radu to smooth his way to the throne and help him take a seat on it. There were only two obstacles: you and your father. But neither of you were unwavering or set in stone.

It was hard to ask around for witches in Târgoviște without raising suspicions unless you were a young girl in need of a man or if you were the mother of one. I was neither. And I wasn't looking for love. I was looking for ways to kill my husband.

I set my old lady to work. I don't know how, and I don't know from where, given by whom or bought with how much, but Maria came back one day with a little bundle wrapped in some dirty cloths.

"They call it mandrake, my lady, the plant. It's a powder the witches make from the roots of this plant. These roots look like a man, and the man screams when it is dug up from the ground, and the one who hears the scream will die on the spot," she said, handing the bundle to me. "It's a powerful plant, but the witches know how to use it."

"And did the witches tell you how to use it, Maria?"

"They did, my lady, they did. If you put a smudge of this powder on your cheek," she said, gesturing with one of her fingers, "it makes your cheek rosy and good looking. If you put a pinch on your tongue, it makes your eyes pop out, and you'll appear pleasing and inviting. But if anything more than a pinch gets into your belly, it will bring your insides out and you will die."

I thanked the old lady, who bowed with deference and left the room without another word. The parcel felt heavy in my hand, heavy with all the venom that was in my life, with all the decisions I had to make, and with the sadness that would come after.

I went to my bed and hauled it aside. I grabbed the rock I had dug out in the wall of my room, behind the bed, scratching a little at a time ever since we moved to Târgoviște. Inside the little hole was the only thing I had come to treasure more than poison: a silver crucifix. I put the rock back in its place and started my wait.

You, Dracula

When you came home after seven years spent with Hunyadi, you were different. You had grown, not only in your stature but in your presence. Your eyes had an even more unreachable depth, which was unsettling. Your arms had a wider grasp, your legs covered more ground, you filled more space and sucked more air from around you, spindly and alert, stealthy and frighteningly self-assured. Your forehead was domed over bushy eyebrows that met over your nose and, together with tightly closed lips, you appeared cruel and unforgiving. It was only on the rare occasions when you talked to me that your stench and your peculiarly sharp teeth reminded me of the child I knew. And because I remembered, I took to carrying the garlic with me again.

"I need money," you said with a voice that was cavernous and flat.

"Why? Are you going away again to serve at foreign courts?"

"No, I am not going anywhere. Not anymore. I have learned while I served; I have gathered knowledge and allies and now I have come back to stay. It's time for me to serve my own country."

I tried to guess what you really meant, to read something from your face or from your eyes, from a movement of your mouth, but there was nothing there to give me an inkling about the implication of your words. What I knew for sure was that, if you really wanted to serve your country as you said, your father might be in your way.

"Gold can't buy you that kind of power. I'll give you money. I'll give you all the money you want if you can bring Radu back," I said, and I could see you flinch for the first time. A shadow crossed over your face, and your eyes were now alive, not vacant anymore but sizzling with rage.

"You two can serve the country together. Keep the peace. You and him."

But you weren't listening anymore. You grabbed the pouch from me with cold and coarse hands, prickling my palm with your long and sharp nails. I felt suddenly cold and out of breath and with no choice but to give in to a shiver that took hold of me while my cheeks were burning hot.

After that I asked Gheorghe, my only faithful guard, to follow you. I needed to know how you were going to spend my money. I knew it was not going to be on women or drink because you weren't made that way. Your needs weren't like other men's needs.

He told me it wasn't hard to keep you in sight since you went out only at night and hid in dark places. You just watched and listened, and when all the people went home and the streets were empty, you went into the woods. And every morning of the week Gheorghe had followed you, he came back to me saying he lost you in the woods.

He said your steps didn't make noise through the

leaves, and the branches didn't snap when you went over them. You were surrounded by a darkness so dense you could cut it with a dagger, he said, and owls and bats flew around you.

"I think he can talk to the wolves, my lady," he said one morning, exhausted from the fruitless chase. "When he steps into the shadows, I can hear howling and I can see wolves answering his call and following him into the pit of blackness."

Gheorghe seemed more frightened every morning, and he wasn't a man easily scared.

"What about the money? Is he doing anything with it?"

For a few days the answer was always no, the coins didn't change hands, but then, one morning, the old man returned in a state of great agitation.

"He killed a man, my lady. I saw him taking out his dagger, and he stabbed the man in his chest and in his belly."

I was relieved you finally decided to take action. Gheorghe told me how you met a hunchback earlier that night in an alley near Sfânta Vineri church, gave him the coins, and then followed him to one of the boyar's houses. It was the house of a *dregător*, an important man at the court in charge of the safekeeping of the country. Then I heard about you hiding in the shadows and watching your crooked man paying a servant of that house. After that, when the deal was done, Gheorghe saw you killing the hunchback, and as if nothing happened, sauntering into the woods.

You, Dracula

When the news of your father's death was brought to me a week or so after, I knew it was your doing. I knew the money I gave you paid for his ending. How, I didn't know yet, but didn't really care, either, as I was sure to find out sooner or later. Very well! It was the first time you were any use to me. You did my bidding well. With your father dead, there was only one man left in front of Radu to the throne of *Valahia*: you.

You worked fast. It was only a few weeks after you came back from *Transilvania* that the news was brought to me. I gave a little cry, and I hoped people thought of it as pain or sadness, whichever of the terrible states a new widow was meant to be in. I felt nothing of the sort. I felt relieved and elated. I felt my lungs were finally deep enough to take in all the air I needed to be properly alive.

"He was stabbed in the back on the battlefield at Bălteni, my lady," the messenger's lips were uttering, but what I heard in my own head was *He's dead, your husband is dead, killed by your son. He did it, your son paid someone to kill your husband.*

"His body is in the *piața* for everybody to see and pay their respects," he kept moving his lips.

But what he said next, I heard loud and clear.

"We need to proclaim your son as the new *voievod* of *Transilvania*, my lady. It has to be done straight away."

Of course they had to do it, the country needed a *voievod*, but I knew it would be hard for me to see you on the throne when it could have been Radu. *All in good time*, I said to myself.

"Let's do what has to be done," I said aloud.

I stiffened myself, put a mask of grief on my face, and allowed myself to be led through the corridors of the house. People ahead of me were opening doors to find you. I knew they did when I heard the words "my lord". You were the only one deserving that title for now.

The men bowed and shuffled and parted to allow me to reach you. I fished in my sleeve for a handkerchief that was going to dry imaginary tears. I stepped into the room in silence, keeping my eyes down, not wanting to look at you. The moment to bow in front of you came too soon and the tears too fast, and that was when I started to sob. But not for the past, I cried for the future. And not for the deceased, but for the living.

I watched you walk outside and stand beside your father's makeshift coffin. I wondered what went through your mind, what memory of him would make you feel something other than indifference or resentment. Did you feel guilt?

Anastasia, Târgoviște, 1456

I jumped out of the bath with the lukewarm water clinging to the goosebumps on my skin and started to shiver uncontrollably. With my whole body trembling in the cold, I was fearful that I would never be able to stop. It felt like my own being wanted to shake all the dirty thoughts and sensations that crawled in my head and between my legs earlier and punish me, or even worse, reveal my secret.

I took the towel from the maid, but I refused her help. What if she was able to tell what I had done in the bathtub and laugh at me, or tell the world about it, or tell my father? I knew I hadn't gone to hell, but the kingdom of guilt and shame was welcoming me with icy claws. I was grateful when she threw a nightgown over me. I covered my body in it, and I hoped the thoughts would stay covered too.

"What is happening?" I was finally able to ask while she was rushing me out the door.

"There is a man at the door, my lady. He says he is the new *voievod* of *Valahia*, and he has business with our master. He came with a few soldiers. He is on a black horse at the door, my lady. I think they killed one of the guards. We have to go out too. He ordered. All of us."

She looked frightened. I was cold. I didn't think I should be worrying. I trusted that my father would keep us out of harm's way. He was, after all, a powerful man, and he saw the old *voievod* all the time, talked to him and advised on the running of the country. He was a *dregător,* and that was important at the court. Surely the new *voievod* needed a trusted man to stay in charge of Wallachia's safety.

It was when we left my room that I began to sense the fear that was running wild through the corridors of our house. Soldiers were pounding on doors and screaming at people to get out. Our servants followed the orders pouring into the halls, tripping over each other and knocking down furniture. It was dark. There was a torch somewhere by the stairs and its pale flicker made our shadows crawl along the walls. I could hear the noise of glass being smashed on the floor. *I should have worn shoes* was all I could think about. *They're breaking my mother's china, and I have no shoes.*

As we turned a corner, I saw my father being pushed down the stairs by a soldier. I called out, but my cry seemed to hardly leave my lips, let alone reach his ears. Pandemonium had taken over our house, and I wanted my father to make it stop.

Downstairs, two other soldiers burst through the doors, and their cries made the windows clatter. There was more light, but there was also smoke, and the lower we came down the steps, the denser it got. My eyes were stinging, and I closed them tight until tears came to wash the pain away. *Is the house on fire? If only I knew… I should have worn shoes.*

"Get out! Everybody out! By order of the new *voievod* of *Valahia*!"

Following my father on the stairs, a rush of servants in their nightgowns, eyes barely opened, a flock following its master and hoping for his protection.

I couldn't wait for this confusion to clear, for the new *voievod* to see whose household he disturbed and seal the good news with a goblet of my father's best wine as it always happened.

The night chill hit me hard when I stepped outside, but I steeled myself against it. I wasn't going to shudder in front of those people like a leaf in the wind. I was my father's daughter, and we knew our worth. It was won with honesty, intelligence, and hard work, he said.

I shook my hand out of the maid's and started to push, shoving my way into the group of people and slipping through them to the front, where my father was. When I reached him, I placed my hand on his shoulder and patted it, letting him know of my trust in him. Only then I looked in front of us and there you were, the new *voievod*, the man who thought he could take on my father.

For a split second, our eyes locked and a shiver went through me like the blade of a knife, for there wasn't anything in those eyes, nothing to tell me about you, your troubles, or your kindness. There was emptiness or maybe only indifference to what was unfolding.

Right before your eyes was pain—didn't you see it? — my father's pain and mine. I needed you to see it, I needed my father to tell you that we were not accustomed to pain, it wasn't something we could bear. To my surprise, my father looked beaten, already defeated by it. A soldier came and pressed on his other shoulder and brought him down to his knees. I saw him falling down, my eyes peeled on the ground he touched, and I retched from the pit of my stomach at the sight of a head, just an arm's length farther on the cobblestones. A human head with its eyes closed and no body.

I could see my father recoiling in disgust, but instead of protesting, instead of getting back on his feet and restoring order, he started to beg. The words were tumbling out of his mouth in what I thought to be a prayer, but if it was, he wasn't begging God for mercy, he was begging you.

The louder my father's begging, the more anger seemed to spark in you, and when you spoke, your eyes weren't empty anymore but full of raging fire.

"You killed my father on the battlefield at Bălteni, stabbed him in the back," you said with a voice like a winter storm howling through the peaks of the Carpathian Mountains. You slammed the words in front of us like hailstones, and they weren't melting, they weren't disappearing, they were just sitting among us, cold and heavy; words like betrayal and Turks, title and wealth and death, words kept falling upon us.

"You don't deserve your title or your wealth. You deserve to die," he said.

I was suddenly taken by rage, a kind I hadn't known before, fuelled by yours and matching yours. If my father couldn't defend himself, I would defend him. If he didn't have the power to protect me, I would find the power myself. And if I failed at these, I would seek help.

"You are not beyond us. And you are not beyond reproach. An eye for an eye!" I spat the words in your face.

You looked at me for a moment with curiosity. When you lowered your eyes, I suddenly became aware of my thin nightgown. You kept staring, and when you reached my shoeless feet, you grimaced in a tentative smile.

"You are not ready for battle."

The soldiers put my father on a horse and took him away. I wanted to fight for him, to scratch the hands that were touching him, to yell at all of them to leave us alone, but my father kept moaning and begging. I was angry at him for not defending himself, for not standing up. I was enraged that he didn't deny any of the poison that came from your mouth. Were any of those accusations true? Could my father have killed a man? And if he did, did he have a good reason? He must have had a reason.

"He did, Anastasia, your father killed the old *voievod* with help from our husbands."

I couldn't believe what the two women were telling

me. They arrived at the house soon after the cortege carrying my father left, marching to the drum of the horses' hooves. The women wore capes thrown in haste over their nightgowns. Their faces were crumpled with lack of sleep and worry. They were scared and I could feel their fear tightening around my throat too.

"Tell me everything you know. I find it very hard to understand what happened."

"You see, one night about a week ago, a hunchback came to your house and told one of the servants that the old *voievod* had a secret order to have your father killed together with our husbands."

"Why would he have my father killed? They were good friends, they fought in battle together. My father was a good man. I'm sure your husbands were too."

"They were, Anastasia, of course they were, but the country is weak, and when the country is weak, everybody wants a slice of it, and rumours run wild. Who knows what the *voievod* heard about our men that made him take such a decision to have them killed? I'm sure they did nothing wrong. But that rumour, that they would be murdered, well, they couldn't forget about that," said one of the two women.

"So you see, on that battlefield at Bălteni, it was the *voievod* against our men. They had to kill him to save their own lives. He was a very cunning man, but your father was a good *dregător* and only wanted to do what was right for the country. Our husbands were loyal to him, to your father. And now they've all been taken," said the other woman.

You, Dracula

We all allowed a heavy silence to settle over that story. I hadn't known any of the things they told me. Too busy with my thoughts of headdresses and kisses, dreaming of Bogdan and marriage, I had been oblivious to what was happening in my own house. I lowered my eyes to the hands in my lap and sat like that for a while. One of the women shifted in her chair and cleared her throat. I looked at them and they looked back at me expectantly. I felt I had to say something.

"Surely the new *voievod* will understand if told the truth. We should tell him, and maybe he will forgive and let them go. They are the most important men in the state. He cannot rule without them," I said with a confidence I didn't have.

The two women seemed unsure, their own uncertainty like a poisonous thought taking residence in my head.

"Maybe Dracula would understand, but his own father died at our men's hands..." said one of the women, and I could feel my hope melting away and allowing room for doubt. There was too much truth in what she was saying.

"I think we should go to his mother. Princess Cneaja is a woman, she will understand us better. She knows how it is to lose a husband, and maybe she will show mercy and talk to her son," said the other woman, but as soon as the words left her mouth, she seemed to know herself it couldn't be right. "I know, it was our men who killed her husband. There will be no mercy there..."

We fell quiet again for a while, then the oldest of the women reached out and squeezed my hand.

"Your father was the highest in rank, and our husbands followed his lead. We will do the same. We trust you to get all our men free."

That was a task of the highest order, and I didn't know how I could possibly succeed. If my father was truly guilty of murdering the old *voievod*, should I even try? Shouldn't he pay for what he did and with him these women's husbands? But what if they didn't kill him? I knew my father as a kind man, magnanimous to those around him, boyars or servants. What if this was a lie? I remembered my father's sadness every time we visited my mother's grave. A man who suffered so much in the aftermath of death could not kill anybody. It must have been a lie.

This gave me strength and determination although no solutions.

"Let's go and see princess Cneaja. We'll try to urge her to sway Dracula's mind," I said getting up. The women were doubtful.

"What if we can't? What if she won't?"

"One step at a time. We'll deal with that when it happens."

When we stepped outside my house, I could see the dawn forcing its way through the darkness and calling upon a new day. The blood from the servant's body, decapitated the night before, was smearing the cobblestones, dry and dirty. I looked away. What was the day going to bring? The uncertainty, the thought of what might lie in front of us was as chilling as the morning air. I wrapped my cape closer to my body and started walking.

Our small group gathered more people as we made our way to Dracula's royal court. The more men the new *voievod* took with him, the more of their women came to us. Their stories repeated themselves, words like unfairness, children, threats, and death kept coming at me from all their mouths, tears inundating their faces. Before I knew it, we weren't just a group of women with an impossible task at hand, we were a procession who refused to walk on the road of mourning.

The old *voievod*'s body was in the middle of the *piața* on a makeshift stretcher. It just lay there, uncovered and unmourned, guarded by a sleepy man. The thought that my father had anything to do with this man's death—or anyone's death—was troubling me more than I could bear. My companions passed by the body without a glance, but I had to force myself to look away before the image of the wounds on his body remained ingrained in my mind, the same way my mother's white face and cold touch appeared sometimes in my dreams and unlocked all my tears.

When we reached the *voievod*'s house, the women in front stepped aside and made room for me to take the lead. I did it because I knew there was no other choice for me. The thought of living my life without my father was more frightening than begging for his life from his worst enemies.

Princess Cneaja received us in her quarters. I had seen her before but only from a distance when my father had business at the court, and on one occasion, I remembered her coming to me and stroking my hair: "It must be hard to miss your mother. I have a son, too, Radu, as young as you, it seems… He is locked in a Turkish prison, and I am sure he misses me. I don't know how he survives without me. His father left him there." And while her whole face was bright and warm when talking about her son, the mention of her husband brought a cloud over her face and a tightening of her jaw. But that was no help to me.

"We came here to mourn with you the untimely death of your husband, our *voievod*, my lady," I said with a timid voice, desperately trying to make it stop quavering. "We have prayed for him, and we will keep praying for his passing into the afterworld. We are praying for you too, my lady, so that you can mourn in peace."

Cneaja looked much older than I remembered her. There was much pain resting on her face and digging into her skin. Her hands were gathered together in her lap, not fretting, not clenching, but docile. In fact, her whole demeanour was yielding, and that gave me hope.

"We are also here to pray for our men. Your son, Dracula, accused them of murdering his father, but it can't be true. I am talking about my own father, my lady, the *dregător* who is in charge of the safekeeping of the country, and also these women's husbands and sons. All important men at the court, my lady. They couldn't have killed their *voievod*."

"I know who your men are, and I know what they did. You shouldn't have come. None of you."

"But, my lady, nobody saw them do such a horrible deed, and I can't stop thinking the rumour was meant to defame such important people. Maybe somebody who wanted to take their place, somebody who would have something to gain from having them locked up."

Princess Cneaja rose from her chair and came to face me. Her appearance wasn't calm anymore but stern and cold.

"My husband was killed on the battlefield. His own people stabbed him in the back. Now, my husband wasn't fighting among mere soldiers, he was fighting among his boyars who were meant to protect him. If they themselves didn't do it, who do you think might have done it? If you can answer this question and point me to the murderers, you can take your men home."

But I didn't know how to answer that question. I had no answers for my own questions or hers. I had only doubts weaving into a growing fear.

She didn't move and her eyes bore into mine like a provocation. The group of women at my side put their heads down with a humility I didn't deem necessary. Surely our men had to be judged and proved guilty first. Surely the new *voievod* knew the law of the land and had to respect it.

"Where is Cneaja?" The cry came from outside and I recognized your voice, thunderous and unrelenting. I thought to myself that if you knew the law of the land, you should call her Mother and not Cneaja, and if you knew the law of the land, maybe you didn't care to respect it, and if you didn't, how were we going to force you?

Princess Cneaja looked sad when she heard your voice. Her self-assured stance of only moments before had collapsed. She seemed defeated and resigned. I knew then that my father's cause was not dependent on her; she was not the one in need of persuasion but you, Dracula.

You marched into the *piaţa* on your black horse, your face lit by a reddish light that was piercing the night sky, your black eyes burning with the darkness from inside you. I remembered my father's kind smile and his warm embrace and the humiliation that overwhelmed me when I saw him begging you.

"Let our men come home," I raised my voice. "They are important men at the court, and they know how to rule the country. You will need them."

You seemed amused by my words. You dismounted your horse and took a few steps towards me.

"What do you know about ruling the country? Go back to your embroidery." A few of his men started to laugh, and he turned to them, pleasantly surprised at their reaction.

An anger I never felt before started to rise from the pit of my stomach and flew to my head, ravaging all the good and obedient thoughts that were nesting there. A rebellious fighting streak started to warm up my head the same way my unclean thoughts about Bogdan warmed me between my legs only hours before.

I stepped forward and the rest of the women surrounded your mother and stood behind me. I could feel their rage, too, and encouraged by it, I spoke with a courage I didn't normally have.

"Free my father and these women's husbands and your mother can go free!"

I didn't know where that thought had come from, how it formed, or in what corner of my mind, but when I said it out loud, I felt for the first time that I was finally doing something for my father. I didn't feel a mere spectator to the drama.

The words were coming fast and easy, and I delivered them to you raw and heartfelt, just as my love for my father felt to me. But you were unmoved, and they seemed to bounce back as they would from a mountain, their echo dying down unheard and uncared for. Nothing seemed to matter to you.

"Your husbands and fathers are traitors," you said. "They should pay for what they did."

And so, in the heat of that moment and empowered by the trust I felt from the women behind me, I grabbed your mother by the hair and shouted: "The only one paying will be your mother."

I didn't know if you cared. I hoped you would. There was nothing on your face to tell me, and you didn't say anything. The women behind me were coming closer together; a current seemed to go through them, the same bold heat that went through me seemed to set their minds on fire too. It seemed like an eternity holding your mother by the hair and not knowing what to do next, how to channel the determination that gave me such boldness.

When I sensed the cold blade of the shears pressed into my palm by one of the women behind me, I took a deep breath, took hold of them, and chopped Cneaja's hair with one single determined cut.

Her hair in my hand looked like some kind of a trophy, but what I had done didn't seem like a win to me. You were undeterred, your mother sadder. I thought it was wrong to make her pay for your cruelty, but it also occurred to me that I had no other choice. An eye for an eye. Your mother for my father.

You mounted the horse and left the *piața*. I could still hear your laughter long after you disappeared from my sight. I stood there with your mother's hair in my hand, at a loss.

When she talked, Cneaja seemed to have read my mind.

"He doesn't care for me, Anastasia. He doesn't care for anybody but himself. This is how my son is, cruel and cold."

I turned towards her. The words didn't surprise me, but the fact that she was sharing such intimate thoughts with me did. What I heard wasn't defeat, it was resignation.

"Come to my house, my lady, please—come back with us of your own will. You are the only chance we have. No harm will come to you, I will make sure of it. Maybe he will remember what he owes you as his mother. He might change his mind. He might regret his words and his actions. Tomorrow is another day. Let's pray for some guidance for our actions and for his."

Cneaja listened to me and kept quiet for a while. The women around me were watching her, impatient to hear the words that would come out of her mouth.

"There is no reason for me to help you and your men, but if I don't do it of my own will, you will make me anyway. I shall come to your house, and we will wait until he is awake again. You see, my son does nothing during the day but hide in the darkness of his rooms. It is only under the cover of the night when he comes out to spread his dark poison. I know he came out of me, he is blood from my blood and flesh from my flesh, but he is not a good man, if he is a man at all, God forgive me."

I didn't understand her words, not then. Fooled by your imposing stature, your fiery eyes, your strong arms, I thought you were a man with a bleak disposition whom I should attempt to sway towards merciful kindness. But your mother knew you better.

And so we left Curtea Domnească, the royal court, just as the sun was taking over the sky, unveiling the enormity of your actions. Your father's dead body looked more gruesome now, lit up by the glowing rays, his white face appearing indifferent from beyond the pale. I wished he could tell me whose face he saw when the knife pierced through his ribs and pinched at his heart.

"If he could only speak," I mumbled out loud.

"Some secrets are better buried and left to rot," your mother responded and moved her eyes from the body to me. "Some people too."

I didn't understand what she meant, but she seemed so sad that I felt a wave of sympathy coming over me.

"I am sorry about your hair," was all I could think of saying.

Knowing you were not going to pursue my father during the daylight, I went to the gaol in search of him. I walked through the busy streets of Târgoviște to the tower. I saw quiet people keeping their heads down, walking in a rush as if chased by something, as if wanting to be unseen or forgotten about. They whispered at the stalls and with hushed tones in the shops, weary, worried, and fearful. The sun was too bright, the light too overwhelming, the night too far.

I pulled my cape around me tighter; the sun was unable to warm my body. The night dress underneath was now frayed and torn at the hem, but it didn't seem important to me. All that counted was to be able to talk to my father, and I was prepared to beg if I had to or promise the riches of my entire house if it came to it.

The tower, when I arrived at it, seemed bigger, taller, and more impenetrable than I imagined. The heavy oak door was criss-crossed with bars made of iron, and a big lock took pride of place to remind everybody the tower was a gaol.

When I knocked at that door, my hope was fading fast. It opened slowly, someone on the inside heaving while moving it. I couldn't see within; the darkness was dense and scary.

"Anastasia?"

The voice took me by surprise. It seemed to retrieve a memory from another life, one that was further away than what was easy to remember.

"Anastasia, it's me, Bogdan." His face came into light for a brief moment, and I felt his hand grabbing mine and pulling me inside. "I was wondering when you would come. I mean when you would come to see your father, not me, of course. Your father was brought in during the night."

I lifted my eyes and saw him lost, willing, so kind. The gratitude I felt for his familiar presence stunned me for a moment, and then I just threw myself into his arms, and the tears that came gushing couldn't be stopped. I had no desire to stop them.

"What are you doing here?" I asked after a while when the sobs allowed the words to form. My eyes took a moment to take in what was there: a dungeon with low ceilings, water dripping on the rocky walls, a chair, a torch, Bogdan in a uniform of sorts.

"I was made head of the guards. I was called for duty last night because of all the important people who were brought in. The new *voievod*'s special orders." He stopped for a moment and looked at me, taking me in from head to toes. If he disapproved of the wretched way I looked, he didn't show it. He pulled me into a wide embrace.

"Your father is well, frightened and weak, but well. Do you want to see him?"

My tears were trying hard again to find their way out of my misery, but I fought them back.

"Yes, please, I want that very much, to see him, if I can, to see him now."

"I can do that. I can bring you. I shouldn't, I mean I am not allowed, but I'll do it for you. I would do anything for you." Bogdan took my hand and pulled me gently through a dark corridor, his torch leading the way with its warm glow.

"I could lose my command," he whispered when we took a sharp corner to the right. "My life, even. People say the new *voievod* is easily stirred to anger."

"What do you think will happen to my father, Bogdan? What will Dracula do to him and the other boyars?"

"Who knows, Anastasia? Nobody knows his mind…"

"Do you think he'll have them killed?"

I could barely say the word, and I chased the image that came with it away. Stopped in front of a heavy door, Bogdan busied himself with a circle of keys, visibly relieved to be able to avoid an answer.

He opened the door and stepped away, allowing me to take in the inside of that room. Out of its darkness, my father's voice came like a soothing balm over a wound.

"Of course he is not going to kill us, Anastasia, he can't; he is not above justice. He has to have us judged, and he has to find people who saw us doing such a deed. He will find nobody. Nobody will talk against me or any of the other men."

There stood my father, the same man I knew and yet so different. His nightshirt was torn and smeared in blood. His greying hair seemed to have gone white and limp, his skin fell thin on his cheekbones, and there was no poise left about him, only a humility that wasn't usually part of how he presented himself to the world.

I stepped into his cell, and Bogdan remained outside with the torch. I couldn't see much. The air was dry, stuffy, hard to breathe. It smelled of urine. I didn't want to think what that meant, I just rushed to hug my father. Instead of the warmth of his hands, I met the cold iron of his shackles. We stayed like that for a while, as close as we could if not really an embrace. After a few moments I asked the question that had been burning my mind the whole night.

"Did you do it, Father, did you kill the *voievod*?"

My father hushed me, throwing secretive glances towards the door. Outside, Bogdan was shuffling his feet in a cadence that seemed to measure the time.

"I did it. I had to. It was us against him. He was going to have us killed, so we did it first. But, my girl, nobody else needs to know. It's our secret. My life depends on keeping it a secret, don't forget that."

I wanted to feel the relief his words were promising, but I couldn't. Instead, I felt my stomach churning and my heart pumping, and I wanted to scream or pray, to beg somebody else to take control of it all and save my father. And me.

"We took the *voievod*'s mother, princess Cneaja, we took her."

"What do you mean, you took her—where is she?"

"She is in our house. She is going to stay there for now, until he lets you go. Maybe tonight."

I could see the surprise building on my father's face. At the same time, Bogdan interrupted his pacing and showed his own face, aghast, through the door. Both men were stunned, fear and curiosity, dismay and dismissal passing over their faces like waves on a sea at storm.

"Are you holding her prisoner in your house?" uttered Bogdan with incredulity.

"I don't think so, I thought I was, but she wanted to come; she said she'll stay there if it helps. But she didn't think so. I don't think she likes Dracula very much. She said her son is a cruel man," I rushed to say and regretted it immediately, seeing my father's frightened face. But I don't think he was frightened for his life as much as he was for mine.

"This is too unsafe, Anastasia, he can have you locked up too. Do you have any support? Who is helping you?" asked my father, looking at Bogdan.

"There are a lot of women with me. The new *voievod* took a lot of men last night, and their women came to me. We are staying together. But Dracula says you are all traitors, and you sold the country to the Turks. He won't listen to us. That's why we took his mother."

Bogdan was shaking his head.

"You need help, Anastasia. I don't mean the help of upset women, I mean help from men, men who know the run of the country," said my father, and he looked again at Bogdan but in a different way, a conspiratorial way that excluded me. It was a matter for men, they seemed to say, but I couldn't stop thinking that men shouldn't have created the matter in the first place.

"She needs Nicoară and Pandele. They are loyal to me, and they would help her run, she needs to escape."

While I was struck by the enormity of my father's suggestion, Bogdan kept shaking his head.

"They've been taken, too, they are here, at the other end of the gaol. We were told to keep you all far apart. I am sorry."

"Their wives are with me, Father, and their daughters. They're all with me. We are many," I said, full of confidence, but my father dismissed me again.

"What about your father, Bogdan? He is *mare spătar*, in charge of the cavalry, he should be able to help her. Maybe even help me get out of here." My father gave voice to some thought that was meant to give him hope. "He has some influence, doesn't he? He can talk to the new *voievod*."

But Bogdan put his eyes down, avoiding looking at any of us.

"He is gone. I'm sorry, he ran away last night after they arrested you—he went to cross the Danube. A few others went with him. They're going to the Turks."

My father began to say something but gave up and sat on the timber planks that were meant for a bed. I went and sat with him, feeling the weight of the time going by, painfully aware of its passing and of my inability to stop whatever it was bringing.

"I'll find a way to free you, Father. If there is a way, I will find it," I said to the defeated man in front of me. I repeated it like a mantra, looking up to Bogdan for some reassurance, and he took my hand and squeezed it, and this time he nodded, his eyes warm and full of longing.

I left my father in that stoney room shrunken, crushed by his own dishonesty, and betrayed by hope.

Bogdan led me out a different way. The underground corridor had a low ceiling, and we had to crouch to pass through it. The progress was slow, my legs tired and heavy like metal. His hand held and squeezed mine, pulling me all the way. It felt like I could finally let go of all the worries of the night through that hand, and he would take them all, absorb them all, freeing me.

We came out after what seemed like an endless journey just outside the town wall, caught unaware by the sun peaking over the Bucegi Mountains. The small bushes around prickled my feet through my nightgown, but I didn't feel the pain, I just felt painfully aware of my body, of my skin longing to be touched and moulded.

When Bogdan turned around to face me, I was ready for whatever was coming, ready to let go of the tension building inside me. When his lips touched mine with infinite gentle care, I felt impatient for more, I wanted all, whatever all was. I suddenly didn't feel small anymore, I felt grown up and courageous, and when I pressed my lips on his, I took our breath away.

Bogdan seemed a little surprised but extremely willing, filled to the brim with my desire. I parted my lips, inviting him to take what he wanted, and my own tongue went to take his offering. I felt struck by a heat that didn't come from the sun but from inside me, melting me away and growing me back like the gold my father shaped into the bullions he kept locked into a wall.

I had never known before what my body was created for. I thought walking was enough, sewing, swimming, skipping, and smiling were what I was meant to do with it, but my body knew better and slid into that kiss with ease and determination. And joy! An abundance of joy that stayed with me long after our lips weren't together anymore.

"You need to be careful, Anastasia. Be careful for me and for your father and be strong."

"You too," I said with the smile that blossomed on my face from inside me.

That evening, when we got word that all the men were being brought to Bălteni, confusion and panic took over our group, despite my attempts at reasoning with them. The women around me came in and out the whole day, our house a bustling beehive. Small children needed to be taken care of, servants needed to be instructed, households to be kept in order, small fortunes to be hidden, security to be sought or bought.

There were people who were doing this for me. Things in my house were being looked after, I didn't need to concern myself with these. As I came to learn that evening, my father had our house organised as a well-oiled machine for times of trouble. Although he wasn't there, his plans were put into action. I was relieved I didn't have to deal with any of the preparation.

Princess Cneaja was in my mother's quarters, rooms that hadn't been used since she died. I didn't like going in there; it seemed to me that they still smelled of my mother, a mixture of musk and lavender, a light touch of love like a pleasant dream and a heavy touch of longing, like a hole in the heart. Too much for me to bear.

"The men are taken to Bălteni, my lady. Do you know why?" The woman in front of me seemed calm, taking her fate in her stride or just resigned to it. "They are all being brought back to the battlefield, and I don't know why. I need to know why, I need to be prepared, to be ready for what's coming, I need to know what I have to do." My plea reflected the urgency I felt, but she didn't seem moved by it if acknowledging it at all. "How can I get my father back?"

"Your guess is as good as mine, Anastasia. I never knew what my son was going to do. I don't really know him. He is a monster."

There was pain in her words, anguish and torment I didn't know how to respond to, what to say or how to feel other than stunned. How could she talk like that about her own child, flesh from her flesh? What had you done to bring this sadness upon her? What monstrous deed of yours had made her stop loving you?

"I don't really understand why you feel this way, my lady—what has he done, why do you see him as such evil?"

"Sometimes it is about what he hasn't done, the things that he isn't capable of, like love, or understanding, or a bond with those of his own blood, or loyalty, mercy, patience, tolerance, joy… He has never shown joy."

"But does this make him a monster?" I asked, and immediately I knew the answer myself. It was yes, of course. Without love and glee, was any being really human? Just like my body that morning discovering the delight of that kiss. It was a body before when it ran and skipped and ate and slept for me, but it only became true to itself and fulfilled when it kissed. Maybe it was like that with you; maybe you needed to discover the joy of being human. I hoped you would.

"Yes, it does. I know it makes him a monster. But I don't know if I gave birth to him like that or if he became one later or if there was anything I could have done to stop it from happening. And why me? What curse has come down on me to make me his mother?"

"But there must be something we can do, something to soften his heart," I pleaded.

"Maybe have him killed before he kills us all," she said, and the coldness of her words sent icicles shooting through my body. For the first time, I asked myself who, between the two of you, was the real monster.

You, Dracula

Darkness came down slowly on the battlefield at Bălteni. The light of the full moon over the deserted plain was smeared with the light flaming red from the torches. Their smoke rose black to meet the black sky. Was that what hell looked like? Quiet and hot? Tangled with fear and stifling?

We were drained in our hearts and weak in our legs from the long journey. The wait made us more determined. Having had all that time to imagine the bleak future, we were now desperate to change it.

Princess Cneaja hadn't said a word since our conversation back at my house, and I was glad as her words and her disposition frightened me. The other women were quiet, too, resolutely quiet. Bunches of people were scattered across the field, and more were coming in a constant stream. The silence and stillness of the night made us more aware of any noise, ready to pounce like an animal under threat. That is why the murmur that accompanied the arrival of the prisoners seemed so powerful to me, deep and loaded with the disapproval we all felt.

The first one I saw was Bogdan at the top of the convoy leading the men who, guessing their fate, seemed already dead. My father was second in line and seemed to have shrunken even more since I had seen him. I started to run towards them amidst a chorus of protestations from the other women in the group. Bogdan and my father shook their heads with disapproval, and a soldier started to walk towards me, waving his sword. I turned back to my flock under the approving glance of Princess Cneaja.

When you descended in the middle of us from your black stallion, the murmur grew and spread itself like a blanket of locusts' wings over the battlefield: heavy, muffled, carrying a sense of dread and danger, a threat. But you weren't the one threatened—it was us, all of us, and there was nothing we could do about it.

You sat on a chair, indifferent and bleak, and closed your eyes. Soldiers from the back of the convoy started to come up carrying long sticks. Were they spikes or were they stakes? The freshly sharpened tops reached for the low moon, and their shadow on the ground made them look fractured, like a broken, dead forest.

The murmur of the crowd subsided, and I heard Cneaja's deep sigh behind me.

"He is going to impale them."

That is when I let the scream go, before I had a chance to see that image in my own head.

"Stop this massacre! Stop now or your mother will die!"

I grabbed Cneaja's hand and dragged her in front of you.

"Your mother will have to die," I said in a cry of desperation, starting to understand at the same time that you would not care, not about her or me and especially not about my father.

When you rose from your chair, you didn't do it for your mother. You did it for me. The women behind me took a step forward and implored. My father and Bogdan took a step forward, too, held back quickly by the other guards. There were entreaties, begging, promises, a chorus of people stripped of dignity who found themselves at your mercy. They were losing faith, and I was losing my head.

Your hand came for ours. It slithered in between mine and Cneaja's, untangling them with your bony fingers. I was repulsed by your touch, and so was your mother. The wiry hair growing from the centre of your palm took me by surprise, but Cneaja seemed to be bracing herself for your closeness. I jumped back; she only shut her eyes tight with a deep sigh.

I replayed what happened next over and over in my head, every time looking to see was there something else I could have done, any other reaction I could have mustered, anything that wouldn't have provoked your backlash. If there was, I never found it, because I could have never imagined myself quiet and subdued before you. Not then, not that early.

When the dagger came so close to my head, I thought it brought the end of me, and the grave gasps from the people around gave legitimacy to my thoughts. In that moment, I knew I preferred the coldness of the blade on my scalp than the slimy touch of your fingers on my hand. The sound of my hair being cut was unnerving, but the pull of your hand on it made it sickening. There was little pain given by your gesture but a lot of humiliation. I screamed like an animal and tried to free myself. You had my chin in a tight grip, and you didn't let my eyes leave yours, no matter how much I wanted them to. My body wasn't listening to me anymore, it was serving you. When you whispered in my ear, "I am going to take you and make you my wife," I knew there was no choice in it for me.

I was grateful when you let go, and I hated myself for that because I didn't want to feel gratitude, I wanted to feel rage. Your mother put her hand into mine and squeezed it gently, and I knew that was the moment when I had to accept defeat.

So, when you had my father impaled, my heart was broken already. I didn't watch. I could avert my eyes from the atrocity, but my ears took it all in: the screams, the wailing, the pleas, the short orders, the crows' caws and the owls' hoots of death. And then the silence. I found the silence to be most frightening, the sound of nothingness. I was humiliated, defeated, and scared.

I only opened my eyes when I felt pushed by other bodies closer to the other women. We had become your prisoners in an instant, ordered by different soldiers, not guards like Bogdan. The sudden thought of Bogdan gave me a glimpse of hope or worry or both. I looked for him in the crowd, beyond our sentinels, desperately trying to avoid the sight of the tall stakes. Cneaja's hand was still squeezing mine, and she kept close to me, stoic and sad.

Bogdan was in another convoy, a prisoner as well now, together with other guards and small boyars. Maybe our eyes met for a moment, but maybe it was only my imagination or wishful thinking. I couldn't tell anymore.

You left the battlefield on your black stallion,

indifferent to the devastation you left behind in your wake. The sun was coming up from behind rolling clouds, unwilling to shed light over that forsaken place. We were pushed to march.

I didn't need to see myself in a mirror to measure the toll the night before took on my face. I knew what it did to my heart, and I could see what it cost Princess Cneaja. We helped each other put on the black dresses we were given by the sentinels and hid our chopped hair under heavy black scarves. We cried and held hands, and we didn't say a word to each other. There was nothing to say about you. As with any curse, we could only ask ourselves, why us? Why did the curse of you fall upon us?

We stayed in the shadow of your throne during your coronation and watched how the jobs at the court were now taken and given, the old boyars forgotten. You formed a new council of men who didn't know the run of the country, peasants who lived in fear of you. You promised the country's independence by enslaving its occupants. You seemed proud of yourself.

I stopped listening for a while. It was none of my concern anymore; the state of the country wasn't going to bring my father back. Then I felt Cneaja's hand squeezing mine hard. You were walking towards us, a grimace on your face trying to pass for a smile. I squeezed her hand back before you demanded mine. You pulled me and turned me and showed me to your new boyars like a trophy.

"I announce I am marrying this woman, Anastasia. The wedding will be three nights from now, together with my father's funeral."

The new boyars came and went, their words a blur, their good wishes unimportant.

When the last of them closed the door of the throne hall, your mother spoke.

"Radu will come, you know—you can't get away with this," she said with spite.

I felt spite, too, and rage.

"I will never marry you!" I spat in your face, and the feeling of that small victory alleviated the pain of the slap you gave me on my cheek. Stunned after that first one, I didn't see the second one coming, and I was even more unprepared. But what really caught me unaware was when you came close to my face, your eyes like a madman's. From your opened mouth, a pointed coarse tongue came out together with a rotten stench, and you licked the blood that was blossoming on my lip, hot and thick. I wanted to relive the memory of the intense emotion I felt when Bogdan's lips brushed over mine, but the reality of you made me recoil and gag.

"Your blood tastes splendid," I heard you saying before I threw up.

Mara, Târgoviște, 1456

"I am taking this woman to be my wedded wife in front of all of you. You are my witnesses, and our union is now just and right!"

Your voice was deep and demanded attention. You didn't need to scream; the crowd fell silent when you spoke as if under a spell or a curse, maybe because nobody seemed at ease in that *piață*.

I climbed onto the cart to have a better look. People seemed fearful, not knowing how to behave at such an unusual gathering for a wedding and a funeral. Sorrow and joy didn't go together well. People would feel them all the time but rarely at the same time.

There was little sadness in the *piață*. Except for the black cloths hanging at the windows and doors, there was no sign of mourning. A *voievod* died, and another one was coming onto the throne. Life kept going. People married and had children to replace the dead. There was unease in the *piață*, too, and the respect for you, their new ruler, seemed wrapped up in fear. Oh, there was definitely no love. No warmth. It wasn't how I imagined a wedding. It wasn't like that at all.

You took the bride's hand and lifted it over your heads.

"Let the celebrations begin!" you said, and your words seemed to melt the ice in the square, and people moved like they had just woken up from a sleep. There was a lot of drink being passed around, and it warmed them up quickly. It took the edge of the fear from them and replaced it with boldness.

Suddenly remembering why they were there, the band started to tune their instruments, and out of nowhere, the *Călușari* screamed their call, lifted their sticks, and broke into their dance.

You weren't taken aback when the crowd surrounded you and your bride. You seemed indifferent and removed from them, focused only on her. Your eyes were connected but not by love. There was something else between you two that seemed to have absorbed your complete attention in a way that made the rest of the world unnecessary. I looked at you and I wished it was me there, in front of you, burned by the intensity of your eyes. I didn't want to be among the other people in the square—loud, unknown and unimportant, poor and needy.

Once the *Căluș*, the martial dance, was over, my father

started to inch the cart through the rowdy crowd. I couldn't take my eyes off you and your bride and kept turning to see you for as long as I could, when suddenly, the two of you were separated. The girl was taken from you, snatched by the women around her, and deposited on a chair in the middle of the square.

I knew the song, the one about the bride bidding farewell to her past life as a girl and welcoming her future as a woman and wife. I had seen the dance of the other women before, slow and hard like the life of a wife, but when they started it with that girl in their midst, a sadness came over me, a bitter regret that I wasn't the chosen one.

I looked at you, watched you as you were watching her, willing you to see me and to regret, too, that it wasn't me. My father kept moving the cart slowly, and I had to keep turning my head to look at the bride, at you, at the dance, at you, at her, at you, so when our eyes met, when you got tangled in my desires for a brief moment, I embraced you with all my heart, and the distance between us didn't matter anymore. I was happy then, even if it had been only a moment, but that had been the moment I was seen for the first time. Such a pity my man was marrying another woman.

These thoughts were spinning a web of emotions from my head to my stomach, and there wasn't a thread of sadness among them. What I felt wasn't happiness either—although I didn't really know how that should feel—but excitement and anticipation. I was giddy with it.

Cneaja, Târgoviște, 1456

I was contemplating my husband's dead body, stiff and cold in the coffin, wearing the same mask of sadness that I donned since the news of his death. I wasn't feeling the sadness itself, only wearing it on my face as was expected of me. Nobody was to know about the real anguish I had felt while being his wife, the heartache I carried through my nights alone, and the loathing that overwhelmed me when he came to me. This was my misery to carry, and it would die with me, not with him, buried in my heart. May he never find peace.

There weren't many people in the church; respect for the dead old *voievod* clashed with the curiosity about the new one, the one who killed the most important boyars in the country and made a spectacle of them on stakes, the same one who made a council out of ignorant peasants and had a funeral and a wedding on the same day, the mad one on his black stallion who was going to rule the country now. That was something people needed to see for themselves. The dead *voievod* and his wife were not important anymore.

I didn't pay attention to the priest and his mass. I had enough of churches and priests and masses in my time but not the joy they promised; none of them brought the peace or the gratitude or even the assurance that my fate would be better in the afterlife. I was just consoling myself with the hope that it couldn't be worse. How could it be?

Looking at him, small and drained in the coffin, stripped of importance by the outside world, it was hard to believe that he'd had so much say over my life, that he touched and stained not only my body but the rest of my existence, and saddest of all, made me your mother. He couldn't touch me now, not ever again. But you could, and I knew I was going to remain your puppet for as long as either of us was going to live.

We started our small procession going out of the stuffy church only to be struck by the noise and the glee outside, the kind of carefree and thoughtless celebration that people have, thinking it might be the last one allowed during their existence. The music was loud, the drink was flowing. A single look at the place was enough proof of the debauchery that ruled the country.

I spotted you in the crowd in your finest clothes. You were taciturn and didn't have eyes for your subjects, didn't seem to think of them as worthy of your attention. You had eyes only for Anastasia.

She was small and pale in her white dress, her chopped hair now covered with the scarf of the wives, the symbol of obedience and surrender to their husbands. She would have no other choice being married to you. She seemed oblivious to what was happening to her, or indifferent. The fire that was fuelling her when she cut my hair was gone. The girl crying for justice wasn't inside her anymore, replaced by nothing—not a woman, not a child—there was nobody living in that slender body.

You were looking at her like a wild black cat waiting to pounce on its prey. And then I noticed someone in the mass of people watching you with your kind of savage intensity, greedy for your attention, wanting to be caught in your vision. A young girl, no older than Anastasia, with eyes sparkling with zest for life, interest, desire, everything that Anastasia had lost. You noticed her in the end; the girl had lured you with the intensity of her stare, and you took your eyes from your wife and set them on the other woman for a moment. Anastasia caught your glance, and she followed it, settling her eyes on the girl too. The two women measured each other for an instant under your careful watch. When you broke the tie, your wife settled back into indifference while the young girl broke into an unashamed smile.

Your father was buried just behind the church in the sacred plot kept for *voievozi*, but I doubt you have ever been there. Maybe you didn't hold him high in your esteem, or maybe you didn't want to be reminded of the murder, or maybe you just didn't care.

I stayed there by the grave until the coffin was lowered into the ground by Ion, your father's loyal guard. I stayed then a little longer watching the soil being dropped over his coffin, big lumps of dried dirt, and I listened to the noise it made when it hit the wooden box. *Thump, thump,* inevitable, irreversible, just like death itself.

Ion was measured and dignified, but a sudden rush descended over me. There was no time left for poise, this was my farewell. I gestured for the man to leave. At first, I dumped the clay with my hands, but my palms were not big enough to hold all the earth I wanted to put between us. Then I pushed it with my feet, kicking the clods faster and faster until I collapsed, consumed by hate and self-pity.

"You were nothing but dirt to me! Your life was muck and your words dust, nothing else. What a fool I was to let you cover me with your dirt. Not anymore. The dirt is on you."

As the anger mellowed, my breaths got deeper, my mind clearer, and I abandoned myself to a resolute calm. Nobody else would make a mockery of my life. With your father gone, it was only you, Dracula, standing between Radu and the throne of Wallachia. And with Radu on the throne, my duty would be fulfilled.

The hiss took me by surprise as I didn't know where it came from. It seemed to come from everywhere and nowhere, a bad omen of a noise, like a threat or a warning. When I turned around to look, a woman was standing in front of me where there was nobody before, as if she appeared from thin air or from the mist that came dense upon the cemetery all of a sudden. I got up from the mound of soil, dusted my clothes, held my head high, and took a good look at her.

As she emerged from the thick mist, I saw this slender

woman, dressed in a dark tunic with a tall collar and a long black skirt. Her face was hidden under a large hat, but the closer she got, the more I could distinguish the sharp features. Prominent bones under her eyes and the cheeks sucked in, pointy nose and thin lips closed tight. There was something familiar in there, folded in the fabric of her dry skin and in the deep wrinkles. And there was something wild in those green eyes bubbling with anger and spite.

"I should have been there by the side of his grave," she said, her voice an echo of the hiss I heard before. "I should have been his wife and the mother of his child. There was no place for you between us, but you came and stayed, and he kept you instead of me."

I recognized her voice from a place in me I didn't visit very often, a place of locked memories that I wanted buried and forgotten. But they were still there, stubborn and obvious, ready to make my life bitter just like the first time they happened. The recollection of her voice brought with it the memory of the night you were born, the dark corridor of our house in Sighișoara, the screams, the sense of betrayal and of warm water running down my thighs.

"I wish I had taken your son that day, at his birth," she said, and her green eyes became deeper with fury.

"I wish you had, Tinca. I, too, wish you had."

Anastasia, Târgoviște, 1456

"What did you do with the convoy of guards and small boyars you gathered in Bălteni? Where did you send them, Dracula?"

The image of Bogdan's legs stumbling over the chains that tied him to other handsome and proud young men, the look of hopelessness in their eyes, the nod of his head saying goodbye to me, they all gathered into a knot in my stomach, a wave of hate and rage.

Who were you, this dark and stark man walking with measured steps beside me, this angry man leading me into a room of your house to make me your wife against my will? What power did you hold over people to force them into submission like that, and who gave you the right to decide their fate…?

"I sent them all to Poenari to build me a castle on the top of the world," you said, deep in thought, walking farther and farther into the entrails of your house without a torch to break the darkness or a noise to alter the silence. "I will bring you there when it is finished. It will be impregnable, this fortress, and it will be our home," you said with pride, as if you could see the magnificent building and our life together right there, in front of your eyes.

"When will they be back, when do you plan for their return?"

"Oh, never, really. I don't have such a plan. They build and they die, there is no way back for them. The mountain is unforgiving."

And that was the moment I got my first glimpse of who you really were. Not when you killed my father who killed your father, not when you cut my hair to cut my words, not even when you had me marry you on a whim, but when you blamed the mountain for killing innocent young men whose death sentence you signed. What a misled mind!

So, I wrapped myself up with layers of hate like a shield, and I added contempt and disdain. I didn't let compassion anywhere near this cloak of mine that was going to protect me against you. And when we entered your empty and cold chambers, I was ready for you.

I was ready when you lifted my skirts with your hands. I don't know if they had always been like that, but they seemed skinnier now, the fingers longer and the nails pointier, the skin on them coarser, like scales on a vulture's claws. I was ready when your eyes went up my bare thighs following your finger and when you grabbed my underclothes and threw them away and when the sharp nails got stuck in the hair between my legs. I made myself feel nothing, and I watched you fumbling with your clothes, for the first time unsure, unbecoming, and undone.

As I was steeling myself for you, you were losing control; as I let my hate take over more of my actions, you let desire take you over. Slowly, I could feel the balance of power tipping in my favour, and I knew you could feel it too. And there was nothing you could do.

"This body is all that's left of me," I said with spite, "and there is nothing inside it, nothing for you to subjugate or spoil any more. Nothing to grab with your dirty paws and hold onto." The more I spoke, the more power I knew I had. "Take this body, take it, have it your way, you monster!"

I took off my wedding dress and threw it where my undergarments were lying on the floor. I wanted whatever was going to happen to be finished while I still had that power over you. That was going to be my satisfaction if there was no other to be had.

You came to me like a conqueror, your weapons at the ready, your flags fluttering, able for battle, but I was prepared for you, waiting to delight in my victory over you. Yet, in the face of it, neither of us expected what we were feeling. I think you were hoping for something extraordinary, something that had the power to transform your life, to enrich it or to give meaning to it, something like real love, maybe, but you got nothing of the sort, because love couldn't be conquered like that. I, on the other hand, wanted to feel nothing, and yet, a feeling sneaked through my armour. Through all the loathing I nursed for you, when you came inside me, you suddenly stirred that summer storm that had taken over my body only nights before in the bath. I screamed in protest of my pleasure, and I wriggled out of your hold, wishing it to stop.

When you came out of me, we both felt ashamed, undermined by our own bodies and cheated by our own expectations. Victory eluded us both. Misery took hold of us, and while you had started to heal your wounds already, I left mine to fester. Misery was what our son was born from nine months later.

Mara, Târgoviște, 1456

We finally left the square with its noise, *rachiu*, music, we left behind the people dancing to exhaustion and the smells of roasted piglets and fermented cabbage, the light that brought to life the centre of Târgoviște. The farther we went, the quieter and darker the alleyways. I wished for silence, but the cart was cracking and screeching on the cobblestones, giving us away. Maybe it got colder in the middle of the night or maybe the thrill of the evening started to leave me, maybe the darkness made me more aware, but that night, after that wedding, I felt lonelier than ever.

My father was quiet and unaware, the mule was dragging his feet the same lazy way he always did, the houses were getting smaller and fewer. I was being brought to some place I didn't care about and didn't want to be. All I really wanted was to stay in the *piața* where the party was, where the glee spread like wildfire, and the dancing got wilder with every screech on the violin. When *tata* said we had to stop for the mule to drink some water from the river, I was glad, maybe for the first time ever, that we had to think of him first.

From where we were, at the bottom of a hill outside the town walls, we could see the shape of a broken tree, bare branches reaching towards heaven like an imploration. We made our way up the path slowly, my father willing us forward. I sat in the cart looking back over the town at the bundle of light gathered over the square and imagined the music band playing a slow song and you, holding your bride close, lost in her eyes and swaying gently.

But you weren't there anymore. I knew it because you had just taken a corner on the path and appeared in front of us riding a big black horse. Five soldiers surrounded you. There was a lot of noise for such a small group, but you all seemed in a terrible hurry, spurring on the horses with your feet in their bellies, coaxing them with harsh sounds and setting the night alight with your torches.

With you approaching, my father made himself small, hiding behind the cart. I didn't want to hide, I wanted you to see me and to remember me from the square, when our eyes locked as if sharing a secret. When you passed by, you threw only a glance towards us. Was there a moment of hesitation or did I just imagine it? Did you really remember me, or was it only my wishful thinking? Whatever might have been, you didn't linger; you just prompted the horse to go faster, and when you spoke to the soldiers, your voice sounded angry, wispy and harsh, like the rasp of a sword.

"We'll have to teach them all a lesson!"

The words seemed to float around in the night air a

long time after you weren't there anymore. I didn't know what they meant, but they sounded threatening.

"What do you think he means, Father? Teach who a lesson?"

"It is not our business to enquire or judge the *voievod*. He knows best how to look after the country."

Maybe it was so, but I was curious all the same. After the mule had its fill of water, we started our journey again, and I kept my eyes on the group of soldiers descending the hill on the other side. They kept galloping until they reached a barn made of freshly cut timber. I could see the soldiers dismount, but not you. Still on your frightful horse, you pointed at the big building with ample gestures.

About to step into the forest, I turned to take one more look at you and your soldiers, and I couldn't suppress a scream.

The barn had caught fire and the autumn wind was playing with the flames, unleashing their savage greed, helping them spread their searing touch. I thought I could hear human screams coming from inside, desperate, urgent, furious, like the screams of animals going to slaughter. I hoped I was mistaken.

"Is this the lesson the *voievod* wanted to teach, Father? Who do you think was inside?" I was afraid to speak the words, afraid they might be heard, that they might bring your wrath upon us. Even my whisper seemed too loud, but the silence was more frightening.

"I am sure nobody was inside, of course, it must have been empty," said my father, but how could he know?

"He said he'll teach them a lesson, Father, but who were they? Do you think they're still inside?"

My father stopped the cart and turned around to face me.

"I said this is not a matter for us to be concerned about, remember? Listen to me, it isn't. We have so many other things to worry about. Now, let's go."

When I tried to say something else, he grabbed my arm, pulled me with a force I didn't expect, and scrambling for my footing, I decided I despised my father. *I hope the wolves will get you*, I prayed in my head.

I went with him, of course. I followed the cart into the woods, deeper into the shadows, listening to our feet crumbling the first dry leaves of autumn. I had never set foot in the woods after dark before, only very near our house, and the vice I felt gripping me grew tighter with every step I took, and it squeezed me, allowing only for small, rushed breaths.

As we were tiptoeing our way among the tall trees with sharp and clingy branches, the mule stopped suddenly and refused to go any farther. I watched my father pulling and pushing, trying words of encouragement first and then the whip. The mule was now stepping backwards and braying, as if terrified of something that lay ahead.

I squinted my eyes and tried hard to make something out of the darkness that was now surrounding us, heavy and sticky to the body and throat. Was the animal scared of something he could see in the pitch black or of what he couldn't? My eyes were of no help, but my nostrils captured something special, and in a moment, I felt surrounded by my own smell, like I haven't felt it before, a warmth and a shifting of the air around me that made me pay attention to myself, enjoy myself. It was as if a butterfly drenched in pollen touched my cheek with its wings in passing and spread my smell, then whispered "Ileana" near my ear. I recognized my smell, and it was good, but Ileana was not my name.

While I was savouring my discovery, the mule and my father seemed to be getting angrier at each other's stubbornness, as if some madness took over their minds. The animal raised itself on the two back legs, taller than my father now, ready to come down on the man. My father kicked the wild creature in the stomach with all his might, jumping then out the way.

"*Tată*, stop, please, you scare me. You're hurting the animal. Please, let's go back."

But my father didn't seem to hear, driven to madness by an angry force into a pointless fight.

"You, monster," he was shouting, "Leave us alone, go away!"

The mule turned his back on my father and kicked him with his hooves hard in the thighs, but my father was driven by a force of destruction that seemed to have taken his mind away. He rushed to the cart and grabbed the axe, the biggest one that he used to cut the tallest trees and started to scream at the animal. When the beast lifted his front legs again over my father, he cut its stomach with one swift movement and jumped out of the way again. But this time, the insides of the mule spilt on him, guts and blood and dark slime, and the two creatures gave a horrible cry and collapsed on the ground like one.

The smell made me gag. My own smell disappeared. I wanted to help my father, but when I reached him, I vomited on his legs. When there was nothing left in me, I lifted my head. The darkness was gone; the thick of it had a transparency now, like a candle behind a veil allowing contours of trees and branches to come into light.

My father looked around surprised. When he saw the mule, he put his face in his hands and started to cry. What was I to say?

"What happened? Why did you get so angry at the animal?"

"But it wasn't our mule, you see? It looked like a wolf to me, a beast from the forest, and it was coming after you, Mara. And a voice in my head kept saying, *Kill the beast, kill him.*

I tried to help him from under the animal's legs. He sobbed and lamented inconsolably.

"What have I done? What came over me? Lord forgive me."

"Lord, please don't let us die in these woods," I echoed.

The straw on my makeshift bed pricked my skin through the night, and I kept turning and sleep kept running away from me. I hoped sleep would wash out the bloody image of my father with the axe in his hand and the smell of the mule's insides and my mother's face stricken with pain when she saw us. I knew sleep could be like that, forgiving.

Your face kept appearing whenever I chased the other memories away. I saw your face sad when looking at your mother, intent when looking at your bride, and curious when you looked at me. I liked the way you looked at me better because there was an openness about it—you were willing to see me.

I didn't know if sleep got hold of me in the end when I felt the same warmth I had felt earlier in the woods, that magical touch of the butterfly in the darkness. I tried to open my eyes to see the source of my pleasure, but the eyelids were so heavy, too heavy to lift. Or maybe my eyes were open but blinded by the darkness of before, which fell heavy and sticky yet again all around me.

I knew the warmth enveloping my body was real, although I didn't know where it came from; I knew the touch of the butterfly wing was real, although I couldn't find it or touch it in return. The mist must have been real because it was gathering on my skin around my goosebumps and my nipples like a tickle. My smile had to be real, too, wide and playful around my lips, my ears, my waist, and between my legs. What about the tremble I felt inside me? What about the desire for something else—deeper and stronger than what I already had— were all of them real?

"Ileana, I was waiting for you for so long."

The voice came from near me, so near that it seemed to come from inside my head, a deep voice, soft and commanding, familiar, unforgettable, a creature I, too, was waiting for. But that name was not mine.

You, Dracula

I wanted to open my eyes and tell that voice—tell you—gently that it wasn't me, that it wasn't my name, but something brushed over my lips and kept them closed with what felt like a sweet kiss that demanded my complete surrender.

Later, when I could open them to talk, it didn't seem to matter anymore. What difference did it really make what my name was? I thought my name could be Ileana if Ileana was to feel what I had just felt for what seemed like a small eternity only moments before. And if the two little marks blossoming in shiny ruby on my neck the next morning were going to make me Ileana, so be it.

Cneaja, Târgoviște, 1457

When you sent me out of your way to the monastery to shrivel and die, there was still plenty of life left in me, and yet there was nobody to live it with; there was love I still held in me and wanted to give, but there was no one to give it to. There was a lot of me left but nobody to see it, nobody who cared to see me for who I was.

In my life, I had been gifted to someone as a daughter, traded with someone as a wife, and disgraced by someone as a mother. Were any of these my making? My choice? Had I done anything to bring this fate my way? No, they were all other people's plans that I had to fit into, their lives imposed on mine, which they cut to measure with their needs and desires.

That is why, when Anastasia came to see me in the monastery with her belly sticking out of her dress and her breasts heavy with the milk to come, I welcomed her the way I wished someone would welcome me: a daughter who had been failed by her father, a wife failed by her husband. And I thought then, while she still had a chance, that maybe I could help her be a fulfilled mother.

"I don't want to be a mother! Not to his baby. I don't want my baby to be a monster like Dracula."

Half a year had passed since the day I buried your father, and you buried Anastasia's future in a forced marriage. Half a year of your reign over *Valahia* had buried half of the country's men. Your battles with the Turks had halved the money in the coffers, and your poisoning the wells and setting fire to the crops had halved our livelihood. Your cruelty didn't know half measures, and neither did your love for *Valahia*. You did it all in the name of patriotism, in the name of the country, you said, but the country grew afraid of your name.

I looked at Anastasia standing in front of me, and I could see every day of that half year encrusted on her face and imprinted in the way she carried her belly. Her youth was lost, wasted along the dark corridors of your house. There was no zest for life about her, only regret and spite, and although there was still fire in her eyes, it sparked only when she talked about the hate she bore for you.

She said she didn't want to be the mother of a monster like you. It still hurt me to hear that, even if I was the first one to call you what you were. Maybe she was right. Had I known who you were or who you would become, would I still have wanted to have you? Could I have stopped you from growing into a heartless and bloodthirsty demon, or should I have stopped you from being at all?

This was all too late for me and you, but what about Anastasia and your baby?

"Why did you come to me?" I asked.

"I don't know anybody to trust with my life, but there must be a way to rid myself of this baby. And you must know it. Surely you know of something or someone. Surely you can help me."

To think that only moments before I wanted to help her become a fulfilled mother while she didn't want to be a mother at all. What about me? Did I have a choice? I was given and taken, a prisoner to a man and a country who demanded a child. The memory of my cheek burning in shame and desperation after you slapped me all those years back, your coarse tongue licking the blood off my wound, that memory was chasing me every day. While it was all too late for me, there was still time for her, and I should be the last woman on earth to judge her. It was her decision to make. But to help her?

"I am a prisoner in this monastery. Nobody comes to see me; I can talk to nobody."

"I am sure you know how the world spins out there, Cneaja. Help me, please."

Her hair had grown back to her shoulders as had mine. The pain she suffered left deep lines on her young face just as it did on mine: childhood, parents, joy, all gone, a mark on our face for each of the losses. But she didn't have to end up like me.

"There is a woman who visits my husband's grave from time to time. She used to be in his chambers a lot, and I know she hoped to take my place in my home and in my husband's bed. She was there when Dracula was born, and she demanded to take him away."

"Why would she want him, why did she want your baby?" Anastasia was taking in my words, her eyes wide opened with curiosity.

"She said she can tell a vampire if she sees one. You see, Dracula bit my nipple and sucked my blood just after his birth, and the women were afraid."

The memory made me shudder and I could see Anastasia's revulsion.

"Look for her at the grave. Tinca is her name, and she says she was born on a Saturday. You will know her from the green eyes. You can't miss her. She will probably help you. She would help anybody who wants to destroy me and my son."

"So she didn't take him…"

"She couldn't. My husband didn't allow it. I wish he had. I always wanted to know what could have been if she took him. I am still wondering, and I will never know."

I think that was the moment Anastasia's thought became her firm decision, because her face opened suddenly, as if a veil were lifted from it. She rushed to embrace me and then she fled, throwing a "Thank you" over her shoulder.

It was true, Anastasia's life didn't need to be wasted bearing your son if it could be helped. And I didn't have to wait around at your mercy. Maybe the desolation in my life could be replaced with joy if I helped bring Radu

back. Maybe it was finally time to take charge of my own
life

Anastasia, Târgoviște, 1457

I went to the cemetery that afternoon, right after I met Cneaja. It didn't take me very long into my life as your spouse to see that you were absent during the day, locked in your room and in the darkness of your misery. You were weak in the sun, and you didn't want anybody to see that. You didn't want them to notice how your eyes became glassy and unable to see, how your breath became so shallow that you collapsed on your bed lifeless and slept the sleep of the dead. No, you didn't want anybody to know your secrets because during the night your powers came into their own, and you went out into the world to do your grotesque work and show your cruelty to whomever dared be in your way.

It was during the night when you married me and

during the same night when you gathered all of *Valahia*'s misfits from its prisons and its streets into a barn and set it alight. It was under the night's cover when you welcomed the Turkish envoys with a nail and a hammer to their heads and under the moon's careful watch when you started to sharpen the swords, melt the gold, and round up your army for the battle with the Turks.

I knew better than to cross your path during the night. That was when I locked myself in my room and nursed my rancour and swaddled my belly tight as if that would make the baby disappear, and that was when I dreamt about Bogdan and hated you even more. Night after night.

Tinca didn't come that day, so I went back the day after and the day after that. The cemetery was small and quiet, the tombstones a constant reminder of death in those tumultuous times. The epitaphs were telling me of important people of state who ruled for many years or were cut down prematurely, of battles won and of lives lost. And then my father with no grave and no stone and his epitaph unwritten. I had plenty of time to think of these things until Tinca came on the third day.

She wasn't what I thought she would be. She wasn't young or beautiful, she wasn't full of charm or allure, there wasn't anything special about her that Princess Cneaja didn't have, something, anything your father might have wanted from another woman.

"Why are you waiting for me?" she said even before she set eyes on me.

"How did you know I was here?"

"You've been here for three days lurking in the shadows. What do you want from me?"

"Princess Cneaja sent me, she said you could help."

Her laughter cut my words short. I was startled because hers was not a laughter like mine or anybody's I knew. It sounded like her throat was a tight, rocky gorge, and the sounds echoed in it back and forth from the end of the world. Cavernous. Harsh. Unforgiving. I was taken aback.

"Why do you hide your baby?"

I looked down at my belly. I knew it couldn't be seen under the heavy cape I was wearing. Yet somehow she knew. I gathered my courage.

"I don't want this baby."

"It's not yours to want or discard. It's his."

"But I'm carrying it. And I don't want it. I don't want to carry his baby. Cneaja said you can help."

"Why would I help you? I don't owe you anything. You are nobody to me."

"I know, but don't let another one like him walk on the face of this earth."

"What do you know about the likes of him?" she asked without curiosity.

I didn't know how to tell her about your stench and your pointy teeth and hairy palms, about the saturnian disposition, the cruelty and the thirst for blood, or your secret life at night, or the power you held over me against my better judgement.

"He is a killer. He killed my father," was all I dared say.

"And now you want to be a killer, too, the killer of your baby. He killed your father, so you want to kill his baby. Revenge for revenge. An eye for an eye. Does it make it better? Does it make you feel better? A child killed for the parents' sins?"

"It is not like that, that is not why I am doing it," I said, and I felt doubt sneaking its ugly head into mine.

"Why, then, why are you doing it?"

"Because I'm scared. He is not a good man, if he is a man at all. I don't want the baby to be like him. I don't want his baby at all."

The woman looked at me with her deep green eyes, but there was nothing in them; they reminded me of your eyes at times, empty when not full of rage or hate or bitterness.

"Go home, girl."

The desperation was crawling all over me, its claws raking at my heart.

"But why me? Why do I have to pay for my father's sin?"

"Your husband is paying for his father's sin too; you are well suited to each other."

I wanted to ask more but she lifted her arm and put her palm over my mouth.

"Go home, girl, and bring this baby into the world. Then I can take him. I'll have your baby. I am the only one who can take care of him, and I will, but once he's mine, you can never have him again. You will never see us."

"Is this how this baby will pay for his parents' sins too?" I said under my breath. The words came out smothered in tears, abundant and unstoppable, the kind that only self-pity can bring about. And desperation.

Mara, Târgoviște, 1457

I saw the two women talking at the back of the church when I came out to beat the rugs. It was that day of the month when I had to scrub all the rugs around the altar and the long one to the front door, and it was always harder after a rain. People were carrying in all the mud on their shoes, and sometimes it came mixed in with straw from feeding the animals, cabbage leaves or fish bones from the market, and feathers of all sorts dipped in blood. But the worst was the dung from the horses and the dogs, which made the whole church stink and the rugs stiff. These were the days when the broom wasn't enough, and they needed a good beating outside.

The two women didn't seem friends; they weren't standing close to each other to share gossip or grief in front of the old *voievod*'s grave. They were measuring each other but not like rivals, just appraising each other's worth. They didn't seem equal, for one was standing tall and unbending while the other's head was down and her body inclined as if in need or in prayer. Their whispers were loud and hurried like a gust of wind through the trees in the woods back home.

I thought that maybe I should just keep going about beating the rugs, finish my jobs quickly and walk through the town as I usually did while waiting for my father to pick me up. But the voices were growing stronger, and I couldn't help hearing words and the curiosity got the better of me.

"What use would you have for my baby? Why my baby?"

There was no more going about my business now, after hearing this, so I just hid better around the corner of the building under the cover of some bushes and listened. I couldn't see the face of the woman who said those words or her belly full of the baby she didn't want. The words seemed big and heavy to me, and the way she said them was more like a whine and a cry for help.

I felt sorry for the woman. Her words were drenched in tears, and she seemed inconsolable.

"It's simple. If you don't want the baby, I'll have it. I'll take your baby to be mine."

The younger woman seemed taken aback by this, not sure she understood.

"But Cneaja said you would help me get rid of it."

"Then Cneaja doesn't know what she is talking about. You don't want the baby, but I do. That's all there is to it," said the other woman, undeterred, and somehow, without me seeing her step away, suddenly she just wasn't there anymore. She had vanished as if swallowed by the dusk, spat into the shadows.

It was only then that the woman carrying the baby turned her head, and I could see her face from under the hood. Oh, what a surprise was wrapped up in that cape! If that woman wasn't the same girl from the wedding in the square, the one who married the new *voievod*! I must have gasped seeing her or stepped on a branch or dead leaves because she looked towards the corner where I was hiding, trying hard to suppress her sobbing.

I hesitated; I didn't know what to do. It seemed to me I was too small for such a big secret. And while there was definitely a thrill about knowing, I also wished I could unknow it.

I went back into the church as quietly as I could and hid behind the door. I didn't want to be seen. I didn't know what I would have said or done.

On the way back home that evening, I kept thinking about the girl, the bride, the wife. She wasn't any older than me yet married to a *voievod* and carrying his baby. I thought about her luck to be born into a wealthy family—I could tell that much because her face wasn't burned by the sun, and her hands weren't cracked by too much scrubbing—to be married to an important statesman and be blessed with his child. And yet, just like my mother used to say, she wasn't counting her blessings because wealth didn't seem to mean much to her. The handsome man she had didn't seem to please her, and his baby was only a curse to be rid of.

I was thinking of the filthy-smelling rugs in the church, the empty bed at home, my mother's children being covered with the dirt from the back yard when they died. And this girl? With her beautiful cape to cover her young body, a *voievod* to look after her, and a baby to secure her place as the most important woman in the country? What was she complaining about? What was she having too much of or not enough? Why was she refusing all these honours and her own baby's life?

Because she was ungrateful, I decided. And people like that didn't deserve the good that was bestowed upon them. Selfish girl. The *voievod* didn't need her.

Following the cart my father had to drag himself since the death of the mule, I was thinking of a plate full of steaming food and a long warm cape, and I imagined for a moment they were just being handed to me. And the *voievod* was smiling when our hands touched, and that evening, when I went to my bed that didn't have the curtain anymore, I asked my mother:

"How do you get rid of a baby?"

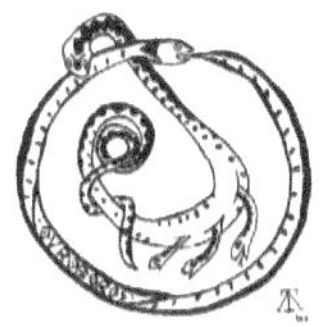

Cneaja, Târgoviște, 1457

"Ion, I asked for you because I need your help."

"Anything for my master's wife and my *voievod*'s mother, my lady."

My husband's most loyal servant had aged too. We all seemed to have grown old, except you. As our hair got thinner, yours got shinier; as our eyes got tired, yours became deeper and sharper; as our bodies were weaker, yours was a model of power and strength.

"I called you here as my husband's most loyal soldier. This has nothing to do with Dracula."

"As you wish, my lady, I am here for you." I had met Ion the moment I set foot in the country. He never left your father's side in the throne hall or on the battlefield, and he was waiting outside my bedroom door when your father came in. I didn't understand how and why he was so devoted to a man who held integrity in such low esteem.

"If your loyalty sits now with my son, you should leave."

Ion put one knee on the ground and bowed to me.

"I see mistakes, my lady, I see revenge instead of forgiveness and fear instead of justice. Revenge and fear and war rule our country now," he said, his head still down. "It is not my place to judge, but the country is suffering. People can't trust their *voievod* if he is burning their crops and poisoning their wells and killing their animals. Too much destruction was brought upon the country in this war with the Turks. Dracula is so taken by his desire to win that he forgets about the people he is doing it for. There will be no man standing to cheer his final victory."

"I see all this too, Ion. I am a prisoner here, but the walls of this monastery have ears and the doors have tongues. People talk. The country is in pain and Dracula will bring it to ruin if he continues like that."

"The war with the sultan will be the end of *Valahia*, but there is nothing we can do. He is the *voievod*."

"He doesn't have to be, Ion." The soldier lifted his head and looked at me straight. His eyes didn't betray his mood. I couldn't tell if he was outraged by my words or pleased. He was waiting.

"Radu can take his place."

Ion took his time getting up, and when he stood, he was looming over me. He was a big man, but the things he must have seen and the blood he shed on the battlefields left deep lines on his face. He looked tired but there was no shortage of determination on that face.

"What is it that you want me to do, my lady? I am no murderer."

"I didn't ask you to murder anybody, Ion. My son cannot be easily murdered, but he can be kept to one side. All we need is a new *voievod* at the ready. This is what I need your help for."

"Tell me what you have in mind."

"I want you to bring this letter to the sultan. I want you to bring it yourself and to never look at it and to never let it out of your sight. I want you to give it only to the sultan and to wait for his response. Then come back safe and never speak of this to anyone. Can you do this?"

"May I ask what the letter will say, my lady?"

"It will say that Radu is now wanted in the country, that he will be honoured as the new *voievod* by its people, and that we hope peace will be protected by the almighty Turkish empire in *Valahia*."

Ion was moving from one foot to the other, his eyes closed. He was rubbing his hands deep in thought.

"I wish there was another way," he sighed.

"I wish there was another way too. But there isn't. Radu will be good for *Valahia*. Peace will be good for *Valahia*—you know it too, Ion."

"Peace will be good for all of us."

I handed him the letter sealed with the monastery seal,

and Ion opened his leather tunic to put the letter inside. I knew he would protect it with his life.

"I am glad he took it, my lady, he seems to be a good man, a loyal soldier," said the abbess that evening. "We should pray for him, for his safe travels and his safe return."

The abbess had invited me every night to her private rooms for dinner ever since I arrived in her convent. I didn't always go. She talked too much, and she was too eager to please. She knew I was no use to her then, but she also understood that I could become useful some other time just as I also knew I needed her help to stay in touch with the outside world. It was a good arrangement for us both, and we didn't have to pretend too much to like each other.

She cleaned her lips of the cream sauce that covered the roasted piglet we had for dinner and took a sip of wine.

"This is good wine," she said, putting away the goblet and bringing closer the Bible and the crucifix we used every night for our prayer together. The metal of the crucifix sparkled warmly in the light of the candles. We prayed in silence, our hands intertwined around the Bible and the silver Jesus.

"I hope he will bring back good news. Amen," the abbess concluded and let go of my hand.

"I hope so, too, Mother, and I am sure Radu will see that your convent is well cared for. I am sure he will look after all the people who helped to bring him back and put him on the throne of *Valahia*. Radu is a very good boy."

As we rose from the table to go to our rooms for the night, the abbess said:

"The sisters found the wood you were looking for. Was it ash wood, I believe? What do you want them to do with it?"

"A stake, Mother. I want them to make a stake."

Anastasia, Târgoviște, 1457

And then we moved. You told me one evening to pack my things. You said we were going to leave the court in Târgoviște that night to go and live in our castle up in the mountains. You called it ours. The fortress the boyars built for you with their hands and their money. The place where you sent Bogdan away from me. The castle you wanted and my father had to die for. You called it ours as if I wanted any part of it, any part of you in my life, as if carrying our baby in my belly wasn't punishment enough.

There wasn't much I needed to pack. There weren't many things I wanted to bring, only memories from before I set eyes on you, memories from a childhood that seemed wrapped in soft cotton and wool, sunny days and love. I regretted not being aware of it back then when my father always had a smile for me and my mother a story.

I only became aware of affection when it was taken away from me together with all the innocence of my childhood. I longed for love only when all I had left was loathing.

The day of the move was blessed with a warm sun, and the carts were waiting at the gates for our lives to be tucked away. The maids were loading the linen and the soaps. The women in the scullery were packing the cutlery and the goblets, the chefs the hams and cheeses. There was a frenzy of activity in the house and chaos outside. Horses were aroused and grooms were flustered. The swords were reflecting the sun, making it spark, and fragments of its light seemed to be flying everywhere. Oblivious to all, you were asleep in the darkness.

When the sun set behind the walls of the city, the bustle of the day died slowly, and people and beasts settled into waiting, anguish and unease on their faces. They knew what they were leaving behind: families torn apart, goodbyes unsaid. But what was it that lay ahead? Only fear and uncertainty. Would they ever see their children growing, their parents getting old, their friends dancing in the *hora*?

You came out of your chambers indifferent. You mounted your black horse and led our procession in silence. Without a choice, we followed in silence, the hooves of the horses on the cobblestones the only sign that we were not a cortege of ghosts and ghouls.

When we came out of the city, the night was pouring over us like black ink. It was quiet and cold although spring was well under way. It was the same in my heart, frosty and bare. Only my belly was full with your child and my mind with hateful thoughts. You had me a prisoner even before locking me in your castle.

We started to climb through the forest, and among the thick trunks of the oaks and the fir trees and under the leaves that were coming out of their winter slumber, it was getting darker and darker still. And quieter. The quieter it got, the more attention we paid to every noise of a bird in the trees, every slither of a small animal out of our way, every howl of a wolf farther up in the woods waiting to meet us. You were keen to keep going, fearless, unperturbed.

I thought we had walked forever and maybe we had. My back was aching from the relentless rocking on the saddle and my belly was pushing forward, heavy with the unwanted child. I was so relieved when a little light made an appearance, flickering through the trees. I held it in my vision as a guide, careful not to lose its warm glow behind the thick trees and warming myself at the promise of it.

When we reached the hut hidden among the pines and covered in ivy, we were all ready to stop for a rest from the punishing journey you inflicted on us. Not you.

My maids were looking at me keenly, begging me to say something, anything that could warm your heart and make you take pity on us and give us a respite from the hard walk. I knew there was no such thing.

"We all need a rest," I said with a softer voice than I would have wanted, a reflection of my hopeless attempt.

"There will be plenty of rest when we get there," you replied, aloof, just as I expected.

I couldn't suppress a sigh, and it seemed to multiply and ripple through my maids and the other servants, quiet and heavy.

As we passed by the front of the hut, its door opened and four people burst out, fighting for a spot at the front, fear and curiosity alternating and mixing on their faces at the sight of us. When the two older people, a man and a woman, set eyes on you, they bowed so low their faces were buried into the rotten leaves that spring had uncovered.

"My lord, what an honour, we are at your service," they whispered.

Not the young girl. Her bow was only of her head, her eyes following you, growing bigger with the recognition of you.

I looked at her, I was watching her watching you in awe. You didn't seem to be aware of the humility and neediness buried in the old people's bows, but the intensity of the young girl's scrutiny wasn't wasted on you. Her brazenness touched you like a challenge; her eyes fixed on you like a provocation. I averted my eyes, ashamed for the two of you. The girl's parents stood there petrified, swallowing hard.

With a nod of your head, you put us all in motion again. The two old people seemed relieved, the young girl too mesmerised with you to show her disappointment, the boy too sleepy, the people in our cortege resigned.

Soon, the trees became sparser and the horses' hooves weren't buried in the moist moss of the forest anymore but hitting hard on bare rock. The path, wide and smooth moments before, became narrow and tight. On one side, the barren mountain, on the other a deep ravine.

At the next turn we got a glimpse of the sun carving its way through the peaks at the horizon. The dusky light started to soften the darkness. The climb around the mountain was relentless and the abyss beside us alarming. The servant holding my horse was probing every step with a long stick.

When the castle revealed itself around the next bend, we all gasped at the surprise of such a sight: majestic, perched at the edge of the precipice and on top of the world, dark and menacing.

A sound like a call to battle emerged from somewhere deep inside you, possessed by a frenzy I hadn't seen in you before, and you drove your boots into the horse's belly. The animal lifted his front legs and neighed in pain. From the forest we left behind, a wolf responded in tune with your call and frightened all the horses. A chilling wind started out of nowhere, carrying with it two vultures who started circling over our heads.

You couldn't or wouldn't control your impatience, and prodding wildly at the horse, you stormed up the steep path. Relieved to be left behind, we marched along with little purpose, step after step, as if carrying our crosses up to Golgotha. It certainly felt like an execution.

"My lady, wait, please, my lady!"

The young voice was calling from below us, down the path in the forest. When I looked back, I saw the girl from the hut, the girl whose eyes couldn't get enough of you earlier and whose sight you beheld.

The servant pulled the reins to stop the horse, but I told him to keep going. I had no desire to talk to that girl.

"Please, my lady, wait, I have something to give you, wait…"

The servant searched for my eyes, again looking for direction. I shook my head, and we resumed our ascent.

"There is something you need, my lady, it's for your baby, from my mother, wait…"

Those words were the ones that grabbed my attention, and curiosity got the better of me, so I told the servant to wait.

Barely out of the forest, the girl leaned against a tree to catch her breath. I looked at her, really looked at her slender body covered in a torn dress and at her broken shoes that were hanging to her feet by a thread. When she moved again and left behind the shadows of the forest, she stepped right into a pool of light, and the first rays of sun got caught in her untamed mane of blonde hair as if setting it on fire.

She was as young as me and as tall as me, but where I was dark, she was fair, where I was full, she was small, and while I carried myself with pride, she carried herself with desire. I knew then what you had seen in her. But what had she seen in you that I was missing?

"Could I talk to you alone, my lady?" she said when she caught up with us, throwing a furtive look at my servant.

"Nothing of what you say to me could be of such importance that I would want to keep it a secret," I said with faltering pride, knowing right away it was a lie.

"Are you sure, my lady?" she whispered, and hesitating for a moment, reached deep in a pocket of her dress and brought out a little bundle covered in a dark cloth. She looked at it for a moment longer as if weighing the importance of it to me, or maybe to herself.

"What is your name, girl, and what age are you?" I asked, looking down on her from my horse.

"Mara, my lady," she curtsied, fiddling with the parcel in her hands. "I am eighteen, I've been for a couple of months now, eighteen years old," she said, her eyes intent on her parcel.

"And what is it that you have for me that you think might be a secret I would want to share with you?"

The servant was fretting a few steps away with the harness, trying to keep my horse steady, and I got a glimpse of my ladies-in-waiting coming back down the path to see what was keeping me. The girl saw them, too, and after a little wavering, she handed me the parcel.

"It is something my mother said you can drink to help you with your baby, something you were looking for…"

I took the parcel in my hand and started to open it.

"I don't know what you're talking about, girl. What could I possibly want for my baby that I don't have already but that your mother has?" I smiled, and peeling off the cloth, I uncovered a handful of powder, deep red, the colour of ripe beetroot. I was unconvinced but curious.

"Well? What is it?" I asked impatiently and put out the

arm holding the parcel.

"I heard you asking for something that will help get rid of the baby. This is what that is. Something to make your wish come true. My mother said it works every time."

Her words made me dizzy, and while looking at her eager face, I became painfully aware of everybody else's—the servant looking away hoping to unhear the words, my ladies-in-waiting with disbelief plastered over distraught smiles.

"It is what? I mean, you think I wish for what?" I was hoping the louder my shouting, the more outraged my protestation would seem. But I was also scared, very scared of having my secret wish exposed like that and being brought out for judgement in front of so many people.

"How dare you?" I shouted again in despair, trying to hold onto a shred of dignity and to the parcel in my hand. But my scream scared the horse, and the horse scared me, and I let go of the bundle and watched the crimson powder being carried by the wind and falling onto the hard rock like blood drops. My baby's blood I didn't spill.

Mara, Târgoviște, 1457

I didn't know what upset her more: that I knew about her secret or that I spoke and gave her the powder in front of everybody—or was it because she wasted it all in the wind? I thought I was helping where the old woman in the graveyard wouldn't. I thought I was doing her a service, a favour, lending her a kind hand. She didn't respond with kindness, and maybe I should have known because every time I saw her, she didn't seem to be happy with what she had. I hoped that luck and all the things that came so easily to her were going to run out.

The path down to our hut was brighter now, the sharp rays of the spring sun sneaking through the branches of the trees. Climbing up, I was light despite the darkness and excited for bearing such a gift. Coming down, I felt darkness despite the light and humiliation for trying to bring it to her. I didn't know what the new *voievod*'s wife wanted, but I hoped she was never going to have it because what she already had aplenty, she didn't seem to care about. Ungrateful.

The days when I had to clean the church in Târgoviște were still the best of my whole week, even if that spring seemed to bring the most rain and wind of all the eighteen I had been alive. The rain was icy and the wind was biting and the mess was freezing on the carpets, but I didn't mind cleaning it as long as I could stay in town afterwards and watch the people go by.

I had watched the people before the new *voievod* took the reins of the country, bustling about in the streets and markets, bargaining with loud voices from under their fur hats, full of zest and ambition for their day. It wasn't the same anymore, not after his coronation. There were fewer people on the streets and even fewer of them were men. The women were hurrying about the place, hiding under their capes, and all they bought was food. No shiny fabrics, no painted leathers, just grains and beer.

I had heard my father whispering in my mother's ear about all the boyars who had been marched up to Poenari in chains to build the castle for Dracula, a fortress that the Turks would never be able to reach.

"They had to build it with their own money," he was saying, and my mother was pursing her lips and crossing herself with worry.

"I don't like it; this is not right."

"And he brought folk from the street to run the country, woman," my father kept saying.

You, Dracula

"No, it is not right, the world turned upside down with the boyars laying bricks and the bricklayers laying the law of the country," said my mother, and she crossed herself and spat three times to keep the devil away.

After a moment of silence, my father continued.

"Do you know what he did at his wedding? He pardoned all the people in his gaol as is customary and then he ordered them all into a barn he had built for the occasion. He fed them good food and gave them good wine, and he went to talk to them. But then he got very angry at them for having stolen and begged and not worked for their keep and for ending up in prison. I heard he went outside and locked the doors and ordered his guards to set the barn on fire with all those people in there." I could hear my mother gasping with horror. "We were there that night, Mara and I, we were coming back home, and we saw him and his fury, and we saw the fire with our own eyes and it was something terrible."

I could remember the flames from the barn and the screams from inside filling the night with terror and dread. Was that what happened? The enormity of that memory had my stomach tied in a knot, but my father wasn't finished.

"There is talk of an endless war too. There is talk that he is not paying his tribute to the sultan, so the war might never end. There are no men left on the streets of Târgoviște… I push my cart along the empty streets, and the stalls are closed and nobody wants my wood."

"What will we do? How will we feed ourselves?"

"Hopefully the blacksmiths will keep forging swords

and the farriers will keep making shoes for the horses so I can keep bringing something to put on the table."

That was what they were saying, but I knew it was me cleaning that church in town that was going to put the food on the table. So I cleaned and scrubbed and prayed for a different life. And sometimes I thought about the new *voievod*'s wife in her warm clothes in her castle with the baby she didn't want. Ungrateful.

"You have to stop coming here to seek me. Go clean the church, or go home, let me mourn in peace!"

The voice came from nowhere and was swallowed back quickly into the heavy mist that descended over the graveyard. She was right, the woman who spoke the words—I was there to seek her. Since seeing her with the new *voievod*'s wife that afternoon, I kept coming back in the hope that she would make an appearance for me. I didn't know if I wanted to be seen or spoken to, if I even had anything to tell her. I didn't know why I kept coming back.

I told myself it was nothing more than curiosity and that I could stop coming anytime I really wanted to, but for some strange reason, I didn't seem to have that desire. The graveyard kept calling me back, drawing me in like bees were drawn to a flower. Yet there was no food for me in it, or joy. No flower wanted to grow in its shadow and darkness, only the weeds covering its soil. Its musty air was keeping the bees away. It was calling me, the graveyard, so I kept going back.

When I heard the woman's voice that evening, I

wasn't scared. I stepped into the mist, and when she spoke again her voice came at me from everywhere, sneaking from the bushes at my feet and flowing over my head from the white moon hanging in the trees.

"Go home, girl, there is no room for you in this forsaken place. Only for sadness and revenge and their sister, death. They travel well together."

I thought this time the voice came from behind a gravestone, but it could have come from inside my head.

"I know a lot about death and sadness, my lady, but maybe you could teach me about revenge."

She started to laugh in a manic way, and her crazy laugh seemed to be everywhere around my head, scratching at my ears and at my mind.

"Revenge can't be taught, you ignorant girl. Revenge doesn't knock at your door, asking to come in. We are born with a seed of it, small, as small as the seed of kindness and of fear, or that of love."

I recognized that noise, my mother made it when her patience ran thin with one of us children, and I imagined the creature in the darkness rolling her eyes at my ignorance as my mother would have done.

The shift of the mist around me was slow, but I could feel its touch change like a dress in the wind, hugging the thighs with one blow and letting go with another. I tried hard to see through it, to guess how close this woman's body was to mine, but it seemed to me that parts of her were scattered everywhere, and at the same time, that she wasn't there at all.

"It is really up to us to decide which seed we are going to water and let grow, which seed of all the ones we have inside us are we going to bring into the light and feed. You are young, there is still hope, I hoped for love when I was your age. It is only revenge for me now, nothing left but revenge to nurture and reap its fruit."

"What happened to love?" I asked the darkness, not knowing which way to turn my head.

But then I felt a faint shuffling at my left foot, a crawling noise through dead leaves, and I looked down just as I felt the coldness of the snake climbing up my leg. I screamed and shook my leg wildly, trying to keep my balance, desperately trying not to fall, afraid of what else might creep under the leaves. I couldn't look at my leg, either, spooked, squirmish, sick with fear and revolt. The more I moved and tried to rid myself of the snake, the more it seemed to grow, its cold scales becoming larger, its body fatter and stronger, clinging to my thigh and working its way up to my waist.

"Make it stop, please, are you doing this? Please take it away, I don't want to die like this. Please," I was begging the mist and the smoke and the darkness, the thick air around that choked me, dire and poisonous.

"Make me a promise, girl, one promise and the snake goes away." The voice was whispered and sweet; the snake, cold and firm, was squeezing my thigh.

"What is that? What do you want?"

"I want your child. I want you to give me the first child that comes out of your womb to be mine and only mine."

I was stunned, my mind had never thought like that

about my body and never about my womb. The only children I ever thought about were my brothers. And they were dead. And the memory of their cold bodies and their stiff smiles sent a shiver up my spine, in the same spot where the snake was headed. I didn't know if this promise to the darkness was binding me, if it was real, if it meant much or could be forgotten. But the snake's tongue, forked and searching my skin, rough and stingy, was real. My fear of it was real. I had never been so sure in my life.

"You can have it. You can have my child. You can come and take the child any time you want. Just make the snake stop, please, make it stop."

"You have to promise," I heard the voice hissing somewhere close.

"I promise, I promise, make it stop, please."

"Say it."

"I promise to give you my child. I promise," I said, and the snake fell at my feet and slithered down under the bushes like it had never been. I kept shaking and turning around, though, the crazy dance of a madwoman, until my limb felt light again and unburdened by that awful animal.

After a while I stopped, too tired to continue, and I could feel tears ready to accompany my sobbing. I was cold and I wanted to run as far as I could, away from that devilish place of terror. When I turned, the mist was gone, the darkness melted, the sunset was spreading a warm light through the trees. And I hoped it was all just a bad dream and that my promise had been made to nobody.

Cneaja, Târgoviște, 1457

I will never forget the moment I set my eyes on Radu again. His fair eyes I hadn't seen for so many years, the sweet smile that made every day with him worth living, the gentle hands that I held when he was sick or sad or sulking and that were squeezing mine, grateful for my love, they were all there. Even the ugly scar you left on his face with your dagger had merged with his beautiful face, like a memory engraved in our minds.

He came, finally free, sent home by the sultan to take over the throne of *Valahia*. It was at the time you went up to your fortress in Poenari with all the soldiers and left Târgoviște unmanned and ungoverned. There were, of course, the peasants you had made boyars in the country's council, but they had no understanding of the Turkish political games. Murad, on the other hand, understood you didn't have the support of the country anymore, or of the boyars, or of your cousin in Moldova. The sultan knew you were weak and alone, backed in battle only by your relentless hate for him. He finally realised what I had long known, that it was time to banish you to your castle and install Radu on the throne.

"You will have to take over, Radu, before he brings *Valahia* to ruin, you have to take the throne and bring back peace for this poor country," I said to him two days after he arrived back.

"There are things you need to know, Mother, things that happened in Turkey with the Ottomans, with the sultan."

"I don't need to know these things, Radu. They happened there and they can stay there. Ours is a different land and we live by the laws that our grandfathers made as they saw fit for us. And these rules are all that matters," I said and reached out to stroke his hair.

He hesitated for a moment and then flinched under my touch. He had never done that before, but no matter, he was going to remember and learn to like it again. The two of us were going to mend all the broken bridges. Neither your father nor the sultan could keep us apart anymore, and if things were going my way, you, Dracula, would be gone soon too.

"I don't know if I am worthy, Mother; I don't know if I can."

"Of course you can, Radu, you are a good man fallen under the shadow of a monster. Where you are kind, he is unmerciful. Where you show diligence, he shows impatience and wrath. Your respect and regard for the law of the land is dragged through the mud by his disdain for anything sacred. Don't let his shadow darken your path."

Radu was shaking his head in disbelief.

"You don't understand, Mother. You talk about mercy and patience, but things are not the same for him. He is unmerciful because he was never shown mercy. He is impatient because nobody does things better than him, or swifter. And you say he doesn't show respect for sacred things, but you know, when your own father betrays you, it is hard to keep anything sacred at heart."

"Maybe it is how you say it is, Radu, but he is still a monster who poisons the wells and kills the animals and burns the crops and spreads the leprosy and impales living people, and he does it in the name of the country."

Radu's eyes were looking down, watching his own restless hands in his lap. I reached out with my hand under his chin and brought it up. He didn't flinch this time, and in the end, he lifted his eyes and gazed into mine expectantly.

Of course he wasn't the same Radu I had lost all those years back. He wasn't the innocent child my husband left at the sultan's court, not the Radu I had in front of me. I looked in his eyes, searching for proof that the rumours I heard about him enjoying the harem life weren't true, but I couldn't see anything beyond tiredness, resignation, and weakness. It didn't matter; there wasn't anything I couldn't heal with bowls of chicken broth and slices of gammon and juicy breasts from young pheasants. He was home now—my Radu came back to me and to his country, the country you were destroying, battle by battle.

But, after all, even a tired and weak *voievod* was better for *Valahia* than a tyrant murderer. I was his mother and if he was tired, I would help him rest. If his trust in himself took a beating, I would reassure him. If he became weak, I would prop him up and lead him from the shadows. Anything to free our country and ourselves from you.

"This war has to end. We have to make it end. You and I, against him."

"There is nothing we can do to stop him, Mother, you know it yourself. He is invincible," said Radu with a sigh.

I went to the armoire in my room that held all my belongings in the monastery. I didn't have many clothes or shoes or other frivolous things, and the few pieces of jewellery I used to enjoy had long been transformed into golden coins to be used quickly and without trace when the need was there. I picked up the long parcel at the back of the cabinet. It was covered in red velvet, which I had cut out from a useless dress I used to own, and I brought it to Radu.

"Nobody is invincible, Radu," I said, uncovering the stake made by the nuns from the finest ash wood.

I should have known better, though. I shouldn't have let my love for Radu blindside my judgement of you or your power. I thought Radu and I could move mountains together and remove you from the throne, but he wasn't the son I hoped he was.

Two days after his arrival, I sent word that I wanted to see you in the monastery. I didn't know if you had heard of Radu's return or the sultan's plans to put him on the throne of *Valahia*. It didn't matter, it wasn't why I had asked for you. I might have made the plan in haste after seeing Radu home, but I had the ash wood stake made some time before. It was, I had been told, a sure way to kill a vampire.

The plan, though, required a particular strength on Radu's part, and he didn't have it. When he had to surprise you in the monastery's inner yard, he failed. When he had to bring out the stake, he failed. When he had to strike you, his will failed him, and you struck him.

Wiping the blood from his cheek, the blood from the second wound you just inflicted on his face in front of me, I saw for the first time that the delicacy that I loved about him wasn't something to admire but something to pity. The softness he displayed in his eyes wasn't kindness but weakness, and the gentleness of his hands didn't come out of gracefulness but of cowardice. My Radu wasn't a fighter or a leader, he was a follower. And that was why Murad chose him. The sultan didn't want a *voievod* for Wallachia, he wanted a puppet with strings woven out of the golden riches of the harem, a puppet he could easily control.

"You should have fought back, Radu. Like we planned. I lured him here in the monastery to reason with him or be done with him. He didn't want to reason, which is why I gave you the stake. You stood close to him, and you had the stake at hand, just like we planned.

Why did you hesitate?"

The blood gushing from the wound on his cheek smothered his tears, and his sobbing smothered his words.

"I…I…couldn't… Mother…I…don't want to. I love him, I am not like you, I love him."

The disbelief got the better of me for a moment, and I just stood there untangling his words with my mind and tangling my fingers through his.

"You don't know how it was in prison, in the Turkish caves, in the darkness and the cold. When there was no hope, he held my hand. When there was no food, his hand guarded my tin, and when there was no water, it was his hand that stole from other people. He looked after me there, in the caves, until we were moved to the harem. And in the end, he wanted me to run away with him. He told me to go with him and I didn't. I didn't want to, not from the harem."

I kept stroking his hand and let his words sink in. The more intense my stroking, the more I could feel my love for him dissipating, and in its place, a hole allowing for disappointment to take residence.

"He was good to me, and I always felt love for him, and admiration. He was like a father to me," said Radu, stopping my hand and squeezing it gently. "I am sorry I didn't become who you wanted me to be. I am good for the sultan but no good for my country. I will always be his *voievod*, not *Valahia*'s."

"What about me, Radu? What about my duty to give a good *voievod* to the country? It is easy for you to say you failed, but me? How could I fail so miserably?"

Radu was asleep now in the cell next door, awaiting his coronation.

Outside the monastery walls was the town of Târgoviște, the cradle of the nation, busily at work, preparing to welcome its newest *voievod*. Just outside the city gates lay the Turkish tents full of janissaries, and among them, in the middle, under the golden crescent, slept the sultan. He led his army all the way to the heart of our country to place Radu on the throne and take the power in his hands. You tried to stop them, but while you had the extraordinary power of one, they had the power of many. You stopped caring and retreated to your castle. They finally prevailed.

I always imagined the joy I would feel when the day of Radu's coronation came. I imagined it so strongly that it always felt real to me, like the comfort of a cold rain on a scorching day or like the joy of the crimson juice of a ripe cherry bursting into my mouth. I knew how I would feel, and my body knew it too, and it was desperately craving that relief. Except today, the relief didn't come. There was disappointment and fear. There was regret and guilt. No relief.

My husband took me from my parents and trusted me to carry his heirs who would carry the flag for Wallachia's independence, and I failed him. My two sons were *Valahia*'s worst enemies: Radu was enslaving it and Dracula was ruining it, and all I could do was watch them while stroking one's hand and hiding an ash stake in my armoire for the other.

Sleep didn't come for me. The night was unravelling its clouds over the moon, and their black smoke invaded my room through the closed window, putting out the candle. I wondered if it was you haunting my cell and if you knew about my treason. I sat in bed waiting for a sign. The silence was as thick as the darkness. And it was as dense outside of me as it was inside.

"I didn't ask to be your mother!" I yelled to the murkiness around me. "I didn't ask to be anybody's mother!" I yelled again, but the murkiness didn't yell back, and my scream seemed just an afterthought hanging in there between memory and regret, choking me. I got out of bed and opened the window, gasping for air. In front of my window, perched on one of the branches of the walnut tree, an owl.

Anastasia, Târgoviște, 1457

The crimson powder flew with the wind like a wounded bird, and the girl who brought that cure was driven away by my pride. Only the baby was still in my belly, heavy and burdensome, unaware of being unwanted. I knew I should feel love for my baby, but all I felt was resentment and shame, my belly—proof of my decline. Will the woman from the cemetery come to claim it as her own like she said? I knew I didn't want the baby to see the light of day, but once born, could I give it away? What if its little face and limbs would talk the language of love and weave me into its intricate web of feelings? What if I wanted to keep it? Surely you would never allow it to be taken away. You would never give away your first born, your own blood, bad or good, saintly or monstrous.

I kept marching towards the castle. For the last stretch of the ascent, I dismounted and began my climb of the one thousand four hundred and eighty steps that led to your fortress. You told me about these steps with pride and endless anticipation. You spoke with disdain about the boyars building them, measuring their worth in stone slabs laid for you, not in the good deeds they did for the country or the families they left behind.

The sun was up now, and you had disappeared for a while, hiding somewhere in the entrails of your castle away from the sun's light and heat. The climb was hard and arduous, and our small procession of women and laden donkeys was advancing slowly. I was the last in our line since my conversation with the strange girl from the woods, who seemed so willing to tangle herself into our story. I was advancing slowly with tiredness, drawn back by reluctance. There was nothing good waiting for me up there. Why rush?

I kept my eyes down, careful of the steps I was taking on the treacherous rocks and taking furtive looks at the breathtaking abyss, which was calling me with enticing promises of calm beauty. I sat on the edge of the precipice and closed my eyes.

Come down to me, the abyss seemed to say, *and lie with me awhile. Rest on the bank of my river and close your eyes to hear the murmur of my wind, the caressing whisper of my willow branches on your face. Come…*

There was warmth in those words, and there was comfort, and I would have happily stayed there to bask in the relief they were bringing me. There was stillness in the air and silence in the breeze and peace was finding its way into my heart when I felt a tender touch on my arm and heard a whisper.

"I never thought I would see you again, Anastasia. It is you, it is really you, thank God for bringing you to me."

I opened my eyes to fingers feeling my skin and to Bogdan's eyes staring into mine.

"Bogdan?" I couldn't stop saying his name, and I started touching him with the same amazement with which he was touching me, with fervour and the joy of recognition. Our eyes, palms, fingers, lips were so hungry for each other that when we finally kissed, it didn't seem like attraction or the intense pleasure of discovery as it had when we stole our first kiss. It seemed rather like desperation, fear of losing each other again.

We hurried, afraid of someone seeing us, worried about what could happen if you found out. We hurried to disentangle our bodies, but we remained tangled otherwise, thoughts and desires unnamed and unfulfilled.

"I heard Dracula ordered all of you here, Bogdan, and I have feared for your life ever since. I am so happy to see you are well," I said, but I could see he was not well. The rags he was wearing revealed a skinny body, a shadow of the towering young man he used to be. He seemed smaller, bent from his waist as if apologising for his survival. His face was rough, burned by the sun and slapped by the unforgiving winds, and the palms of his hands bore the marks of the rocks they carried. His hair was long and matted, and his face, sad now and resigned, was hidden under an unkempt moustache and beard.

"What did he do to you, sweet girl?" he said when he finally allowed his eyes to leave my face. "You are carrying his child." The words came out stifled somewhere between regret and anger, and they filled me with dread.

"I had no choice in it, Bogdan; it wasn't what I

wanted."

He listened to me full of tenderness, but his calm blue eyes were gathering the dark clouds of storm.

"I know, it isn't what I wanted for us when I threw the headdress at your door. I wanted the dancing, the kiss, and the swim under the midsummer sun, and I was hoping for a happy wedding and for a child of our own. Instead, he gave me a shovel and he gave you his child, and everywhere we look, there's death that he has brought upon all of us: our parents and other people's children, animals, wells, crops—all sacrificed on a whim, only to satisfy his need for destruction."

His hands continued to touch my hair and my face, my shoulders and then again from my head down but never as low as my belly, as if I wasn't a whole person but a portrait of me hanging on a wall.

"I think I should go, Bogdan, before they know I am missing. I will try to come and see you again, anytime I can, if I can at all. Stay around the castle, I will try to look after you, send you some clothes and some food. Stay strong for me, please."

"I don't need food or clothes, Anastasia," he said with bitterness. "I need a dagger or a sword. I need to face the monster and kill him and spill his blood on every step of these one thousand four hundred and eighty that he made us build. I need to show him that his blood is not worth any more than that of all the people who died here. He is not in charge of death. Death doesn't listen to him."

"Sometimes I think it does, Bogdan, he is not like me and you. Things that count for us don't matter to him because he does not take his power from the light of the day like the rest of us, but from the darkness of the night and from all the evil creatures that are lurking in it."

"Look after yourself, Anastasia, and stay away from him. I'll find a way for us to run away from here. You'll see."

I wanted to believe him, I wanted to be as naive as I was when we first met, but that part of me was broken. The naivety that produced hope broke sometime between my father's impaling and my husband's indifference.

When the big wooden gate opened and then closed behind me, and I found myself inside the inner yard of the castle, I knew that was the end of my world.

Mara, Târgoviște, 1457

I woke up that morning with the feeling that something had happened, but I didn't know what. I felt strangely joyful but weirdly ashamed, as if my joy was something I should hide. I was hot from the inside as a fever might make me feel, and my skin was prickly on the outside, as if touched by the wings of a swarm of bees at the height of summer.

I started to get dressed and when I touched my skin it sent an ache, a flash of pain, right down in the centre of my belly, but not something that hurt—on the contrary, it was like a flash of sweetness, and it reminded me of the one time I licked honey from a jar that was left unwashed in the church.

Would my mother be able to see what I was trying to hide? Would she know from looking into my eyes what was going on inside my belly? I came out of the hut with a spring in my step and a song in my head. My mother was outside, hanging out a few rags to dry.

"It's nice to see a smile on your face," she said,

busying herself with the job at hand.

I didn't say anything, afraid the words might betray me. I grabbed a rag from her basket and went to the line to hang it up. Why was I suddenly so happy?

"You're humming," said my mother near me, eyeing me up and down with warmth. "What song is that?"

"I don't know, I don't think it's a real song, I'm not sure…"

I could feel my cheeks being set on fire from that spark inside me. Could she see it too? Maybe she could because all of a sudden, she dropped the clothes and the pegs and came even closer. Her eyes were fixed on me, and I could see the warmth from before disappearing and fear spreading on her face to replace it.

She brought her hand to my chin and turned my face away from her, examining my neck. She gasped, and the air coming from her throat sounded like terror and panic.

"Oh God, oh God, not her, not my girl. Please, don't let that happen!"

Her fear rubbed against my skin like sand in a storm and invaded my mouth, making me choke.

"Mother, stop, please, you scare me, what is it? Please, stop…"

My mother was crossing herself with rapid movements, as if trying to get ahead of something, as if her quick devotion to God was going to stop whatever was to be happening to me.

"Talk to me. What is it?" I asked as she took another

look at my neck.

"A bite is what it is, two small holes in your neck is what it is, and dry drops of blood hanging off them," she said, spitting on her thumb and rubbing my neck with it. "And they won't go away, they are not going away," she kept talking, spitting, and rubbing.

I wasn't sure I knew what she meant, but I knew it could not be good.

"Are you sick? Are you in pain?"

Her questions and her worry took me by surprise because she wasn't one to fuss about us children, and even when my brothers were dying, she would just sit by their straw bed prostrate, laying cold cloths on their foreheads and murmuring prayers.

I wasn't sick and I didn't feel any pain, but my sweet secret was disappearing from my belly, leaving an empty spot there like a hole or like a cloud that had dropped all its rain and was melting away, consumed and finished.

"I don't feel sick, Mother, I feel fine, will you tell me what it is? What are you scared of? What is the meaning of what you see on my neck?"

"I think it's a *strigoi*, girl, a vampire, an undead feeding on your young blood, a *zburător* maybe, if we are lucky."

I had heard of *zburător* before, a dark spirit of the night, showing up as a handsome man to young unmarried girls and torturing them in their dreams. Was that what my shameful happiness from last night was? The joyful secret that was lingering in my belly? None of it felt like torture, though. There wasn't anything that I wouldn't want to feel again and again and hide it from my mother again and again.

"I don't know what you are talking about, Mother, I didn't feel anything, and it doesn't hurt at all."

I touched my neck and rubbed it as hard as I could.

"See? No pain, it doesn't hurt."

My mother pulled my hand away and took a closer look. She spat again on her thumb and rubbed some more. I could feel my neck becoming hot and sore and prickly, but I stayed there like a log in the storm, unmoved and unknowing.

"Maybe it was a spider or a scorpion," she said in the end. "Go and strip your bed and open the doors and the windows and sweep the whole house."

I was glad to do it, so glad to free myself of her touch and get myself out of her sight.

I swept the floors and shook the cloths from the beds. I even changed the straws from underneath them and couldn't find anything to show my mother. She came back again and again to look at me, searching my eyes and looking me up and down like that would give her a measure of what happened to my neck. She kept sighing and muttering and making me go over things I had already done, gloomy and unhappy.

In the end, when everything was turned and turned again, when even the ashes in the hearth were sieved and thrown away, she gave up. I sat down on my bed and covered the marks on my neck with my hand. I was feeling the two small lumps gently, asking them to tell me the secret of their story when my mother barged in again.

"Go into the forest and fetch some garlic. Go on, hurry up," she nudged me.

I got up from the chair reluctantly, but she would have none of it, pushing me forcefully through the door. She seemed angry with me, and I didn't understand why, because I hadn't put the marks on my neck by myself and I didn't know who or what did, and my joy and my secret from my sleep were now ruined and it was her fault. It was all her fault.

"I can't wait to leave this house and this misery behind!" I said through gritted teeth and slammed the door behind me.

The forest swallowed me quickly into its mossy stillness, and I dumped my anger on the moist leaves at my feet and hung it from the bare branches that were touching my face. And yet more rose up from inside me, and more was clutching at my head like a madness I couldn't control or stop.

Only one thought seemed to be able to soothe my rage, and I kept saying it in my mind—*I will leave this life behind*—and I ran through the woods as fast as I could, churning that thought—*I will leave this life behind*—as my feet were churning through the leaves on the ground.

As I was reaching the end of the forest, my soles started to feel the rock underneath and my eyes started to see through the sparse trees the rocky way ahead and my nose started to take in the crisper air of the higher mountain. The thought grew stronger in my mind like a storm gathering all the dust from a field in a crazy swirl, blowing it around with no purpose or direction, just rage.

When I stepped out of the trees, I found myself on the edge of the precipice, breathing hard from the running, tired of it and of my life, tired of the misery it carried with it. The Târnava River was raging beneath, its muddy waters carrying the misfortune of other lives like mine. I wanted to jump, I badly wanted to jump and leave everything behind, my life and my parents' hut. I wanted to cause my mother the sadness she caused me, but the sudden memory of my dead brothers made me freeze. I didn't want to die, I suddenly remembered. In fact, I truly hoped I would never have to die, but what could I do that would help me leave my unfortunate life behind?

I stepped back from the edge of the precipice and took a moment to look around me at the old trees and the ancient mountain and at the never-ending sky. Up there, ruling from the top of the mountain over the river and the forest and the villages underneath, sat the *voievod*'s castle, indifferent to all, sturdy and domineering, a victory of man against nature.

I imagined the sulking young girl, the *voievod*'s new wife, carrying her belly along the castle's long corridors and in its throne hall, her ungratefulness caked all over her surly face. The tumult from before started to settle, my mind started to free itself of the poisonous thoughts, and a grain of hope started to sprout.

Maybe I should be the one living that life in that castle, I said to myself with more determination than hope.

You, Dracula

"No more pulling this cart for me from tomorrow," said my father, trying to get it over a hump on the forest path. "I was talking to the priest tonight when you were finishing the washing." The coldness of the cleaning water sent shivers through my tired back, and my hands felt again the painful tingle I always got after dipping them into the icy bucket.

"And what did he say?"

"He said the butcher is getting a new donkey because the old one is too old even to sell the meat off his bones, but he was going to give the skin to the tanner."

"So what does this have to do with you not pulling the cart tomorrow?"

"I am going to go to the butcher and give him some wood to give me the old donkey," my father said with some pride.

"What about the tanner? What if he wants the skin?"

"I will give him some wood too. I have plenty of wood, I just need a donkey to haul it."

The cart seemed to be ripping apart with every tug my father was giving it. The shrieking sounds echoed in the murky forest and kept startling me. We made this journey back home from town almost every night, yet any noise coming from the dark could send me into the depths of fear and desperation.

"You might need a new cart too," I said just to reassure myself I wasn't swallowed by the tar night.

"Just new hinges, I think, but these can still do good by us for a while."

My father's gasp the next moment heightened my fear even more, and I looked where he was looking, trying to make out what he was seeing. Nothing. The darkness was dense and when I opened my mouth, it rolled on my tongue, covering it like butter would cover a slice of bread.

"Isn't that strange?" murmured my father to himself. "I thought we should be home already."

"Can you see anything?"

"No. Make sure you keep your hand on the cart, don't get lost. The darkness should lift any minute, and we'll be on our way."

I stepped closer to the cart, but when I reached for it, my fingers didn't feel the grain of the wood, polished and worn and reliable. They touched something else, alive and surprising, both smooth and coarse, liquid and solid, hot and cold. *This couldn't exist*, I told myself while moulding it with my hand, *but I wish it did*. I tried to pull back from it, but a gentle force kept it in place and caressed it with slow and reassuring touches, and since fighting it seemed useless, I abandoned myself wholly to that caress. My hand was swallowed bit by bit by whatever it was, and suddenly the ground at my feet was covered in it too. Neither slimy nor metallic, hard or soft, that feeling, playful and delightful, my feet were sinking in it. It seemed as if I was drowning slowly and I wanted to scream, but I couldn't hear my voice. I couldn't even hear it in my thoughts. My voice and my thoughts were drowning, my mouth filling up with something that couldn't be. I kept telling myself, *If only it were real.*

I didn't know how long it was before my father's cry reached me. At the beginning, I was urging him to go away, voiceless, hopeful, but then, as his screams became words and I recognized my name, I took two gulps of air and opened my eyes.

"What happened?"

My father was standing in front of me shaking his head, frightened. "You turned weak and pale, and you were trembling."

"I wish I knew," I said with disappointment when my fingers touched the wood of the cart.

"It's time to go, the darkness is gone."

I looked around me and I could see the veins of the oak leaves and the ants on the bark of the trees and the blades of grass trampled by the wheels of the cart. The darkness had lifted like it had never been.

"I don't believe it! It was here all the time, just in front of us, right under our noses."

My father was pointing at something between the trees. I looked in that direction and right there, in front of us, stood our hut, darker than the night and quieter than silence itself.

"What's that smell?" my father asked before we set eyes on all the garlic that hung from every window and door.

"I'm not putting it in my mouth!" I said coming into the house. "You can't make me. I saw what you did to Gheorghiţă, but I'm not having any garlic stuffed into my mouth, I'm not dead."

"Nobody is asking you to, that is, if you want to die…" said my mother, rubbing some garlic leaves around the hearth.

"What is all this, woman? Our house smells of stew from miles away. What happened?"

"Show him your neck, Mara, show him the bite."

I touched my neck where the lumps should have been, but I couldn't feel anything. The skin was smooth and soft, and my fingers couldn't find the bite.

"It's gone—there's nothing here, look." I went towards my father, but my mother grabbed my arm and looked for herself. She rubbed. She scrubbed. She spat on her thumb, and she rubbed again.

"Stop, you're hurting me! It's gone, leave me alone."

"It can't be gone just like that, vanish into thin air. It was here this morning."

My father came closer and touched my mother's hand gently.

"It's like you wish it to be there. If it's gone, it's gone, leave the girl alone."

My mother took her hand away and cleaned it on her torn apron.

"Tomorrow we might be getting a new donkey," said my father, pulling a three-legged chair from under the table and sitting on it with a groan.

My mother pulled out the other and settled on it, resting her elbows and her eyes on the empty table.

"Less food for us," she said, picking up an imaginary crumb between her fingers.

Sleep wouldn't come. I lay there and tossed about on the freshly changed straw, hoping to make it settle around me, trying to nestle myself into it so it wouldn't poke me at every move. I didn't think the straw was the cause of my sleeplessness, though, or the coldness that entered into me once the fire in the hearth died down. It had to do with the thoughts that circled my head about the strange day I had had and the crazy stir of fear and excitement, fear, and curiosity, fear and desire for all of it to happen again.

When my parents and my brother were fully asleep, with heavy breaths from chests free of the deadly disease that killed the others, I opened my eyes. It was dark in the room, but bright outside, with a sweet light that didn't shine like the one from the moon. It was a light so warm that it brought a smile to my face and a giggle to my heart. The house was still dark and cold, none of the lustre from outside was penetrating our citadel of misery. I looked at my family, snoring, unaware of the wonder outside. They wouldn't understand anyway.

I closed my eyes again and my right hand found its way to my right nipple and squeezed it gently. The more pleasure was bursting out of it, the more I wanted it to keep coming, so I kept squeezing. When my other hand clasped my other nipple, the pleasure was coming in small waves all over my body, screaming at me to do it more, to touch myself more, to search my body for more.

I didn't need to search hard, though, because my body was showing me every spot that wanted to be crushed, every bit of skin that wanted to be pinched, every opening that needed filling with that joy, only to make more of it. When my fingers started to circle around one point between my legs, I became scared that I couldn't contain all that pleasure anymore, yet I wanted to keep making it. That was when it all stopped. Abruptly. Like my body wasn't in tune with my mind anymore. Like I wasn't in tune with that part of myself anymore. Like I was dead and unnecessary.

I was just about to close my eyes and try again to go to sleep when a movement outside caught my attention. None of the light of before was left. It was as if someone blew it out over the forest one moment and then sucked it back in the other and spilled out darkness instead. The same way the light before was warm and inviting, the blackness after was impenetrable. But it wasn't just like a wall had grown at my window. It had depth like the water in a well, and it shimmered as if stirred with the light of a candle. It was bubbling. My eyes couldn't get away from it, caught in its dance, following its wafts of smoking shadows, trying to see what lay behind.

The face wasn't clear at first. I didn't know which part of the blackness were eyes and which part were ears. I didn't know how much murkiness goes into making skin and how much it takes for hair. But the face cropped up nonetheless on the other side of my window like a memory or a dream, both familiar and new, someone I should share secrets with and run away from.

"Who are you?" I asked the shadows without saying the words.

"You know who I am."

I looked back in the room to the bed where my family was sleeping, but they were undisturbed. The face outside shimmered in silence, but I could hear its laughter.

"They can't hear me."

"Why?"

Suddenly, the mist swirled around and gathered two eyes, darker even than the darkness before.

"Because I am somewhere in your mind."

I knew then it was the truth. I understood it was in there yet not all woven by my own thoughts. I accepted that somebody else was taking place in my head, and I was becoming a spectator at their play.

"Should I be scared?"

The eyes disappeared into the swirl of shadows and then gathered at the window again.

"You should be grateful."

A wave of gratitude wrapped itself around me. I opened the window and ripped all the garlic that was still hanging around and threw it as far as I could, then I sat back on my bed.

"Now, let's finish what we have started," the voice of darkness said.

You, Dracula

Without another word from the shadows, I brought my hand to the point between my thighs where all the pleasure from before was still waiting, and I made more room in my mind for my guest.

Cneaja, Târgoviște, 1457

And so, the day of Radu's coronation arrived. Nobody knew where you were, hiding in your fortress in Poenari or lurking in the woods around Târgoviște with your soldiers, ready to strike and to stop Radu and the sultan from taking your throne.

It had been a long journey for them from Istanbul, and you made it a hard one too. You harassed their troops by night with erratic attacks, and you starved them by day. You paved their way into *Valahia* with burnt crops and carcasses of rotten cows and pigs so they wouldn't find a crumb to eat. As for water, there wasn't a well left unpoisoned in the whole country.

If all these stories were true or not, I didn't know, but I believed Radu when he told me that all your attacks stopped just a few days short of their arrival in Târgoviște. "It was so quiet everywhere we went," he said. "There were no people around, no animals, no birds. For two days we marched in the scorching heat, and we didn't meet a soul." I remember his eyes tearing up and avoiding mine when he said, "Only then we got the stench. There was no wind to carry it away so, when we took in that putrid air, laden with death, we feared for our lives for the first time. Because you see, the smell came from decaying bodies, and these bodies, half eaten by vultures and worms, with their insides spilling out of their bones and no skin or flesh to hold them together, these bodies, Mother, were hanging high on stakes over our heads. And they were many. As many as I could see with my eyes, and the more I left behind, the more appeared in front of me. And we had to walk like that, with these leftover people staring down on us all the way to Târgoviște. It is hard for me to think Dracula did that, Mother," said Radu. But for me, knowing you the way I did, it has never been hard to think the worst of you.

There were rumours you were going to attack the day of the coronation. I didn't think you would, not with all the Turkish soldiers swarming around Târgoviște like ants over a slice of melon forgotten in the sun. The sultan had guards with rifles peeping out from every opening in the battlements around the city. The view from there was the best there was, and they wouldn't have missed a badger if one tried to find its way under the leaves. I didn't think you had any soldiers left to strike the Turkish army. I tried to imagine you in your fortress, planning to take your throne back from my son Radu, and Anastasia beside you, planning to take your son away from you.

The dress I was wearing was scratching my skin, too tight and too heavy with all the embellishments required to be worn by the *voievod*'s mother. I wasn't the same mother I had been at your coronation, deemed insignificant by you and your greed for power. I wasn't the same one you threw in the monastery—childless, lonely, unheralded, clad in the black smock of widowhood. I was now the mother of another *voievod* praised by the sultan himself but whom, sadly, I deemed insignificant. I felt sad to have mothered two sons but neither good for the country.

Murad didn't get up when I came in. He was sprawled on the throne, his head barely emerging from under the heavy golden silks and green velvets of his gown. He, a Turk, sitting on the throne that cradled your father's shameless betrayals and your incessant thirst for blood. The forefathers were sure to roll in their graves at the shame of all the Turkish crescents adorning the hall. Their flags guarding the sultan to his left and right, the turbans popping out from all corners. The hall became foreign to me, it didn't hold any trace of Christian mercy, so I resolved not to expect any. For once and just for a brief moment, I would have wanted you to prevail in your battles with the Turk and wipe the smile from his smug face.

"We meet again," said the sultan, changing his position on the throne, as if trying to reaffirm his legitimacy on it. He had none. He had done nothing to earn it except for holding prisoner the rightful *voievod* and using him. Radu and I owed him nothing.

I bent my head just enough so he wouldn't take offence.

"You got the son you wanted in the end," he said, clearing his throat.

"I did," I said, but in my mind, I knew I got the son the sultan was done with. "And you put him on the throne of *Valahia*, just like I begged you a long time ago. You could have spared a lot of time and the suffering of a lot of people."

"The time has come now." He shifted position again, bent forward, and summoned me to him with his finger.

I took a few steps forward and stopped, but his finger kept moving, calling me closer. My feet seemed to have taken roots, refusing to move. I shuffled with great reluctance until he seemed satisfied.

"What about your other son? The one you didn't like? Where is he?"

"I don't know. He doesn't like me either. Dracula doesn't like anybody well enough to tell them anything."

"He's putting up a great fight against me."

"He likes his battles, and he feeds on revenge. One doesn't want to be on the wrong side of Dracula."

His laughter filled the throne hall, and for a moment, I thought the guards were loosening their grip on their weapons and relaxing, but when he stopped abruptly, the ice in his voice froze them again.

"There isn't much of a side to take. I wouldn't want to be on the loser's side. Soon he will have to admit he has lost this battle, and others, all the battles. He will have to come and surrender."

"Dracula didn't know how to love me as a son, and he doesn't know how to love his wife as a husband, but he loves his country as a *voievod* and he will never surrender it to you."

Murad sat back on the throne again and rested his arms on it, settling into his position of power.

"That might be so, but his father declared Wallachia a vassal to the Ottoman Empire, and Dracula should have kept it this way. Instead, he didn't pay the tribute, and he refused to send me the five hundred boys he owed me every year, and then he sent my envoys back to me with their turbans nailed to their heads. And he thought I would be scared and run or hide. Look at him now! Tell me who is hiding now and who sits on the throne? To be a *voievod* you need to have a country, and his country is now mine. But you, Princess Cneaja, you are still the mother of a *voievod*. Be happy—Radu will do what's right for all of us!"

I went back to the monastery that day. There was nothing for me to be happy about when the celebrations unfolded the night of the coronation. After months of war and your destruction, there were no cows or pigs left in the country to feast on nor chickens to lay the eggs needed for the cakes, and the wheat for the bread lay burnt in the field. There was no barley to make beer and no water to pull from the poisoned wells. There were no prisoners to be released and no men to dance the *căluș* as it happened at your coronation. There were only women like me crying to see the devastation you left behind.

The Turkish trumpeters didn't know our songs, and their singers couldn't understand our *doina*. Their camels didn't taste like our lambs, and the gold crescent on their flags seemed empty of life compared to the eagle on ours.

You were gone, hiding God only knew where, looking, maybe, for your next prey, like the wolves you kept for company. Or maybe you were planning your next move in the war that brought so much destruction upon the country you said you loved. But this love of yours wasn't ordinary, it was intense and obsessive, like a curse you couldn't help spread. And you always demanded to be revered and cherished in return.

What you took for love was poison that destroyed everything it touched. It crushed me, it killed your father, it sabotaged Radu, and it wiped out the country. How blind were you not to see what you had done? How misled by your own mind not to feel ashamed? How many more lives were you going to ruin in pursuit of your imaginary love?

When the last of the Turkish soldiers left Târgoviște, when the dust settled over the wax that sealed Transylvania's fate as a vassal of the Ottoman Empire again, when the sultan wasn't asking for Radu anymore but for his money, and Radu got sadder and more disheartened and hated himself for his weaknesses and his country for its demands, I called on him to see me at the monastery.

"You should come back into town, Mother, the town

house is your home, not here. This is… so sparse…" he said, looking around my cell with a mixture of disbelief and pity.

"And what is waiting for me in town, Radu?"

"The life that you left behind, Mother, your memories. You have been the lady of this country and its mother for a long time."

"But this is not my country anymore. It isn't the country your father and brother tried to protect. It doesn't belong to us anymore; it belongs to the sultan."

"I thought that was what you wanted, Mother. You wanted Dracula gone and me on the throne of *Valahia*, regardless of who gathered its taxes in their coffers. Isn't this what you wanted? There's peace in the country now."

"I wanted you to be a true *voievod*. I wanted you to rule for the good of the country and bring prosperity back to people's homes. Peace is good but poverty isn't. The poor of this country are poorer now, and they are worked harder by their boyars than they have ever been, and their children are sicker and their patience is running thin. Do you know what this means?"

Radu's eyes were on me, but they were empty of emotion or care.

"I told you I am not cut out for this, Mother. I don't know how to say no to the sultan or lead a country against its enemies. I can hardly look after myself since I left the harem, let alone an entire country. I wanted to please you and fulfil my duty as you taught me to. I thought I should be able to do it, but your will is not enough. I can't be the man you want me to be, the man who stays on the throne of *Valahia* and tends to its prosperity and keeps its people willing. I am a simple man."

His subservient and dejected words made me suddenly aware of the air my son was surrounding himself with and spreading around—a dead air, still and dull, with no movement, no intent or purpose, an air stinking of breezeless marsh that made one want to go away and leave it behind.

"Radu, it is not in my power to help you anymore, if it has ever been. Go and fight or go and hide. I am staying here to wait for my end in peace. A widow of a heartless husband who gave me two sons with no heart between them. What is left of me but the carcass of a woman broken inside? I failed my mother by failing as a mother. And I failed my duty. I couldn't raise children worthy of this country as she taught me."

"Never mind the country, Mother—does my love for you count for nothing? The love I had for you as a child and carried with me in the Turkish caves? Always wanting to please you, always wanting to be held in your high esteem and always failing? You never saw me as your boy, you only saw me for a *voievod*. Well, I never wanted to be one; I just wanted to be your son. Does that count for anything?"

Radu murmured all that with sad eyes, but the air around him didn't move—dead and unnerving like the stillness of blackness—and ultimately, his words didn't move me.

When the door closed behind him, I sat down on the narrow bed in my cell and looked at the Virgin Mary's image hanging on the wall, pained and ageless, looking at her child. What did she feel, mothering that boy? Was it love or duty? Did she want that child to be hers or to share him with the world? Was she proud or full of regrets?

I covered the painting with a shawl and turned the small table away from it. Radu's stillness was hanging heavy in the air, so I opened my window to let the night breeze in. The owl was there, perched on the same branch of the old oak as it had been ever since I moved into the monastery. At the beginning, I had tried to shoo it away, afraid of the news of death it was carrying. But death was now a part of my everyday life. There was nothing to be afraid of.

I sat down, unscrewed the bottle of ink, and sharpened the quill. The paper felt thick under my fingers and its ridges soothing, ready to collect my hurt, my disappointment, the love I didn't receive and the love I still had to give. I was going to put it all on paper, my story, the story of my life. Not of what I did, but of what I felt. Not of how I made history, but of how I didn't. And, most of all, not for me, but for the other mother left in your aftermath. Anastasia didn't need to repeat my mistakes.

I didn't need to think for long; the words seemed to find their way onto paper themselves.

"I will soon be forgotten, and my name will never be known. Will you, Dracula, remember me, your mother?"

Anastasia, Poenari, 1457

There wasn't much joy in my life up in the castle at Poenari. I longed for a chance to be close to Bogdan, to feel his fingers parting my hair and his lips brushing against my ear. While I hoped for this to happen every morning when I dragged my heavy body out of bed, I still had to go to sleep every night with only my secret memory of his touch.

We set eyes on each other a few times in the inner yard of your fortress, the small distance between us a source of both joy and sorrow. I wanted so badly to tell him of the pain my mind bore for bearing your child in my belly. About the secret place between my legs that his kiss on *Sânziene* night made me discover and of the emptiness that my father left in my heart. I wanted to tell him about how I wished for the two of us to grow old together and what the name of our children should be, but mostly, I wished I could sit near him with no words between us and no need for any. Blissful silence.

Instead, a furtive look, a glance from under my hood, quick heartbeats full of longing. All I could do was take my eyes off him quickly, afraid that someone might see, someone might tell you in a moment of terror. Because people were scared of you and your punishments on a whim; your cruelty was now widely known. Your subjects would admit to anything if they thought it was what you wanted to hear. I was afraid that if you found out about Bogdan, you would have him killed. And in the end, you did, didn't you?

Small funerals were happening all the time without any pomp or sadness or fuss. Bodies covered with mountain rocks but no gravestones. Prayers were murmured in a rush, but no priest. Young lives lost and wasted with no memories left behind. The last of the boyars, who had barely resisted the winds and the frosts of winter while building your castle, were now no longer useful to you and were left to die slowly of hunger and thirst, weakness and disease.

This was not how Bogdan died, my love for an afternoon, my hope for a lifetime. His body might have been weak or diseased, lacking food and drink, but his hunger was for revenge, and his thirst was for your blood. The winds and the frost didn't kill him. He was killed by you, if not by your hand.

After not seeing him for a week, the agony became torture, but I was too afraid to ask about him.

One evening I was in the book room, the place where

I spent most of my days knitting by candlelight. It was a vast room, but it seemed small, diminished by shelves upon shelves chained to the stone walls, laden with codices, letters, and papyrus scrolls. The huge table in the middle was piled with your most recent state documents, maps for your wars, and correspondence, most likely from your numerous enemies.

You liked it there because there were no windows. The air inside was stale and imbued with the smell of old paper, its dusty slow decay drying the nostrils of visitors upon arrival. But guests were rarely tolerated there when you were in an ill disposition. Except me. It was, in fact, my duty to be there when you came at dusk after your sleep.

Usually, we would spend a few minutes in silence, the shuffle of paper when you checked your new letters the only sound in the room to fill in our estrangement. But that night, the worry for Bogdan made me let down my guard.

"There were no burials in the last few days," I said to you half question, half affirmation, unable to contain my anguish.

"I don't think so, no burials," you replied dryly, uninterested.

I hoped you were going to say something else, to add anything that would end my misery, but you kept looking through the papers left for you on the table, and your lips remained closed.

"Are they all dead then? All the boyars? Not one left?"

"I wouldn't know, Anastasia; their lives lived in

treachery are not my concern anymore."

"Not all of them lived long enough to lie or sin," I mumbled with my eyes in my knitting.

"Do you know of one who didn't?"

I said nothing more and busied myself with my work. You came towards me and handed a scroll you had in your hand.

"My mother sent words to you."

I looked at the seal and saw the monastery's mark imprinted in the wax.

"To me? Why to me? Who brought it?" I didn't know if I should hide my surprise or, on the contrary, let it show. What would your fickle nature want? "Are you sure it isn't for you?" I asked just when I turned the scroll and saw my name carefully calligraphed on the paper.

"I got one from her a few days ago."

"And what does she say?"

"I didn't open it. I am not interested in what she has to say to me… Not anymore. My mother has said enough. Cneaja is dead to me."

You went to the table and shuffled some papers around. I was fiddling with my scroll, curious about it, eager to open it, but held prisoner by the worry for Bogdan. I couldn't stop myself.

"So no deaths then," I said in haste and too hopefully.

You lifted your eyes from the table for a moment and then dropped them again, but in that instant when you looked at me, I felt naked, stripped of secrets and dignity. I could feel tears running down my cheeks, hot with longing and frustration. I turned my face away from you, trying to stifle my sobbing.

"There was one death. No burial. A young lad fell to his death trying to put up the flag of *Valahia* on the tower. I sent him up there. I wanted everybody to know whose land this fortress defends."

"What happened to him?"

You laughed and shook your head.

"He fell into the water, and I told them to leave him there, that he wouldn't be missed."

I wanted to be able to stop, to hide my distress, maybe preserve some dignity but the sobbing got the better of me. You came close again and lifted my chin with your scrawny fingers. I felt your pointy nail scratching my cheek.

"He wouldn't be missed, Anastasia, would he?"

You squeezed my jaw and then let go. You turned around to leave the room and, as you closed the door, your words still found their way to me.

"He will not be missed by me."

The air stayed still afterwards. The smell of the books continued to envelop me like a familiar blanket. The candles were still burning, and their light was still warm and comforting. Nothing collapsed around me but everything inside me did. I was finally free to cry, and I allowed the tears to run free. I cried for the one kiss we'd shared and for the many we missed, for the love that blossomed but wilted away unopened, for the dreams I had and for the future that never happened. I cried for Bogdan, but mainly I cried for me, for everything I could have become but would never be.

Much later, when the tears dried up and hope was no more, I opened the letter from Cneaja.

"I will soon be forgotten, and my name will never be known. Will you, Dracula, remember me, your mother?"

She wrote about her childhood memories in Moldova with gentleness and about her mother with reverence and admiration—a woman in whose footsteps she had strived to follow and not disappoint. The pages about being a wife talked about the humiliation she felt being beside a man who only used but never loved her. Agony was in every word written about being a mother. She believed she had failed at everything.

There was much talk about the country, and the ink was splashed and the paper thinned in her rush to blame herself on those pages. Words like duty and shame were underlined and love was mentioned only as desire, an aspiration never to be reached. It broke my heart to read those words, to know of her struggle and of her loneliness, of her distress of failing her mother by having failed to raise good children for the country.

I could feel all her pain coming through those words on paper, I knew well how it felt to think you disappointed your mother and to have to live with that thought. How many times had I gone over that one memory I had of her in the bed and me laden with the guilt that only a child can feel for lying about a broken vase? If only I understood death then as I knew of it later. If only I didn't think she died because of my dishonesty. If only I didn't think I had to be perfect to be loved.

Was it even true? Would my mother have stopped loving me the moment she found out about the vase? Is love so shallow and fickle, limiting itself only to perfect people? It didn't feel like that with Bogdan. Whenever I thought about him, I didn't see his imperfections—did he have any?—I felt only an infinite warmth, and I knew he could do nothing wrong.

The candles in the windowless room were dying. How many hours had I been in there pondering over Cneaja's pages and twisting the knife of guilt over and over in my wounds? Two hours, three, maybe more, because torment takes its own time, doesn't it, when it has agony as a faithful companion.

I gathered the pages on my lap, ready to leave the book room and take myself and my heavy belly to bed when I noticed one last page that had fallen on the dusty floor. I picked it up and brought it near the only candle that was still burning, its weak flicker bringing to life weak ghosts of darkness.

That page was different, the colour of the ink was darker and the writing more rushed. There were smudges, like water had spilled over it or maybe tears. I started reading with trepidation, hungry for more of the things Cneaja wanted me to know.

It is a long letter I wrote, full of many words and many thoughts, full of regrets and guilt. It took all this time and all this paper for me to understand how mistaken I was about giving my love and how misled I was about doing my duty. How sad to see how I wasted my life trying to fulfil my mother's wishes and commitments. And what did I get in return? Not her affection. Surely she didn't have much for me, because if she did, she wouldn't have sent me away with a man I didn't want, to live an empty life I didn't deserve. If she cared for me, she would have kept me and she would have listened. The same way I should have listened to my boys when they tried to tell me they loved me. They tried hard when they were small, but I didn't think their love was enough. I didn't want boys, I wanted voievozi. *I should have simply loved them for who they were, not for who I wanted them to be. Such a waste. Such a pity we'll never know how life could have been for me and for them. And for the country.*

I stared at that page for a while without seeing it. The tears started again to gather and ran freely on my cheeks. They were tears of hope splashing over Cneaja's regrets. Maybe it wasn't too late for me and the child I carried still in my belly.

So what if he was not going to be perfect? Was he not worthy of my love? Just because I lived my life thinking I was not worthy of my mother's?

The enormity of my previous thoughts, wishing to rid myself of the baby, started to descend upon me. The memory of that old woman, Tinca, with her mean green eyes burning holes through my skin whenever she looked at me seemed now like a threat. The thought of her spidery hands holding my baby suddenly terrified me. What was I doing giving my baby to her? No amount of hate I held for his father should allow me to do that. My baby deserved to be loved by me.

Putting the papers away, one last sentence caught my eye on the back of the page:

Love comes with forgiveness. And forgiveness gives back love.

Oh, Cneaja, how right you are and how wise to write all of it down.

I knew my realisation was important to me the same way Cneaja's was important to her. I knew I had to share it the same way she wanted to share it with me. Our stories, our misfortunes, our mothers' misbeliefs that led us to ours, but most importantly our realisations—all of them had to be shared.

I looked for a new candle and lit it. I pulled the chair towards the table and threw away the embroidery that was lying on it, useless. I picked up the quill with trembling hands. The ink was drying as fast as I could put the words on paper.

"I thought I knew who I was before you, Dracula, made me your wife."

Mara, Poenari, 1457

The butcher's donkey was old and skinny, and we were making very slow strides with it pulling the cart along the forest path. It was the day my father got it , and when I finished cleaning the church, he was already at the steps outside waiting for me.

"This donkey has a name! Have you ever heard of such fancy? To name the donkey…"

He was truly amused at the idea. We never gave our animals a name, they were just the dog and the mule. We gave them food, and that ought to do. They weren't like a brother or a sister to call when you needed help with something or to remember them by when they were dead. And they kept dying. All of them did, animals and brothers.

"What's his name then?"

"*Tunet*, Thunder, would you believe it? To call this old

hag Thunder," said my father with a wholehearted laugh.

I didn't care for the creature's name, I just wanted to go faster. I didn't want to be caught in the darkness of the woods again, but at the same time I thought I did. I wanted to feel the darkness coming and surrounding me, but at the same time I knew I shouldn't. And surely, I didn't want to give my mind and my body to it again, but if I did, was I bad?

When one wheel of the cart ended up in a puddle, it was my father who pushed and pulled it. The donkey seemed to have given up months before, but my father refused to see it.

"We'll give him something to eat and let him rest for a few days, and he will be like new," he mumbled more to himself than to me, fighting to get the cart out of that puddle.

"I'll push, you pull," I said and put my hands firmly on the cart.

It took us three shoves to see it out, and when I saw my dress all dirty with the splashes of mud, I thought that another wash might put a hole in it, because it was that flimsy.

After that, my father insisted on pulling the cart with one hand and the donkey with the other. He seemed deep in his thoughts, giving nothing away. If he was sorry for the deal he'd made or the wood he lost, he didn't show it. After a few steps, I slid my hand in his, took the rope tied to the donkey, and went slowly ahead with the animal.

You, Dracula

When we arrived home, my mother was boiling a pot on the fire outside the house. The smell of mushrooms and garlic, at other times appealing to my empty stomach and my hungry mind, was now repulsive. Its steam reeked of poverty just like our house and like the appearance my parents had about them all the time.

"You are late," she said, stirring the pot.

"But hopefully not too late," replied my father, searching for something in the cart. He moved a few logs about and took out a little parcel, holding it with an expression that resembled a victorious smile. He took the paper off with care, layer by layer, and when he was done, he revealed a bone, a big-enough bone, which he held high, pointing it a little towards my mother, like one would a trophy.

"From the butcher!" he said with confidence to her. She went and grabbed the bone from my father's hand and threw it in the pot whole, stirring it with a new-found vigour.

"I'll only boil it here for a moment to leave some juices, and then I can boil it again tomorrow in a stew."

"And what is it that you're boiling today?" I asked with scorn.

I could see a flicker of sadness passing over my mother's face, but she stopped herself from mouthing it.

"Today is mushroom soup," she said, taking the bone out of the pot.

I knew the mushroom soup tasted just like the mushroom pie and the stew like the soup and they were all the same, because if you threw mushrooms and garlic in a pot, they weren't going to make roast chicken, but I said nothing more. She could call her brews whatever she wanted. At the end of the day, it was only something warm to go into the belly and keep hunger at bay.

Thunder collapsed the next day with a big thud. I thought the butcher gave us the bone because he knew. He had to know about the animal, didn't he? Why would he give a bone to my father if he didn't know the donkey was dying?

"I'm sure he knew, father."

"The butcher is a good man, and I gave him plenty of good wood. How was he to know? If he knew, he wouldn't have given him to me."

"Well, he was sending it to the tanner, wasn't he? Why do you think that was? He knew the donkey was dying. I'm telling you, he knew."

The two of us were looking at the animal, which had collapsed just outside the town's gate all of a sudden. He had foam around his mouth, and the teeth showing from under his foamy lips were rotten. Lying like that, on his side, his mouth half open, he seemed to laugh at us and at our credulity. *The butcher knew*, the dead donkey seemed to tell me.

"He couldn't have known, I'm telling you, nobody could know, only God," said my father, leaving us on the side of the road and going towards the guards at the big wooden gate at the entrance of the town.

There were four soldiers standing, old like my father, too old for the *voievod*'s wars. There were no young men left in the country, only their bodies and blood feeding the burned battlefields. The black cloth that announced death was hanging outside every house now, sometimes two or three or more were pinned to the outside walls of the small and big dwellings alike. "Death doesn't choose," my mother would say, "death takes tall and short, smart and stupid, old and new. You can't run away from it. You say a prayer if you have time. Soldiers should say their prayer every morning. And so should their mothers. Day after day after day."

I could see my father moving his hands in big circles in front of the soldiers, then lifting them on his head, then pointing at us, at the cart, and at the dead donkey on the ground. Two of the soldiers started to laugh and push him around with their swords, but my father didn't budge. He turned to the others and started again waving his hands, explaining, begging, pointing back at us.

I was so embarrassed, so ashamed, I wanted the earth to swallow me whole. When the two soldiers followed my father back to the cart, I hid behind the pile of logs on top of it, pretending to look for something.

The soldiers laid their swords on the ground, the bows and arrows on top of them, pushed their sleeves up, and grabbed the donkey by its legs. My father was frantically moving the logs in the cart to make room for the animal while the men swung it a few times. It landed almost on top of my father.

"This poor animal has nothing left in it; it's light as a feather. No wonder it's gone. Only skin and bone," said one of them to me. I turned my head and continued my search, pretending not to hear.

"What are you doing with it?" I asked my father when the soldiers were gone. "You should bring it back to the butcher and show it to him. Ask him to give you some meat for all the wood you gave him."

My father was throwing some rope around to tie the animal on top of the wood. I got up, caught one end of the rope, and looked him in the eyes, willing him to listen to me.

It was hard to see my father so beaten and humble. He was getting smaller by the day, shrinking like an accordion that hasn't been played for a while or like a grape left out in the sun for too long. He was only a shadow of the man he used to be, but I couldn't feel sorry for him. He was too weak and wouldn't ask for what was rightfully his, too modest and fearful, too gentle for the world we lived in, and the world found it easy to leave him behind.

Side by side, we pushed the cart along the narrow streets of Târgoviște until we reached the church where my bucket and my rugs were waiting for scrubbing. I slipped away from my father, and he didn't turn to say goodbye.

When I reached the door, I shouted to him:

"To the butcher?"

"To the tanner," he said without turning. "It has good, solid skin. It'd make some good *opinci*, sandals for someone, this donkey."

"It would do as much good for someone as thunder does," I mumbled to myself.

Anastasia, Poenari, 1457

After Bogdan's death, I stopped walking around the castle, stopped measuring my cage; I only wanted a measure of the time until the baby was out. As the day was approaching fast, I could already feel the tantalising taste of revenge on my tongue.

I had known you only for a short while, for as long as it took the baby to grow inside me from nothing at all into something. But this didn't mean my need for revenge was small or short or weak, because you spent every day since our encounter adding misgivings to doubt, weariness to distrust, piling reason upon reason to nurture my hate of you.

Before reading Cneaja's letter, I kept dreaming of the day you came back from one of your outings before the sun could uncover your deeds, fresh and glowing, imbued with the delights you grabbed from the depths of darkness. I imagined you arriving at the door, ready for your slumber and oblivious, your child gone, given to the one creature who wanted him: the woman at your father's grave, Tinca.

I had hoped you wanted the baby. Maybe you had plans to show him fatherly love or how to put an arrow through an enemy or tame horses. And if you wanted him, I was making sure you were never going to have him. Not as long as I was alive. You took away so much from me, everything I cared about: my father, Bogdan, my hopes to ever love or be loved. If you thought you could have a child to cherish and be cherished by, I was going to take him from you. It was finally in my power to take something of yours and I couldn't wait to do it.

But then Cneaja's letter arrived, and although my hate for you was as consuming as ever, it wasn't enough anymore to make me give my baby away. I wanted a chance now, for me and my child. I didn't want to repeat Cneaja's mistake or my mother's, choosing to give my love only if my baby was deserving or worthy. I had churned these thoughts in my head for days until my mind was made up. I was going to run away with him.

When you came home the next morning, I thought your face was darker, your eyes deeper, your smile even more absent. I was waiting for you in the book room, where you wanted me to be every dawn, embroidery in hand. The letters, mine and Cneaja's, were safely hidden behind a stone in the wall. You seemed preoccupied.

"My mother is dead," you said with indifference, throwing a piece of paper on the table.

I was taken aback by the news. After reading her letter, I wanted to see her, to bring over her grandson, to tell her I understood what she meant and that I would keep my child and love him no matter what.

"When is the funeral? We should go to the funeral. You have to go and pay your respects, and I want to come with you."

"I didn't go to see her when she summoned me a few days ago. She was still alive then. Why would I go to see her dead? What good would that do?"

There was no pain or sorrow on your face and no regret in your voice. There was no glee either, only indifference. You were flipping through papers at the table in the middle of the book room as you did every day, although nobody was writing to you anymore since you had left the throne to Radu. But I wanted more. Did you know of her change of heart? Of her regrets?

"Was she asking for you? Why didn't you go? Maybe she wanted to say something… what if she had something important to tell you?"

"If it was important to me, she wouldn't have called Radu too."

"Did Radu go? Did he talk to her?"

"No, he didn't. Why would he? I think we both understood a while ago we were never going to be good enough for Cneaja. We both tried, in our own way, but Cneaja was a hard woman to please. She didn't want children, she wanted *voievozi*. Why go there to be reminded?"

"What if there was something else? What if she saw things differently from her deathbed? Maybe she wanted to say she loved you after all."

"If she wanted to say she loved me, she should have tried harder. But she wouldn't. Instead, she drank mandrake to kill herself."

I was taken aback by your words and your apathy, talking about your dead mother like that. You really had no heart.

"You can't know. People see things in new ways in the face of death."

"Really? What do you think your father saw in the face of the stake?"

The cruelty of those words sparked a rage in me that I hadn't known before, and I started towards you, screaming with disgust and hate. When I got close enough to shout my fury in your face, I became suddenly aware of something I had never seen in you before. You seemed pleased with yourself. Gloating.

Only then I felt another woman's smell surrounding you like an aura around an angel, and my anger grew. But it wasn't the woman you brought between us who drove me mad with fury, it was your joy. I didn't care about who made you feel that way, I cared that you did. Because if I didn't have a chance at feeling joy, then neither should you.

I screamed. I scorned. I spat at you. I wanted to wipe the joy off your face, but you were quicker to wipe the anger off mine. The first slap took me by surprise, but I didn't give in to the fear of being slapped again. I threw myself at you and tried to bite you and scratch you, to leave my mark on you. I couldn't leave you unscathed, smug with joy. I wanted you to feel anything else but. So, you slapped me again.

As I was gathering more force out of my fury and readied myself to strike you again, I felt an awful pain, a sudden blow that split me into two. My legs were gone from under me, folded into my belly. I fell on the ground, and as the pain waned, I scrambled to the table and rested my back on its wooden leg. I knew the baby must be coming, and I closed my eyes to unsee you.

The second wave of pain was even harsher, as if the knife that had split me into two before was now poking around my insides to make sure nothing was left untouched and unhurt. I screamed again and the scream seemed to help. It didn't make the pain go away but smothered it, silenced it and, ultimately, empowered me. I felt ready.

By the next wave, I wanted the baby out. The desire was so overwhelming that if the child hadn't come out by itself, sliding on the floor between my legs, I would have torn it out of me with my bare hands. I was hot and wet and lightheaded. I lifted myself just enough so I would be able to lean against the wall and breathe. The pain disappeared but had already been replaced by a sort of exhaustion I hadn't felt before. I wanted to close my eyes, but I also wanted to see the baby. Was it a boy?

You stopped and looked at us with curiosity. There was nothing in your eyes beyond that, no affection or love, no wonder, no sense of celebration.

I never thought you would be together with me when

the birth came. You were usually never at home if one didn't count the hours of the day when you locked yourself in your room and slept your ugly life away. I always imagined I would have the time to bring the child to the green-eyed woman and leave him with her. I never planned what was going to happen after that except for hoping to see your pain when I told you the baby was gone. But that? That indifference? That misplaced curiosity? I never imagined it was going to be that.

You moved towards us, and I grabbed the tiny thing from the floor. My heart sank when I saw the caul enveloping his body, and I scrambled to free him from it. I knew what a caul meant. The feel of it on my fingers, slimy and repugnant, the coldness of it, the bloody smoothness, were sending shivers of horror up my spine. I knew why people feared babies born in cauls. Did you know? I wondered if you knew, and were you going to say the word *vampir*?

I was holding the little bundle with one arm, freed the baby from it with the other, and threw the caul in a corner of the room, faltering and hesitant for only a moment. That was when you snatched him from me. I started to kick and hit you because seeing him in your hands opened a longing in me like a wound. My body wasn't ready to part with my boy; my mind screamed with desire to hold him and with fear of losing him and with the knowledge I needed to protect him from you and from the world and maybe from himself. And that was when I understood what love meant for a mother.

I tried once more to take the baby back, but you kept me at arm's length, and without as much as looking at your son who was screaming—red with blood and blue with cold—you said dryly:

"Make preparations for a baptism. Let's christen this child in the name of God to protect him from evil."

Mara, Târgoviște, 1457

I don't think I had seen a body so small in a coffin before. I mean my brothers were small when they died—they looked like dolls I saw later in a shop in Târgoviște, clumsy and lifeless and white with empty eyes—but that woman's body seemed really lost in the big box in the middle of that small house of God.

I hated when there were funerals in the church. People were loitering about the place, wives wailing, children playing, men spitting on the floor tobacco chewed with *rachiu*. I couldn't tell them to stop or to move, I wasn't allowed. I did it once — "Move to the side so I can clean" I said to a belching man—and the priest said that people were grieving, each in their own way, and I should let them at it because it was their right to be with their dead in any way they wanted. And that was all very well for the priest to say, but during these days, the cleaning took longer, and it shortened the time I could go to see the rich ladies hurrying through the streets of Târgoviște as if they didn't want to catch a disease, like the plague of being poor maybe.

It was different that day, though; the church was empty, the body resting alone and in peace, nobody crying over it and nobody tearing their hair out, grieving, or flaunting. I finished cleaning the front of the church quickly. Although it was late in the autumn and cold, the rain kept at bay, and without rain there was no mud. The leaves blown in by the wind were easily swept. All I had to do was pile them at the back of the church so they didn't get blown back in, like the bad news in our house.

Every time I passed by the coffin, I closed my eyes or looked away. Seeing the lifeless body made me weak, light in my head and wobbly on my legs. I couldn't wait to be finished and leave that place.

I was dusting around the statue of Virgin Mary near the altar when I heard steps coming through the door, and two long shadows crept along the floor, reaching for my legs. I turned and I saw two nuns, small women clad in black from top to toe, fingers interwoven with their rosaries and eyes down, taking small steps inside the church. I stopped the dusting and looked at them, mesmerised, because they seemed to float under their long garments, their movement fluid like the gentle flow of a river on a summer afternoon.

The nuns stopped by the coffin, and one took out a small bunch of flowers from inside her sleeve. They were forget-me-nots, and their light blue came through delicately against the gloomy background. Her simple gesture of putting the flowers into the dead woman's hands, which were joined together on top of her still chest, startled me. It was so unlike what I had seen before—my mother stuffing the garlic into Gheorghiţă's mouth.

I suddenly felt like a thief or an intruder sneaking up on them, and although I knew I wasn't, I cleared my throat all the same to say something and alert them of my presence. It was their turn to be startled, and they lifted their eyes quickly like two deer alarmed at new sounds in the woods.

"I am sorry, don't mind me, I am just cleaning the church."

They kept looking at me, slowly coming back from their world of prayer, kindness, and forgiveness.

"The priest knows I am here, he tells me what to do…" I continued stringing together my words and my excuses.

"Lord have mercy," said one and "Bless you," said the other. "You should do your work as you were told."

I busied myself for as long as I could at the back of the church because I didn't want to disrupt their benediction, but my work was quickly done, and I wanted to get out of there as quickly as I could and go about my other affairs.

When I passed by the coffin, I crossed myself three times as required by the tradition.

"*Dumnezeu să o ierte*, may God rest her in peace," I said quickly.

"Isn't she peaceful?" asked one of the nuns and invited me with her eyes to look.

"She seems very peaceful to me," I said at a loss for more words.

"God is merciful, giving her rest after such a troubled life," said the other nun.

"Who is she? What happened to her?"

"She is Princess Cneaja, daughter of a *voievod*, wife of another, and mother of two more."

"She must have died a proud woman," I said wondering why there were no *voievozi* by her coffin, only two small nuns who looked at each other for a brief moment and then back at the woman in the coffin.

"I am going to go now, I am finished for the day," I said but their interest in me was gone.

Out on the porch, I emptied the bucket of dirty water and stuffed it with leaves I had piled there from inside the church. A cold wind was swirling them around, and every new gust seemed to multiply them, the porch too small for their crazy *horă* dance. I kept pushing them in, scrunching them with my fist, trying to fit them all into the small bucket, and their smell reminded me of the forest back home, musty and old.

All of a sudden, my fingers dug into something firm but mushy and cold that made me jump, and I withdrew my hand quickly as if bitten by a snake. Nothing moved in the bucket; the leaves were as dead as the woman in the coffin. I poked at them with a stick, trying to see what startled me. There was nothing in there, but there was an urge in me to keep poking and stirring, and the more I did, it seemed like the leaves were disappearing or melting into water. Maybe I had left some water and I didn't remember. It was there now.

I kept stirring and marvelling at what was happening until all the leaves disappeared and there was only water left. Then I stopped, and as the surface stilled and became a clear mirror, I saw myself. I had to gasp because the creature in the water, although it looked like me, exactly like me, wasn't really me.

I could tell because I knew I was staring into the bucket, but my reflection wasn't staring back at me from down there. The other me had its eyes closed, and its hands were locked together as if in prayer. And although I was wearing a headscarf, the girl in the bucket wasn't, and her hair was bountiful, parted in the middle and dark.

I kept looking at her—there was no choice in it for me but to look, until she slowly moved her hands away from her mouth and opened her eyes. Now she was staring back at me, which made me uneasy because it felt like she saw right through me, unlocking my secrets and my desires, door after door of my mind. And then she started to smile, a lovely, timid smile, encouraging and gentle, which turned suddenly into a mean grimace. She wasn't smiling anymore, she was laughing at me, and when her lips parted, they revealed two long teeth on the sides of her mouth. I screamed and pushed the bucket away and ran, while a viscous, muddy water spilled out on the ground behind me.

Around the corner of the church, the wind was

ravaging the trees, and I could hear its howl through the old creaking branches. The air was heavy with rain and darkness, and the woman's voice coming out of that chaos, guttural and rasping by my ears, didn't take me by surprise anymore. I knew it. I had heard it before.

"You are playing with the darkness, I see."

"I am not, I really don't like the darkness," I said with a shudder, and I looked about me trying to see her. All around me, the rain was pouring down, dense and stifling. My clothes were drenched and felt stiff, foreign to my body. So did my mind.

Her laughter came as a surprise because it sounded crazy, and it messed up my thoughts just like the wind messed up the leaves on the porch.

"Really? You don't like the darkness?" she asked again in tune with another squall of the wind.

The words came first, the rancid breath after, and her withered face last, so close to mine that I could dig deep into the emptiness of her green eyes.

"Do you like the warmth between your legs?"

With only one look she seemed to have swept away all my other thoughts except the memory of that warm spot between my thighs. I was desperate to touch it, but I didn't dare move.

"Do you like the slow, painful pleasure that builds inside you when you squeeze your nipples?"

She was circling me now, her head bobbing in and out of my vision, and I felt sleepy and painfully awake at the same time, completely surrendered to her will. Without ever touching me, she was building something inside my ribcage that was screaming to burst out and scratch my skin.

"Do you like his voice in your head, full of promised delights?"

I was too scared to talk, afraid that I might break the spell she had me under, and although I knew at the back of my mind that I should run away, I also didn't want to.

"Do you like what you do in the darkness?"

Her face was now close to mine, scraping my cheek.

"Do you like what the darkness does to you?" Her tongue came out with a hissing kind of noise, long and sharp like an arrow with a split head. I wanted to be repelled by it, but I wasn't. I wanted her to go away, but I wanted the memories she was unearthing to stay.

"Do you like the darkness?" she whispered in my ear.

I closed my eyes, tightening my legs, my fists, my belly...

"You have to say it. Say it! Say it!"

"Yes, yes, I do, I like the darkness!" The words found their way out of me like a prayer, an imploration, a song ready for the chorus, but the chorus never came.

"Don't play with it, though. Darkness can blind you," she proffered and then she stopped talking abruptly, suddenly indifferent and uninterested in me, attuned to the wind as if it carried important news.

"The baby has been born," she said, "my baby is here." I watched her features mellow, the green of her eyes becoming lighter together with her disposition, words tumbling out of her mouth with ease.

"She promised her baby to me; she said I can have it right after his birth."

"Who said? What baby?" Just as I voiced my questions, I knew there was only one answer possible. "The *voievod*'s wife promised her baby to you?"

She pulled her black cape about her and stepped away from me.

"Where are you going?" I whispered in fear of her answer.

"A promise is a promise. I'm going to take what's mine; she promised me her baby."

The wind had stopped at sometime between feeling my pleasure and living my guilt. The rain held off; the clouds dispersed. And then she turned:

"I will come to take your child when it's time, just like you promised me, too, that night in the graveyard," she hissed, and I suddenly became aware again of my wet clothes, my drenched hair, of my muddy bare feet, and of the cold that descended all over me.

Anastasia, Poenari, 1457

What can I write here about loss? I could put down a lot, or I could scribble a little. I could choose words that would tear anyone's heart apart, and I could drain these pages in my tears or in my blood. Yes, that would be talking about loss, and you would know I've suffered, you might even believe me and spare a sad thought for me. And what good would that be to me? Could your sad thoughts bring back the gentle touch of my mother's hand on my hair before bed, or the way my father's face opened in a smile on seeing me? Would your sad thought make Bogdan rise from the Argeş River to whisper something sweet in my ear and melt my insides? Would this thought ever bring back my son?

Loss is not the absence of someone or something. It is the missing of them and the longing for them, the emptiness you carry around that you fill with the memory of them and that it is never enough. Day after day after day.

I lived with the memory of my mother's touch lingering in my hair and my father's smile reflected somewhere at the back of my eyes. I longed for Bogdan's whisper in my ear because I had the memory of it. But what about my son? I have nothing from him, only a desire to have known him. There are no memories that I can cling to, only an irresistible urge to love him. There is an emptiness in my belly and in my soul where my baby should have been. My baby is gone.

In the end, it was you who gave him away. I was hoping Tinca wouldn't come, that she would have forgotten about me and my child, that my rushed promise had been swallowed by the darkness that surrounded her and disappeared together with her like it had never been. All that time when I wanted to get rid of what was growing inside me—if I could only go back to it and erase it!

But Tinca did come for my boy. She came stealthily, unheard, and unnoticed behind me at the church door. "You need to know!" she said. "What good is not knowing?" and the priest repeated it, and I also thought for a moment that we should know if our child was like you, but only for a moment, until I remembered my urge and my promise to love that baby no matter what. I sang a lullaby to him, and I tried hard to never let go of him, but we didn't matter to you. It was never about me or him, it was about you and Tinca. Whoever she was and whatever power she held over you, it wasn't for me to understand. It was for me to obey. I wasn't the queen in your chess game, I was the pawn. And so was my boy. Dispensable.

You, Dracula

You gave him away when I wanted him most. To think there was a time I didn't want him makes me sick with loathing of myself. To think I would never have him to touch his hair and smile at him and see him growing up makes me sick with loathing of you. To think I have no memories of him—what did he smell like?—and nothing from him to fill in the empty space he left in me except a name, his name, Mihnea.

How could I wake up like that every morning and go to sleep every night and see you every day, day after day after day?

Well, that could not happen, I know it cannot happen.

I know I won't allow it.

There is nothing left here for me.

Mara, Poenari, 1458

I went to bed every night hoping the darkness would come, hoping to hear its voice like the sound of a horn calling from the mountain's peak, deep and full of yearning, calling my heart to join in its rhythm. My days were spent in a haze, half abandoned to dreaming but also trying to hide it from my mother.

Those secret thoughts were hard to bear in the daylight. While they made me giddy with the anticipation of what night could bring and with the flutter of a thousand butterflies in my belly, they also brought a kind of worry I had never felt before, heavy and gloomy. I felt I had no grasp and no handle on whatever was happening to me, and while I liked the hope and the joy it brought, the worry had my mind and my stomach tied in knots, and my shoulders slouched under its weight.

These thoughts were churning while I was cleaning the church, picking up mushrooms, dusting the saints, filling the pail from the river or pulling the cart. There was no reprieve, no rest, no stopping them. And when the night came, the waiting would begin.

My hearing became painfully sharp, caring not for the rustling of the leaves or the sneaking of the fox or the hoot of the owl. It was something else that my ears became attuned to, something like a whisper or a soft whistle, a murmur or a ripple that started outside my head but invaded it quickly like a summer rain, a chatter, a pitter-patter, and ultimately, a noisy flood, a tumult that took me over and left me breathless and gasping for air.

When I could hear it coming, I became paralysed with joy and dread, both pulling me apart, both taking residence in my head and fighting for supremacy. And then, suddenly, silence, stillness, darkness, the moment I was neither inside me nor outside of me anymore, the time when I was floating like a good dream among nightmares.

This is when the darkness was talking to me, sweet nothings of sunshine in my hair or raspberries on my lips or honey on my nipples, and my whole body blossomed in a smile although I knew it wasn't true. My hair was fair like a dull day, my lips were red like tomatoes, and as for honey on my nipples, well, I wasn't too sure what to think about that.

But sometimes the darkness would be different, like a storm, and wouldn't look for room inside me but would press on top of me like the wind that brought the snow in the winter. The whispers would be thunders, and I wouldn't smile inside but cry with fear. The sunshine would be drenched in clouds and the raspberries crushed and the honey sticky on my nipples, making them painfully hard. Even so, I still had the urge to touch them, and the more I touched, the more pain I allowed to penetrate me and the more I cried. But what was really hard to believe was that every night, I would be lying on my bed hopeful, waiting for it to start all over again.

I didn't know what it was at first, a fright, a bad dream, or was it the darkness choking me? I woke up in a panic with a dry mouth, and the back of my throat felt like paper. My mother was calling from outside, her voice all worked up and urgent.

"The castle is on fire, the blaze is huge, come out, look at this, God help us all! Come out! Come out!" she kept screaming.

My father got up from his bed with a grumble, taking his time to put all his limbs in working order again. His arms, worn out by the axe splitting the oaks and the fir trees, his back, forever bent under the weight of the logs, his legs, shaking while pulling the cart, his whole body was always stiffer and more painful when the weather outside was colder.

My mother came into the hut like a storm.

"It's burning, come out! Whatever happened to catch such a fire, I don't know…"

"Wait, woman, wait, I'm coming," said my father, finally standing.

The heat struck me at the same time as the reddish light had our hut surrounded. I had my hand on the doorframe, and it was warm, strangely warm in the cold night. Was it still night? I couldn't tell. The smoke was rolling dark and dense through the trees, but the reddish light that was coming through wasn't the dusk or the dawn, it was the tail of a ball of fire that was sitting on top of the mountain.

We started walking towards the end of the forest, my mother first, driven, her rushed steps frightening the badgers and the rabbits who dug deeper under the mountains of dead leaves. My father followed in a slower fashion, his pace measured, his pain holding him back. Every now and again he stopped for a moment to catch his breath and to look at the birds shooting through the branches away from the heat. I was last in line, stepping with ease through the trees, led by curiosity. What could have happened at the castle?

When we reached the end of the forest path and stepped onto the rocks at the verge of the precipice, the blaze was setting the whole sky on fire. The rocks were warm under my feet, and the air was burning my nostrils and my throat when I breathed in. I could hear my mother's cough in front, but I couldn't see her anymore, her body swallowed by the smoke. My father was only a step ahead of me, testing the rocks with his feet with caution. Without a word, he reached out with his hand, and I gave him mine and we kept going a few more steps until we heard a shout in a deep voice.

"Stop right here, you can't go any farther."

"Oh, you gave me the fright of my life! Dear God,"

my mother's voice reached us before we saw her stop in front of a broad man, a soldier or a guard by the look of his clothes and his dagger.

"What happened? Is the castle burning?" asked my mother quickly, trying to pass the man. He moved one leg to better steady himself and blocked the whole path.

"People will be coming down now to save themselves; nobody in their right mind is trying to go up. The path has to be free. You need to go home, wherever you came from."

He hardly finished his words when people started to rush down, running, tumbling, falling on top of each other, screaming and cursing. My father pulled me by the hand he had been squeezing hard all along. I grabbed my mother's hand, too, and dragged her with us.

We had a head start of only a few steps, but we managed to stay ahead, unscathed, until we reached the trees where the path widened into the forest. Behind us, people kept coming, and as soon as they made it under the canopy of branches, they allowed themselves to collapse on the grass, exhausted and spent, with sighs of relief that came from deep in their lungs.

"Is there any water? My throat is scorched," asked a woman, pulling what was left of her skirt to clean her face of soot. Her voice was firm, and she looked at my father expectantly, as all people with rank look at people beneath them. My father understood that, too, and assumed his humble voice, the one he used in town when he delivered his wood.

"Only from the river, my lady, no other water here in

the forest, only from down below, from the Argeș."

The woman gave a cry then, a cry that split the smoke and the heat around us, a cry that came from pain and desperation.

My mother took the few steps towards her in a moment, but the woman was waving her arms wide and wouldn't allow herself to be touched. Her cry started to mellow after a short while, and words started to come out.

"She's gone," she said again and again, "My lady is gone." Her words were smothered in sobs.

We were all looking at her for a while, petrified, incapable of moving, drowned with her in her grief without knowing its object.

My father approached her with timid steps.

"I will go down and bring you water, my lady. Wait here, I will be back soon."

"No," she jumped up and became agitated again. "We can't drink water from there. She is in there, her blood is spilled in that water, don't drink!"

At the sound of those words, a few more women started to cry and lament, surrounding her with care.

"Who is in the water?" asked my father, echoing my mother's question.

"Princess Anastasia," cried the woman, and the name Anastasia seemed to open the dam for another flood of tears. "She jumped! She took the torch to the curtains and the beds and climbed the stairs to the tower, and she kept tripping on her skirts, and she still wouldn't stop. I cried to her, and I begged her to bring down the torch and to come back to me, but she didn't listen, she wouldn't listen."

The women around were trying to console her. "There was nothing you could do," "You tried," and "She wanted to die" they were saying until her tears ran dry.

My mother waited to hear more, and when the ending didn't come, she had to ask. "What happened then?"

"The princess climbed out the highest window of the tower, and she jumped straight into the river," said one of them, and then she turned again to complete the circle of suffering.

I went to them and I kneeled with them and I put my arm around one of them, and although I didn't feel like one of them, I knew I could pretend:

"What happened to the baby?"

I wasn't allowed to take part in the search for Anastasia's body. I had to go back to the hut with my mother. I didn't know if I wanted to see that girl's body smashed on the rocks, feasted on by the wolves. She was only my age, and I didn't want to die. I was afraid of death, and I had seen enough cold and soulless bodies in my life. Hadn't she? What made her want to jump?

My mother talked a lot that evening before she fell asleep; she wouldn't stop talking.

"He drove her to her death, it must be because of him, of the *voievod*, whatever life she was living with him in that castle," said my mother, pursing her lips. "Why else would such a young girl jump to her death? He has a reputation, you know, that he is not of this world, that he was born different, not like us simple folk, but he has powers and needs that people like us don't have," she said, putting her head on the pillow and pulling a rag over her small body.

"Let's go to sleep now. We need our strength for tomorrow. Tomorrow is going to be a sad day," I said.

She turned her back to me but kept talking.

"People said he was a good *voievod*, fighting the Turks to keep the country free. And that although he is unmerciful, he is just and wanted to get rid of the lies and the stealing and the bad things in the country," and after a little more tossing and turning, "Did you hear that people were so afraid of his punishments that a goblet made of gold was put in the middle of the square in Târgoviște and left there, and nobody dared to steal it? That's how powerful he was."

After a few moments of silence, I thought she had gone to sleep, but she suddenly turned to me.

"Poor, poor girl, a poor little dove in a vulture's claws. I wonder why she jumped?"

"You heard the women from the castle, Mother, her child was gone. The *voievod* gave her baby away to another woman. She must have been beside herself with upset and sadness. Only think about it."

"Maybe you're right. No mother wants to lose a child. God rest my boys in peace."

She crossed herself with a sigh, and when she finally went to sleep, I went outside and sat on the three-legged stool where my father carved the walking sticks that nobody wanted to buy.

The night was quiet now, the screams stopped, the flame was gone, and the smoke was lifting above the mountaintop, revealing the remains of the castle, darker than the dark sky, looming over the valley like a call for death. The cold was taking over the forest again, and I could hear the small animals turning in their winter beds under branches and leaves. We were alive in this world, and we all had a place in it.

Why did that girl want to leave this world? Why did she beg Tinca to take her baby that day at the back of the church only to kill herself when her wish came true? Did Anastasia have a change of heart? My mother's words sprang to mind—"No mother wants to lose a child." Was that what happened, what she understood when she held her baby in her arms? That she couldn't live without him?

Then I also had Tinca's words to ponder over: "The darkness can blind you," she said. Was it a threat? It sounded like a threat. And why did she make me promise my baby to her, not that I ever intended to fulfil that promise if I ever had a baby. Maybe now that she had Anastasia's, she wouldn't care for mine anymore.

As the dawn started to unravel the darkness, my thoughts started to tighten; my understanding became clearer and my resolution firmer. I would never have a baby. Not one for me, not one to give to Tinca, not one to love so much that I would kill myself for it.

Relieved to have grasped that thought and made peace with it, I was getting ready to head back into the house when the darkness shifted its shape and consistency, became heavy and almost solid around me, suffocating. I was struggling to breathe; my chest felt squeezed tight, my heart unable to do its beating. I wasn't scared, there was nothing to be scared of, I understood I just had to let go, so I did. One breath was all it took, one breath to suck out of me, that was all the darkness wanted. I gave it willingly and then I watched it scatter like the sparks from a fire, but these were black sparks, and their shine was like that of the raven's feather. And, just like a raven, wings open wide, the darkness fluttered away from me and onto the remains of the castle, settling there in a nest.

After Anastasia's funeral, you descended on our porch almost every night. I didn't know the howl of the wolves could be you, the same way I didn't know the blast of the wind could be you, or the fire dying in the hearth by itself, or my parents' snoring getting louder while the cat's purring got softer. I didn't know it then, yet all those times, it was you.

Sometimes I think I must have known before, but that knowledge carried with it a lot of shame, which made me hide the joy I felt and the longing, too, and the two bites on my neck.

I sensed my mother's alarmed stare on me all the time. Inspecting my face and searching into my eyes when I was close by, examining my walk from afar, pondering over my sighs or my singing, questioning everything I did, intrusive, painfully annoying. Her prying kept me in a state of perpetual agitation, feeling guilty all the time without knowing why, trying to disguise things that didn't need disguising, irked and bitter.

"Show me your neck, Mara," my mother said one evening after having glared at me all day around the house, tutting with disapproval.

"There is nothing special to see on my neck. It's just a neck, surely you've seen necks before," I said, feeling the two marks burning my skin.

"You know what I mean and what I want to check," she said, making her way towards me.

"There is nothing on my neck, I'm telling you."

"Let me see then."

"Stop doubting me, leave me alone, go away."

I pushed her slightly, and she gave a cry of surprise and pain.

"You are not yourself, Mara! Please tell me what is wrong, maybe I can help."

"I don't need your help. I need you to leave me alone."

She didn't ask me to fetch garlic anymore, but she was

picking it herself, hanging it around the windows and hiding it around the house, smearing the empty mule's shed and my father's cart with it.

Some nights I just dozed into a dreamless sleep, but other nights, tired of waiting and torn apart by a searing longing, I would get up, pull the garlic from around my window, and stare into the darkness, hoping it would swallow me. Most nights it did, and the day after such a night, I would just lie in bed, prostrate and happy.

"Get up, Mara. I know a way, come on, please, we have to try."

My mother was pulling me out of bed with a force I didn't think she had. I felt heavy; my mind seemed full of iron and my legs loaded with lead. She dragged me by my arms until I stood in front of her and then pulled me again all the way to the door.

I hadn't been out for a few days, and the crisp air sneaked through my nostrils, making me dizzy. I opened my eyes and rested them on the moss that grew at the roots of the old oak tree in front of our house, the green, soft, velvety moss that had lived there for as long as I had been alive. It had a soothing call; it wanted me to lean my face on it and go to sleep. But my mother was also calling.

"Put your palm out. Hold it out, open wide, please, Mara."

I could see her fingers meddling with mine, but I couldn't feel them. I couldn't feel my fingers, either—they seemed to belong to somebody else, somebody who wanted to be me but didn't know how.

You, Dracula

My mother poured something black in my palm.

"They're poppy seeds. Aunt Valeria gave them to me, she said to spread them from Gheorghiță's grave to the house. If he is rising from the dead and wants to come in, he will stop to count the poppy seeds because that's what they do, you know, vampires, they have to count things. And if we have many and they are spread out, he will be kept busy and he will never make it to the house until dawn, God rest his soul."

I could see her making the sign of the cross and I could hear her talking and I could see the black thing in my palm, and none of it seemed to bear any weight. I saw her fingers leaving mine and the black thing leaving my palm through my fingers, and I just dragged myself back to bed. Behind me, I heard my mother cursing.

I became forever tired back then, weak and placid, and for the first time, uninterested in food or nice clothes. I stopped cleaning the church first, and then I stopped picking mushrooms in the forest. After that, I stopped getting out of bed, and finally, I stopped talking. I didn't know what my parents thought. I didn't know how to care anymore. None of these things held any importance for me, and trying to do any of them was a waste of vigour and a chore. The only time that counted, the only time I wanted to save myself for, was the time when you came to me at night because that was when I felt alive.

So, when you asked me one night with your cavernous voice born out of the depths of darkness to come with you, I said yes. I said yes wholeheartedly, gladly, as if you had asked me if I wanted to keep living.

"Come with me to the castle, just the two of us far away from the world, come, my princess."

Now, having the knowledge that I have, knowing you the way I came to know you, I wonder if that was an invitation at all, if I could have refused, if there had ever been any choice in it for me. I have to ask myself that much. But back then, at the beginning, doubt was not a friend. So I moved into the castle with you.

I don't remember much about those days. I think I slept a lot of the time. It is possible that I may have dreamt about lying in the sun on a warm beach, and it is also possible that it was, in fact, true. Was it my imagination when I felt myself wrapped up in silk or in black feathers, which you said were from a princess swan? If you said it was the truth, I saw no reason to doubt you.

There was always plenty of food for me to eat. Sometimes I wanted to, and many times I didn't. There was always too much, and my mouth would not open for me. It opened for you. You opened it for the chickens you cooked, for the pies you baked, for the milk you stole, and for the juice of the peaches you squeezed on my lips. You said it was for my own good and I believed you.

But when you said I was beautiful, when you said my hair was shinier than the sun, my eyes deeper than the sky, my skin smoother than a cherry, and my smell better than a field of jasmine, then and only then, I knew you were lying. Had I never seen my face in a lake before, I would have been happy to believe you. But as it was, there were still plenty of things to be happy about. Were they real?

Was my name even real? Sometimes I thought I knew it was Mara. I thought I remembered my mother's voice calling me Mara, but when you called me Ileana, for all the pies you fed me, all the feathers you tickled me with, all the sand that warmed my body, real or not, I was Ileana. Your Ileana.

In the haze of the first days in the castle, imbued with the joy of being there like a cloth absorbing spilled wine, I was thrilled to discover my aroused body and eager to let you stir in me every joy and every pain. And you did.

You did it every morning when I opened my eyes and your face was close to mine, so close that I thought my breath was yours. My eyes saw the room with your eyes, my nostrils smelled nothing else but you.

If I wanted to say something, your finger would touch my lips with haste and would press on them lightly, gently, circling them until I felt the urge to part them and take your finger between them and run my lips along it, all the way from the rough palm to the long, pointy nail.

If I was quiet, the finger would find its way down my neck, swirling around my nipples and then down again, between my legs, until I felt the urge to part them, too, and take your finger between them and rub it slowly and gently first and more urgently after, until my body discovered a new place of wonder, pleasure, and pain.

All the same, I was always sorry when these moments were over because as much as I thought I could die from the intensity of such delight, being without was even worse.

You, Dracula

When our play was over and I could sense the dawn knocking at the window, you would succumb to a sleep that reminded me of that of my brothers on the table in the church before their burial, and it scared me.

First time I saw you like that, white, pale, cold, with protuberant cheekbones, aquiline nose, and pointy chin like an angry eagle ready to pounce on its prey, I didn't dare move from the bed the whole day. I kept my eyes closed and looked at you only every now and again, hoping to see a sign, the bat of an eyelid or the lifting of the chest. There was nothing. I stayed petrified beside your stiff body for a long time, until I saw the sun going down and I knew the day must be coming to an end. As a sense of panic was taking out its claws and starting to get hold of me, your eyes opened slowly, and when you saw me, your face opened with an imperceptible grimace, which I thought might be a smile. Then the play started again.

After a few days of watching you sleeping the sleep of the dead for the whole day, I understood that you really couldn't know what I did during that time, so one day, I got up from the bed and opened the door, curious about what lay beyond it. The growl that met my trespass didn't alarm you, but it terrified me. Four young wolves curled up on the floor leapt up and blocked my exit, their bared teeth ready to teach me a lesson.

"Did you try to get out of the room when I was asleep?" you enquired with a sombre tone when I asked you about the animals.

"I didn't know I shouldn't," I said timidly, hoping you wouldn't know I was lying.

You, Dracula

"You're lying, aren't you?" you asked simply, looking straight into my eyes. You didn't seem to mind too much; you seemed rather amused. "The cubs are here to protect you when I am asleep. You see, I get tired, and during the day, I have a deep slumber. You are safe with them unless you go where you are not allowed."

Your words took me by surprise because they were the first that spoke about rules and retributions. It was also the first time you didn't call me your princess, the first time I didn't think I might be dreaming or imagining or wishing for something. The wolves must have been real, as real as your sleep and my wakefulness.

The castle wasn't very big—it was in fact a fortress that had no beauty, elegance, or comfort, but it had a strategic position, thick walls, and plenty of ammunition. There wasn't much for me to do there apart from visiting Anastasia's small rooms, which I liked to sit in. I even tried some of her dresses, but they were all with large waists to fit her growing belly, and I didn't like wearing them for fear I might somehow catch that disease, get a belly with a baby inside. Her pomades I liked, and I put on a bit of chalk powder on my face and a bit of berry powder on my lips as was in fashion, but you didn't like it. You said I looked like an angel as I was, that my beauty didn't need any enhancement, which I doubted, but you said you loved me, and I didn't have any reason to doubt that.

Only sometimes I wondered. Like the time I asked you to allow me out of the castle and into the village or maybe even into Târgoviște to see the new dresses and fabrics and to look at the shoes. You said there was no need for me to go because you were happy to bring me anything I wanted. I got shoes and a cape, dresses of silks and velvets, and the new mittens matched the colour of my new emerald brooch. But I had nowhere to go dressed like that, so after a while, I didn't ask for clothes anymore.

There was also a time I asked for bonbons and honey, doughnuts and marzipan, things I saw only in the merchants' carts and had always craved. The bonbons I liked a lot, and I could have eaten a few, but the honey was too sweet and the marzipan too chewy, and I got tired of them quickly.

The first time you locked me up in the dungeon, I was scared I would never see the daylight again. The darkness there wasn't like the one in the forest—sweet, vibrant, full of promise—that I craved for and welcomed. The darkness in the dungeon was damp, and it smelled of rotten fish and rat piss. It was noisy with flutters and crawls that made me sick, and every time I thought something touched me, I cried and I begged you to let me out, and I promised to obey and do everything you asked me to.

You laughed and said I was already doing everything you asked of me, but locking me in the dungeon was for my own good, not a punishment, and I should be grateful. It was only after the third time that I understood how much you hated my womanly bleeding every month. Without fail, the day before it even started, you picked up the huge key of my prison, pushed me gently down the stairs, and sighed.

"What a waste of magnificent blood."

After three days in there, I could hear your steps, the key turning in the lock, the screech of the old door, and your voice like the chirp of a robin.

"I missed you, my dove."

And this was how I knew it was real.

I think I probably had everything I wished for. Food aplenty, clothes to cover every part of my body twice and three times over, a bed in a room of my own in a castle of my own, and the *voievod*'s full attention and love. Nobody asked me to scrub anything, to pick anything, to mend, to push, to dig—there was no work for me to do.

Every once in a while, when I could stand on my own two feet without fainting, you asked me to dance for you. I liked dancing, like all the people down in Poenari liked it on a Sunday after church when the *lăutari* would come to play their instruments. When I could, I sang my own songs that I remembered from those days, and I moved my body the way I used to when I knew the young men were watching. They had liked it, and you couldn't have enough of it.

Entire nights passed like that, a flicker of flimsy memories under the flicker of many candles, your eyes, your pies, your wolves, the sand, the honey, the dolls... I wasn't sure which of these were real—my pleasure, my dreams, my parents, the raspberries? Was I even real?

I kept having this dream about being naked and

rolling in a bed of raspberries, crushing them and drinking their juice, but I had never seen so many of them and so big. Back at home at the edge of the forest, I used to pick them from their bush, careful not to squash them and waste the miraculous liquid, eating them one by one to make the taste last longer. I liked them a lot and sometimes I would stay there to eat them all and didn't bring any back to the hut.

Your raspberries at the castle were different, you called it raspberry crush, but it tasted like blood to me. I didn't like its taste; it didn't burst fresh in my mouth, it was only sticky like sour honey, but you kept saying it was special, a raspberry crush that would make me younger and stronger. So I said to myself, *If it keeps me far away from death, I'll drink anything*, and I gobbled the red liquid you gave me and said it was good.

By the time the gipsies arrived, my wishes had come true. I was mostly happy—dreaming or awake and definitely rich, although I had no one to show my riches to—and very much alive, although when I couldn't get out of bed with weakness, I wondered about that.

I knew I must have become your wife, the blessed wife of a *voievod*, sometime since I came to the castle, but I had trouble remembering our wedding, and memories of it, if there were any, were missing.

"Of course we had a wedding, Ileana, a most wonderful one. There were *lăutari* playing loud music, and the *Călușari* danced their hearts out."

Why can't I remember any of it? I kept asking myself, searching for the smallest clue.

"Many people came, and you looked like a little dove in a white *ie*. So beautiful."

Only when you said that, I suddenly remembered Anastasia in her long white blouse at your wedding, and I didn't think you were telling me the truth. I opened my mouth to say it, but you covered it with a kiss. When you lowered your lips to my neck, a wave of warmth invaded my body, and when you took your bite, a wave of memories invaded my mind. I could finally see myself in the middle of a crowd, wearing an *ie* and dancing the women's dance. *Maybe it was always me, never Anastasia*, I said to myself just before collapsing in your arms.

"So, why are you here alone?" asked the young girl who came with the gipsies while I was showing her how to play with the wolf cubs without getting bitten.

"I am not alone!" I laughed. "I have the cubs."

"But they are animals, they are for play and for guard. I am talking about people, you know, like parents or brothers, people to talk to, who look after you."

"I have my husband, don't I? He's here with me all the time. He talks, he reads to me, buys me clothes and bonbons. He looks after me. He even taught me how to read and write," I said with pride as this was something that I had always wanted to be able to do.

"He is a little scary," the girl said timidly. "He doesn't

smile, he has hair on the palm of his hand, and he is very smelly. He is not like other men I've seen, you know, normal, like my father and my grandfather."

"Well, he is. And he would do anything for me," I said with conviction, but at the back of my mind I tried to remember the hair on your palms, and I couldn't really grasp a memory of it. Was it there? As for the smell, I always thought it was all the roasting and the boiling you did for me and that maybe some of the meats had gone off.

"Do you ever leave this castle?" she asked when we sat down, and I started to plait her hair the way my mother used to plait mine, and the thought of my mother combing my hair was very comforting and I couldn't stop asking myself, *When was the last time I saw her?*

"No, I don't need to go anywhere; I have everything I need right here, brought to me."

"But do you not miss your mother or your father? You have a mother and a father, don't you?"

"Of course," I said, and as she asked, I wondered about them—where were they and how long had it been since I'd seen them last and what did they look like after so long, and I thought there might have been a brother and a mule too.

I liked it when the gipsies came that first time and stayed for a few days in front of the castle. They brought life with them, a free life I didn't know anything about. There was talk of other towns, other fashions, strange animals I'd never heard of, fruits and spices I'd never tasted, seas and oceans I would never sail on. They knew it all, they had seen it all, they were coming and going as they pleased to see and do more.

I didn't pay much attention to the men; they went about their business in a calm fashion, and their faces didn't give away much under the thick moustaches. The women, on the other hand, were a joy to watch with their colourful skirts, the blouses with large sleeves and deep necklines showing the many necklaces that were sitting comfortably on full bosoms. They were svelte, with beautiful shiny skin and long black hair that shone like ebony in the sun.

Anica, the oldest of them all, was serious and thoughtful all the time as if the fate of all that world far and wide rested on her shoulders. Under the large red kerchief tied at the back of her head, she had her eyes on everyone, and everyone had their attention on her, searching for approval. All the other women were respectful and quiet around her and met me with a lovely smile on their faces. The children seemed to see no end to happiness and carried a sort of devilment and joy in their eyes, which I loved.

And then, of course, was Doina, the girl with many questions and untamed hair, a little younger than me—if I even knew for sure my age anymore—who proclaimed herself my pearl sister when she gave me a necklace she had made out of tiny white stones.

You seemed fond of the old man too. His name was Căldăraru, Anica's husband, father and grandfather to them all, chief of his family, incredibly proud and protective of it when he spoke about them. You started looking for this old man's company when you woke up, after dusk, around the fire they always made.

The two of you stayed late into the night surrounded by the smoke from Căldăraru's pipe. With his white hair and his long white beard, he looked like one of the saints painted on the walls of churches I seemed to remember. With your raven hair and turned moustache over thin lips, you reminded me of the devil. I didn't know what the two of you talked about into the night, but you became thoughtful and melancholy.

While I was mostly content or simply idle, there were times when a veil seemed to lift off my face or a dense fog that appeared to hold my mind seemed to scatter. I wasn't really aware of them being there until they were disappearing, but those were the moments when I could remember something else beyond you and the walls of the castle—and long for it too. Yet every time I asked you about the outside world, the veil would come down again and the fog would cloud my mind and my limbs wouldn't listen and I would take to bed and drink the raspberry crush you were pushing through my lips.

When the gipsies weren't there, the two of us spent a lot of time in the book room. I liked it when you read to me; I liked it even better since you had taught me how to do it myself. I was reading about and imagining things I was never going to see, people I was never going to meet, voices I was never going to hear. They were all taking pride of place right there in the book room every night: planets, trees, maps, wars, winds, kings and queens from afar were all coming out after dusk from their hiding places on shelves and scrolls, with their strange clothes and tongues battling each other or other extraordinary creatures of the earth.

Reading was good and embroidery was good, and you were good to me and maybe we could have kept going on like that for all eternity: sleeping, dreaming, feeding, singing, swaying. Maybe we could have stayed as we were. But we didn't.

When the gipsies came for the second time, the old man brought you a book. That one book, although it was you who read it, changed my life. Because my life—I finally understood then—wasn't mine to live, it was yours to play with. That book taught you about bloodletting and taught me that your love was selfish and limited to yourself and your needs. Your love wasn't for me, Mara, the girl I was and who stood in front of you, with mousy hair and beady eyes but for Ileana, the girl from your dreams whose hair was like the sunshine and whose eyes were deeper than the ocean. And even at that, your love wasn't for Ileana herself but for what she meant to you, what she did to you, how she made you feel.

Who was this girl, anyway? It had been complicated for me to ask, since you thought I was her and I was happy with that for a while, but as time went by, I started to believe she was no more than a figment of your imagination. You said she was a girl who came to you in the depths of the Turkish caves when you were kept prisoner there, and she was good to you, kind and warm, and it gave meaning to that dark existence. Listening to your stories about her, I knew that she couldn't possibly be me if she was real at all.

But all these thoughts came later, a few weeks later, when I finally started to recover from the wounds you inflicted on me when you cut through my skin and into my veins and gathered the blood that was gushing out of me into your vials.

"It is for your own good, Ileana, I read it in the book. It's called bloodletting. It's for healing, but I was doing it all wrong before, taking blood only from your neck. We'll let some of your blood out from some special points… healing points…" you said, showing me the book with excitement.

I shuddered seeing the woodcut of a man with his insides open and lines with letters going outwards from many points of his body. What were you going to do? There were cuts on the arm and legs but on the eyelids, too, and on the soles of his feet.

"Please, no more blood, don't take any more of my blood!" was all I could say. You were oblivious to my begging, and in the terror of the moment, I could see your nails growing and your gums parting to make room for sharper teeth. The woodcut seemed to laugh at me, a toothless and raspy laugh that sounded like a swarm of bees. I closed my eyes, and I could feel their stinging all over my body. I tried to run and fight until my limbs got painfully stiff and tender and my ears were screaming in protest of the roaring buzz. And then, all of a sudden, silence. The bees turned into butterflies, and the gentle flutter of their wings was soothing. I sighed, relieved it was over, but when I tried to open my eyes, you closed them with your hairy palm. Between your fingers, a bee.

"It's for your own good, Ileana—you know I'd do anything for you!"

As much as I wanted to believe you, with the pain crippling my entire body and hammering at my mind, unable to walk or talk, I looked death in the eye and wished it would take me wherever dead people went, in a land without pain. I wished for it so badly that I soaked myself in it, covered myself with its comforting blanket and rested in its shade, waiting for it to take me. It didn't.

Anica, the old gipsy woman, cured me, potion by potion, wound by wound, tear by tear, and day by day. Doina, my pearl sister, stayed with me, changed my dressings, gave me things to drink, to eat, to look at, told me stories from outside the castle and outside the world, and she kept you away when she could, pretending I was asleep.

That was the only time my mind was clear of you, and I had the room in there for my own thoughts about my life with you. Without the sandy beaches and the raspberry crush that you poisoned my thoughts with, without the consuming passion that ate my body and made me burn with desire and delight, my life in the castle had seemed bare and lonely. Now I knew I was in danger. Surrounded by Anastasia's things and a prisoner within burnt walls that reminded me of her fate, I finally had to face mine.

"I will need your help, Doina, I need to get out of this castle," I told the only friend I knew one day while she was cleaning my wounds.

The young girl stopped. She lifted her eyes from my wound and looked at me with fear mixed with pity. Then, without a word, she continued her work.

"You have to help me get out of here. My life is in danger, and I don't want to die. He will kill me soon, I know it. I will have to run away with you—maybe you can hide me in your cart, it's the only way."

Doina put a finger on my lips and shushed me gently.

"You have to stop. I can't hear anything about this, please."

"Why not? You are my only hope, there is no other way for me."

She shook her head with a sigh.

"You don't understand, I can't betray your master. He is our master now, we all declared loyalty to him. We can't do anything to betray him. I can't help you. Not by lying to him."

My head was spinning. That was not the kind of answer I was hoping for. The next moment, I forgot how to breathe, caught in between surprise and desperation. The gipsies were my only way out.

"I really, really don't understand, Doina, please, I thought you were my friend."

"Of course I am your friend, but our tradition won't allow it."

"When did you declare loyalty to him? And why? What does it mean?"

"You were asleep, hell, you were nearly dead after he…" Doina looked me up and down with pity and didn't finish her words.

"And?"

"And a woman from the village came here, she knocked on the door of the castle, just like that, banging it and shouting to open. We were outside looking at her and minding our own business around the fire, and Master Dracula came out and the woman was shouting at him to give her back her baby boy. She was very upset, and it upset Master Dracula too. He shouted back at her that he has taken no child and she should go on her way and leave us all alone, but then little Mihai started to cry—you know, my sister's baby, started to cry—and the woman thought it was her boy and shouted more and beat herself up and tried to get to the baby and grab him. Master Dracula told her to go away and she went, but she was yelling back at us that she would come back to take him and she would bring help. She called us all baby thieves."

"How come I didn't hear anything about this until now?

"You were very sick, Ileana. We thought nothing of it anyway, no need to bother you with this."

"My name is not Ileana, you should know this, it's not my name. My name is Mara, but he called me Ileana all this time and I let him. I let him do whatever he wanted for some food and some clothes. I should have known better. Please, call me Mara."

"I don't think I can," said the girl with sorrow, and seeing the fright that cropped up in her eyes, I felt almost sorry for her.

"You see, that night the woman came back like she said she would, but she didn't come alone. She brought the whole village with her, and they came to take Mihai, my sister's baby, because they thought it was hers. We showed her it wasn't, but they didn't believe us and they said we hid the baby and we were baby thieves. There was a fight, they all started to fight with each other, and our men are strong and fearless but the men from the village were many. That was when Master Dracula opened the gate of the castle and let us in, all the women and children safe in the courtyard. And he helped our men fighting outside. It was a fierce fight, we could hear from the inside the roar of the wounded, but there were more of them than of ours. When they saw that, you know, that they were losing the battle, they went home because they were getting no babies from us."

It was hard for me to believe that it had all happened just under my window, and I didn't know anything about it. How sick was I? How out of this world had I been? What was happening to me?

"When did this happen, Doina?"

"Three nights ago is when it happened. After they went away, my grandmother cleaned the wounds and mended the bandages, and my grandfather gathered us all and told us we were now Dracula's people because he saved one of us and that it was our tradition to swear loyalty to a master and serve him if he served us."

I was listening to her, and a sad thought crossed my mind: I was nobody, I had done nothing for anybody, so why would I matter? Why would somebody help me when I didn't help anybody? You, Dracula, were the one with all the power and the knowledge. People were always going to listen to you, help, follow, believe you. After all, I had done it myself for a long time. But that time was coming to an end.

"I am sorry, it's our tradition, this is what we have to do," I heard Doina saying softly, like a consolation.

It wasn't her fault; it was nobody's fault but mine. I was the only one who allowed myself to be trapped like that.

"It's not your fault, Doina. You do what you have to do, and so will I."

When they left the next day, she gave me a hug.

"I hope to see you again. If not here, somewhere else."

Something shifted in you as well after the gipsies left. You came to see me in my room, you gave me the broths and potions Anica left for me and changed my dressings. Every time you saw my wounds, you winced and seemed full of regrets. You never said you were sorry, but you didn't touch me anymore the way you used to, and seeing my body seemed to make you ashamed, not enchanted.

You retreated from my mind, too, or maybe you just didn't push into it anymore. The fog was dispersing, and I was starting to see things as they were. I started to see you.

Your eyes were there, in their place, but there was nothing in them, no flicker of love or anger, just an absence of feelings. The eyebrows were covering most of your bony face, stark, bringing out your aquiline nose like that of a vulture ready to rip apart its prey. You were white and your face seemed to be made of chalk powder, ready to dissipate in the air with any breeze. The long fingers had pointy nails, and the skin was rough on them like a vulture's claws, and the thought of those fingers on my nipples made me want to scream my revolt and revulsion from the top of every mountain. But I couldn't be on any mountaintop, could I? I couldn't be anywhere outside of my castle that had become my prison.

The more you stayed away from me, the weaker you became, and the stronger I was getting. You were sleeping all the time now, and I was rattling around inside the long and empty corridors of the castle with the four wolves, taking in the smell of the smoke that marked the end of Anastasia's life and the beginning of my end.

I looked for the key to the front door in every corner and every nook. I looked on top of things and under them. I searched inside boxes and pans, stuck my hand into bags of grain and barrels of beer. I just hoped there were other keys around because, if there was only one, you had it. I could see it hanging from your belt, right in front of me, the key to my freedom.

I was waiting for a miracle. Searching. Waiting again and searching some more.

A week later, I decided I was done. I stepped into your room in the tower, the one Anastasia threw herself from. The wolves wagged their tails at the sight of you. They were happy to play with me and guard me, but you had always been their master. Their love and obedience belonged to you.

I sat on the bed where you lay unmoving, pale and dry like the papers in the book room.

"I trust you are well, my lord."

I was listening for a reaction to my voice, for a sign you were still alive, but none came. What was happening to you? The wolves were licking your arm and your face, and I thought that might trigger something in you.

"We ran out of supplies, my lord. There are no eggs to make a pie, no milk to drink or meat to stuff in the cabbage for *sarmale*."

That was a lie; there was plenty of food in the larder, maize for *mămăligă* and cheese in salty brinc. I didn't care much for eating anyway. I waited a little, but there was no proof that you heard me.

"I thought maybe I could take the key and go down in the village to get some food for us."

Nothing. Your chest was not moving, there was no flutter behind your eyelids as I'd seen on sleeping people before. You looked like death itself. Empty and cold.

I could see the key. It was so close to me, so full of temptation and promise. It didn't seem secured in any way, just hanging from a ring that could be easily opened. I reached out with my hand and touched it. No movement, no reaction from you, no breathing, no blinking. I came closer to the bed to make it easier for myself but, by God, I didn't expect that.

The wolves jumped me at the same time, as if you had given them a signal from the depths of your slumber. One had my hand that touched the key. Another was pulling my dress, and I could feel the sharp teeth of another on my calf. The fourth patrolled in front of the door. Their menacing growl scared me; I felt I was no playing partner anymore and I could claim no friendship. I was the enemy, and although they hadn't bitten yet, I knew they would without hesitation.

I let go of the key slowly and they, too, retreated one by one. When I put my hand in my lap, the wolf at the door came and sat at my feet. I stood up carefully and shuffled to the exit, ready to sit back if they didn't want me to move. I didn't need to. The wolves followed me cheerfully into the corridor as they always did and as if nothing happened. And indeed, nothing had happened. I was still a prisoner.

It took me a few days to recover from that incident, but when I did, I started my search again: another room, another wall, a new book or a new chest.

That was how I found the letters. They were rolled into another scroll of no importance and hidden at the back of many other scrolls in the book room. I had taken to reading these scrolls, one by one, hoping I could find something about you, what made you strong and what made you weak, what could cure you and what could kill you, something, anything to set me free.

I unrolled the first, one and Cneaja's words jumped at me from the page:

"I will soon be forgotten, and my name will never be known. Will you, Dracula, remember me, your mother?"

I recalled her tiny body in the coffin in the church, and it seemed like a whole eternity had passed since that day, and I wanted to shout at the paper, *I remember you, Cneaja. I will always remember you—how could I forget?*

I wanted to read that letter all at once, to engrave its every word in my mind with fire, but I also wanted to see what was in the second scroll. I unrolled that one as well, and Anastasia's words revealed themselves to me as she herself had to the whole of the world on her wedding day to you: small, timid, helplessly sad.

"I thought I knew who I was before you, Dracula, made me your wife."

I read their words for a full day and a full night while you slept your deadly sleep in the tower. The more I read, the more I couldn't stop and the more tired I got, the more I didn't want them to end. I felt their pain, their worry, their sorrow, and their guilt on every page. I saw them losing themselves and losing to you, and my heart melted when they finally understood. I heard about love and hate and about regret, there was so much regret on those pages, and it was smothered in tears.

And I told myself I had to be heard, too, and I started to write my own letter straight away.

"I wanted to be your lover, but you, Dracula, took me for a fantasy and made me a slave."

The words were pouring out of me, and with them, my anguish, my torture, my determination. I wrote with joy about sorrow and with courage about fear because with every word retelling the past, I knew I was writing my future. I needed to know about my weaknesses to learn how to be brave. I reminded myself I was Mara, and this was the only girl I knew how to be. Nobody could tell me otherwise.

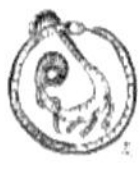

The night the gipsies returned was a happy one for me. You didn't trust me with the precious key, so you gathered all your strength to walk down to the door. When I came to tell you they had arrived, you opened your eyes and looked at me undisturbed, as if none of this time passed. It had been a fortnight since I last saw you moving about the house in the normal rhythm of your lonely existence. When you got up and walked, it was as if it had been only a day. And maybe that was all it was for you. Maybe you were the same and you would always stay the same, but for me, well, I felt as if I had risen from the dead.

When you opened the door, I gulped at the sight of them with infinite joy, their faces touched by foreign winds, their eyes wild with curiosity, their colourful skirts and the smoke from the old man's pipe.

Before I had a chance to spot her in the small crowd, Doina jumped, and we locked in a long embrace.

"I am so happy to see you are so well," she said with a simple and contagious joy. I was truly happy to see her too. Having understood that nobody could help me but myself, I was more at peace with the world. I was only waiting for the right time or waiting to make it the right time for me to escape.

"I am so happy you are back," I answered and meant every word of it.

Căldăraru stepped in front of his family to pay his respects, and while you and he were patting each other's backs, all of a sudden, you collapsed in his arms.

It was the first time I wished death on anybody. Death used to scare me so much. Its stillness, its coldness, its pain and irreversibility, they were all heart wrenching to watch, but I had been through all, and I survived. Now I wished them all on you and I hoped you wouldn't. I wanted the ground to swallow you whole and leave no trace of your rotten body. But the ground didn't want you.

Căldăraru and one of his sons lifted you and brought you back into the castle. Anica rushed to their cart and emerged a short time later with a vial, and she told me to give it to you.

"What is it, Anica, what are you giving him?"

"Bat blood is what it is," she said, shaking the small jar and looking at the thick liquid in it.

"What does it do? Will it bring him back to life?"

"He was never dead, girl, and he will never be dead, not like you and me. But he needs blood to nourish his body and mind. Get him to drink it."

I took the vial and started to climb the stairs to the tower. It was warm in my hand and prickly. I looked closer, mesmerised. I shook the jar as Anica did earlier, and I looked at the liquid, smelled it, and put a drop on my tongue. It tasted sweet. I didn't like how thick and viscous it was, but it tasted like an old wine forgotten in a bottle.

I contemplated spilling it on the steps, never giving it to you, but I knew Anica would make another and another until you got better. The thought of me walking along the corridors of the empty castle all alone, the key at your belt and the wolves guarding my every move was scarier. The time for my escape hadn't arrived yet.

You fed on that blood as one would feed on a gleeful memory and rejoice. You drank slowly, thoughtfully, and I could see life taking hold of you bit by bit.

That evening, you sat with the old man by the fire as if it had been the only thing you ever did.

When I saw the green chest with the sun on one side

and the moon on the other, I knew it meant the old man was bringing more books to you. I recoiled at the sight of it, as the last time it came through the door, you learned about bloodletting. I was not going to let you do anything to me anymore. No number of books would make me allow you to hurt me.

"I am learning alchemy for you, Ileana," you said the next day with pride and hope. "I am going to make ichor—I read about it in a book Căldăraru brought."

"No more books. You can't test what's in the books on me. Not anymore," I said with all the determination I could muster.

"This is different, you don't understand, it is the blood that runs through the veins of gods and makes them immortal. I want to make you immortal. I want to spend the rest of my life with you."

I looked at you, at your confidence and your persistence. You said you were doing these things for me, offering me some kind of privilege, a gift I should want, crave, and couldn't be without. An eternity with you.

"Stop hurting me. I can't spend a moment more with you if you are going to hurt me."

"I won't, my love."

You didn't hurt me, but you hurt plenty of other creatures. For days you locked yourself in the dungeons of the castle and built a laboratory with retorts and alembics, crucibles and cucurbits. You were consumed by your work and imagining our life together after you had made your chimerical blood for me, centuries of that life, fuelled you with a passion I had never seen in you before. You bought pots and pans from the gipsies, and you spent all your time cutting, smashing, boiling and God knows what else you learned to do in your books.

You spent time away too. You disappeared night after night, and you came back at dawn laden with more badgers, mice, owls, fish, and all manner of living things to sacrifice on the altar of alchemy, on the altar of me. I thought I ought to be beholden for your dedication and grit, but although living forever was something I had always wanted, living forever with you made the possibility of death more bearable.

I didn't come into your laboratory. Desolation lived there. Shelves with jars full of insects, jellyfish, spiders, and snakes. A dog's head staring in the distance, a bat sprawled between nails. Buckets of intestines and boxes of skins and bones. A graveyard and a torture room dedicated to the search of a chimera. And you kept saying it was all for me.

When I saw the vials of blood in your hands, I had to ask if I could ever trust you to tell me the truth. You said they were from cows and mules, wolves and chickens, and other women too.

"Are these women dead now?" I asked with worry, panic, and revulsion.

"No, of course not," you laughed. "I just take their blood for the laboratory. You know I'm doing it for you."

"Stop saying that. You are doing it for you. It isn't me who wants to live forever here, it is you. You are doing all this so you can have me until the end of all days. Locked in here for you."

"You are not locked in here. I keep the door closed to make sure other people don't come in. You know, like the woman looking for her baby who brought the whole village with her and tried to take the gipsy boy. That is why the door is closed. Of course you are free to go out," you said as if there were never a question in your mind about my freedom.

I was stunned. My heart raced ahead of my words, and for a moment, I could smell the moist earth of the Old Forest back home and my mother's garlic and mushroom stew.

"Can I go now?" I asked, weary that haste might make you change your mind.

"No," you said simply but categorically.

The disappointment slapped me in the face, and I felt tears pushing the boundaries of my fortitude.

"Why not?" I dared.

"Because there are more babies missing from the village, and people might think it is us who take them."

"Is it? Is it you? Are you stealing babies to bring them here and kill them for their blood?" My head was spinning.

"No, I don't kill babies. And I don't take them either," you said, rather hurt by my suggestion.

"You're lying," I said, bringing my face close to yours. "You lie to me all the time."

You took a step back and looked me up and down with unhidden pity.

"I don't take babies. I had a baby taken from me, and I know how it feels. It's too sad."

What was that? You, sad? Did you even know what sad meant? You had never talked to me about Anastasia and your child with her. Or about the sadness you felt. Or that you even thought about it. I spent years with you alone in the castle, and there was still so little I knew.

"Who takes them then, if it's not you?"

You hesitated for a moment, considered maybe, if I was worthy of your secret.

"The same woman who took my boy. The same woman who wanted to take me at birth. Her name is Tinca."

What good would it be to anyone if I told you I knew her? Or that she even made me promise my own child to her? No good could come out of it, so I kept my mouth shut.

"Why is she taking them? Why does she want other women's babies?"

"Because her own were taken too," you said and stepped into your laboratory.

There was a lot more I wanted to ask, but I knew the door to that conversation was now shut.

So, three nights later, when you brought back to the castle three baby girls, I knew you must have taken them from Tinca.

"What was she going to do with them?"

"Look after them, I think, maybe nothing else," you said doubtfully.

I looked at them in their little basket, with their tiny fingers and their toothless smiles, and I thought to myself, *If I am not going to have children of my own, they could be mine to look after and play with.*

"I will look after them," I said. "I will raise them well, but we need milk. I know from the gipsy baby that he drank milk. Go fetch the best milk you can find, please hurry, they'll start crying any moment now, they will get hungry."

You wanted to say no, and then you changed your mind. You wanted to humour me because you still wanted me. After all, you were killing for me in your laboratory, so with shoulders bent and a wavering step, you went.

The baby girls were cooing in their basket, moving like ladybirds flipped upside down, their tiny limbs agitated. The irony of taking Tinca's children when she wanted to take mine wasn't lost on me. I was smiling in my mind, and that put me, for the first time in a long time, in a cheerful disposition.

I had just started singing a lullaby to them, one I remembered my mother singing to my brothers, when I felt a sudden chill coming into the room. The two candles on the table flickered and died. The moonlight, golden and lazy, took over and surrounded the baby girls with a sweet glow. I felt a shadow growing over me and dread overcoming me.

"You came."

A beautiful woman appeared from the shadows, with ebony hair over shoulders. She was holding her head high, but she couldn't fool me. A look into her eyes, green and deep, reminded me of our meeting in the forest.

"Of course I came. I always come to take what's mine; you know that." Her laughter was loud and unsettled the girls.

"Please, leave them with me, I will look after them well. You don't need them. You have his son, Dracula's son. You have Mihnea."

"How do you know about Mihnea?"

"He told me. He misses his son. He is sad. He doesn't even know if Mihnea is alive. Is he?"

She started to laugh again, and one of the babies started to cry. Tinca stopped, went to the bed, and picked up the little girl. I thought she might harm her, but she became careful, attentive, and protective like a mother should be. She made a gentle rocking movement and the girl stopped as quickly as she started. Tinca deposited the baby back on the bed and came towards me.

"You know he is going to kill you," she said without emotion.

"He might try, but I won't let him hurt me anymore."

"You are so naive," she smiled. "How do you think you can stand up to him? With your bare hands?" She suddenly grabbed my arms and pulled me closer to her. "You have no chance!"

"What can I do then? I don't want to die, but even

death is better than living with him. He wants to make me immortal and live with him forever. I would live forever if I could, but never as his prisoner."

I was trying to release my arms, but Tinca was holding on tight.

"He is going to kill you soon, I can feel it. He is weak. He can't make you immortal, and he doesn't want you to grow old. He is scared, he doesn't know what to do about you."

I knew you were never going to accept defeat and let me go. Tinca was right.

"His love is not for the woman you are. His love is selfish, if it is love at all. He has a dream of who you should be, a fantasy which he bestowed on you. Fantasies don't grow old, you know, they stay the same. It is only the mind that conjures them that grows old. But not his. He will never age, his mind will never age, and neither will his fantasy."

I knew I had never existed for him more than inside his imagination. I had come to see that for a while.

"Why is it that he doesn't age?"

Tinca laughed again, and the baby girls stirred in their sleep.

"He is a vampire, Mara, surely you knew that."

Did I? Did I ever say that to myself? The mornings I woke up with two marks on my neck? The evenings I went to sleep with a drink of raspberry crush? The days I spent in a haze of weakening dreams and devastating desire? What about your long nails and sharp teeth and hairy palms? Did I just think you were an ugly and cruel man?

Tinca was waiting, looking at me intently.

"I should have known, but I didn't. I don't think I did. Can you help me? Please, I don't want to die at his hands."

"Silly girl, naive… Do you want to escape him, or do you want revenge?"

My desire to escape was so overwhelming that I never thought about revenge. Did I want to hurt him back? Did I want to lock him up as he did to me? To cut him in a thousand places and let his blood out if he had any? To make him dream and eat and see only what I allowed him to? The taste of revenge was filling my mouth bittersweet. The memory of the two letters hidden in the book room, Cneaja's and Anastasia's, appeared in front of my eyes too. Did I want my letter to end like theirs, with my death? To talk only about the misery of my life and never about courage or hope or pride?

"I want revenge," I said with poise, as I had never been more sure of anything in my life.

"There is only one way," said Tinca with glee. "When you say yes, there is no return. Ever."

"Yes, I say yes." The words came out without hesitation. Whatever she had to offer was better than my life with you.

"I will turn you into a vampire. Just like I had turned him at his birth."

She paused, searching my face for a reaction. It was

the most astonishing thing I had heard all my life. Me, a vampire. I could feel my face opening in a grin as thoughts about immortality and power were flooding my mind.

"He will kill you sooner or later, and he will bury you without remorse, but I will come and dig you out of your grave and you can start a new life. You will have all the time in the world to get your revenge."

"What if you don't come to dig me out? Will I die there, underground?"

"I will come. I always keep my promises."

Her face opened in a gentle smile. She looked beautiful that day. She wasn't wearing her black tunic that made her look like a man at war. She wore a shimmery dark green dress with a wide cleavage that made her breasts round and full and her skin white like marble. When she whispered to me, "I will make sure you never regret your decision," her breath smelled of ripe peaches, and I knew nothing else would ever make me happier.

She brought me to the bed and brushed her mouth against my ear, but she didn't stop at my neck. She continued her journey down, her tongue soft, her lips full, until she reached my breast. My heart was beating underneath in the rhythm of her breath. She rested there for a while and listened with eyes closed. She smiled.

When she lifted her head, she had a wild look in her eyes, primitive, like that of an untamed animal. She brought a hand to her chest, and I saw her nails had become very long and sharp. With one of them she made a cut to her breast, and we both watched a little crimson stream blossoming on the white skin. She put her other hand under my head and lifted it gently until my lips touched her blood. I sipped from the hot liquid with reverence. It had a complicated taste, heavy like my mother's mushrooms and the old wine from the church, and light like thyme and apples. Tinca lowered my head back on the bed gently and dried my mouth with her fingers. Her nails were no longer sharp.

"Welcome to my world, Mara."

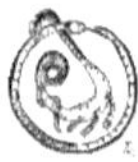

I didn't want to wait any longer. And I didn't want you to have discretion upon my death in the same way you ruled my life. It had to be my decision. I wanted to at least own my death. The next day, early in the morning in the desolate throne hall, with the three baby girls safely asleep in their basket up in my room and the four wolves near your throne, I knew the time had come.

We hadn't used that vast hall much. It was too empty of life for me, it was too full of death for you. But, since your alchemy work had taken nearly every other room in the castle, you would come here to brew your evil thoughts, and I would have to follow.

The embroidery was tedious as always. The colours of the wool, dull. Your mood was saturnian as you kept scribbling on some papers, unhappy, just as every other night. But that evening my heart was racing. Trepidation was running through my veins instead of blood. I was giddy, stirred by worry, awakened by hope. I was eager to meet my demise.

When I pricked my finger with the needle, I gasped to draw your attention. I knew you were going to hear me and look. I knew the smell was going to reach you. You hadn't touched my blood since the night of the bloodletting, but I knew you wanted it. You always did.

I lifted my finger slowly. I watched the expression on your face changing from indifference to worry and from worry to want. When I licked the blood drops that were oozing from the small cut, you jumped from your throne and reached me in a moment. The slap came hard on my cheek. I could have felt helpless and trapped as I had many times before, but this time, the heat gathered on my face fuelled my anger.

"Don't you ever do that again! Do you hear me? That blood is mine," you shouted and slapped me again on the other cheek.

My heart crumbled with shame and humiliation. My mind screamed for revenge. I could feel a trickle of blood finding its way down from the corner of my mouth, and I was grateful for it. I licked it with my tongue, watching you closely. When you came towards me again, I pushed you away as hard as I could, and I shouted back.

"Stop hurting me! Stop taking my blood and stop wanting me to live forever with you. I don't want this life!"

You seemed surprised, as if you didn't know. Maybe you didn't. Maybe you were so tangled in your own lies that you couldn't tell where reality ended and the deceiving began.

"I am doing it for you, Ileana, for the two of us," you said with a new expression on your face. You looked hurt and lost. I was beaming.

"My name is not Ileana, my name is Mara!"

The wolves snarled at me, ready to attack, but I didn't care. I finally allowed the tears to run down my face. They weren't tears of humiliation anymore but of victory and satisfaction. It felt liberating to say my name. I ran upstairs to my quarters and waited for you. Your steps came soon, heavy, laden with desire. When you opened the door, your yearning filled the room like a bad stench. I was ready, inflamed by anticipation.

It didn't hurt. I was afraid it might, but your bite didn't hurt. I was conscious of what you were doing for the first time, my mind free of you and your poisonous thoughts of feathers and beaches and raspberry crush. I felt calm, ready for it to be finished. You took your time and savoured every drop. When you drained me of my blood and sucked all the life out of me, when I saw your sadness for killing your creation, your fantasy, I smiled and closed my eyes with delight. Your fantasy was dying, but my fantasy was only coming to life.

Tinca told me my funeral was beautiful. She said my parents were crying and the gipsies were crying and your mood was dark like the ink drying on a scroll. She said my pearl sister put a pearl necklace on my grave. A day later, when she finished digging me up, I looked for the necklace and found it. I put it around my neck, and I went to the well in the cemetery to see it. There was no reflection of me in the water.

I turned to Tinca:

"What is happening now?"

"Whatever you want. You have an eternity to spend it as you wish."

With these words, Tinca's limbs started to diminish, her skin changed colour right under my eyes and, slowly, scale by scale, she turned herself into a snake. As she slithered away through the golden autumn leaves, I wondered, *How will I learn to do that?*

The End

Acknowledgements

A world of gratitude

to my husband Patrick, for his unadulterated trust in me and in all the worlds of my imagination

to my children Louis, Andreea, Kevin and Adelina for teaching me the lessons in motherhood which made this a better book

to Eileen and Christine whose patience for my dark side has no limits and who made this book possible with me page by page

to Maddy for our shared love of gothic and Romanian authenticity

to my copy editor Amanda, careful with my every word, for conversations about abbesses and sultans

to Chris (thisisreallychris) for the striking, new look of the covers

to my beloved and precious friends Therese K. and M., Aurore, Nicola, Olive, Vivienne, Nuala, Carol for laughter, care, fun and for indulging me

to the wonderful community on TikTok and Instagram who cheered for me and for my book and took time to talk about it

to my amazing readers, bombarded with many books, chose to read mine

<u>www.idraculabook.com</u>

@d.s.crowe_author

About the Author Daniela Stoian Crowe is a native of Romania and a graduate of the University of Bucharest with a joint major in English Literature and Journalism. She has worked as a news broadcaster, magazine publisher and TV producer. Daniela moved to Dublin in 2007 and lives there with her husband and four children. 'You, Dracula' is her second novel in the 'Dracula's Transilvanian Chronicles' triology.

Don't miss...

My Dracula,
The third book in the
'Dracula's Transilvanian Chronicles' series

Coming out soon